G. M. Malliet attended Oxford U   graduate degree from the Unive   She is the author of the bestselling St Just Mysteries and Max Tudor novels, of which *Devil's Breath* is the sixth. She lives in the US.

Visit her online at http://gmmalliet.com.

Also by G. M. Malliet

The Haunted Season
A Demon Summer
Pagan Spring
A Fatal Winter
Wicked Autumn
Death at the Alma Mater
Death and the Lit Chick
Death of a Cosy Writer

DEVIL'S BREATH

G. M. Malliet

CONSTABLE · LONDON

CONSTABLE

First published in the USA in 2017 by St Martins Publishing Group

This edition published in Great Britain in 2017 by Constable

1 3 5 7 9 10 8 6 4 2

A CIP catalogue record for this book
is available from the British Library.

ISBN 978-1-47212-516-3

Original book design by Omar Chapa
Printed and bound in Great Britain by CPI Group (UK) Ltd, Croydon CR0 4YY

Papers used by Constable are from well-managed forests
and other sustainable sources

Constable
An imprint of
Little, Brown Book Group
Carmelite House
50 Victoria Embankment
London EC4Y 0DZ

An Hachette UK Company
www.hachette.co.uk

www.littlebrown.co.uk

This book was written in fond memory of two greatly missed masters of the literary crime novel, P. D. James and Ruth Rendell.

And for Jo.

CONTENTS

ACKNOWLEDGMENTS

More people go into the making of a novel than can be imagined, but I would be remiss in not again acknowledging Vicky Bijur, Karyn Marcus, Andy Martin, Louise Penny, and Marcia Talley for their starring roles in seeing the first Max Tudor into print and for their continued support and encouragement. These five are among the many who helped make my early career at Minotaur possible, with the later able assistance and enthusiasm of Sarah Melnyk. Currently, it is Pete Wolverton, Emma Stein, and Jennifer Donovan who have drawn the short straw. My thanks to all of you, and to Debbie Friedman for her eagle eye. When I kill off characters, Debbie makes sure they don't come back.

My thanks again also to authors Donna Andrews, Rhys Bowen, Deborah Crombie, Peter Lovesey, Margaret Maron, Julia Spencer-Fleming, and Charles and Caroline Todd for their gracious generosity and support.

And to Rhys Davies for putting Nether Monkslip on the map.

Thanks, too, to Bill Krause and everyone at Midnight Ink, for their unflagging belief in DCI St. Just.

A host of others, too many to list for fear of forgetting the most important, have been unstinting in sharing their insights, experience, and wisdom.

And all this goes double for the members of Sisters in Crime.

AUTHOR'S NOTE

If you look closely at a map of England's southwest coast, you may find a small strip of land wedged between the counties of Devon and Dorset. Or then again you may not, for this is the county of Monkslip, home to Nether Monkslip, Monkslip-super-Mare, and other villages mentioned in the stories concerning "former" MI5 agent the Rev. Max Tudor and his partner in crime solving, DCI Cotton. You can enter this county only by believing it exists, or perhaps by walking through the back of a Narnian wardrobe.

Even given that the county of Monkslip *might* one day be real, every place mentioned in this novel, with the possible exception of London, is imaginary, as are all the characters.

CAST OF CHARACTERS

FATHER MAXEN "MAX" TUDOR: A peace-loving and divinely handsome clergyman with a talent for solving crime.

GEORGE GREENHOUSE: His former boss at MI5.

PATRICE LOGAN: An undercover MI5 agent who insists only Max can help her sort what looks like a hopeless case.

DCI COTTON: The detective from Monkslip-super-Mare under whose jurisdiction the case falls. Cotton welcomes Max's assistance in solving another high-profile crime.

MARGOT BROWNE: An actress of stage and screen whose once-shining star began fading long ago.

JAKE LARSSON: Margot's latest young escort.

ROMERO FARNIER: Margot's former lover, a famous director of blockbuster films, and owner of the scene of the crime: the yacht *Calypso Facto*.

TINA CALVERT: Romero's current young flame.

DELPHINE BEECHUM: Cruise director and yoga instructor on board the *Calypso Facto*.

MAURICE BRANDON: A hair and makeup stylist traveling on the ill-fated ship.

BARON AND BARONESS SIEBEN-KUCHEN-BÄCKER: Guests on the yacht. No one seems to know why they were invited.

ADDISON "ADDY" PHELPS: A scriptwriter penning a story based on Margot's life. Her dramatic death provides a perfect roll-the-credits ending.

CAPTAIN SMITH: He commanded the ship on a star-crossed night.

CHEF ZAKI ZAFOUR AND HIS SOUS-CHEF ANGEL TORRES: In charge of gourmet food and wine for passengers on the luxury yacht.

CLARICE MERRIWEATHER: Margot Browne's cousin back in the U.S.

HAZEL AND BEATRICE: Hotel employees who have seen it all.

Hi-diddle-dee-dee
An actor's life for me.

Honest John, *Pinocchio*
(Lyrics by Ned Washington)

PART I

All at Sea

Chapter 1

AN ACTOR'S LIFE

The yacht, which could be seen from the tidy beaches and coves of Monkslip-super-Mare, had all the villagers talking. Even in an area accustomed to having luxury yachts from around the world moor off-shore, this yacht, the *Calypso Facto*, was something special. The fact that it was owned by a famous film director just added to the thrill of it all. Young people, learning of the ship's approach, spent extra time applying their hair products and wielding their curling irons, or perfecting the art of outlining their eyes with little wings at the outer corners to achieve that year's desirable cat's eye effect. For it was a known fact that directors often cast their latest films by spotting bright new stars just walking down the street, going about their own business, or perhaps eating grilled sardines or a crab sandwich at the Seaside Café. That was probably the very reason Romero Farnier had sailed to such an obscure place as Monkslip-super-Mare, they told one another: he was on a talent spotting expedition. And where better to look for raw, hidden talent than Monkslip-super-Mare?

Wealthy residents observing the yacht from one of the refurbished mansions or monasteries on the hills ringing the harbor, and hikers looking down from atop the site of the Iron Age hill fort, were awestruck by the evident wealth floating below them, in particular by the pool and the hot tub sparkling like cut diamonds on the yacht's sunny deck. Tiny tanned figures could be seen wearing teeny strips of colorful spandex as they lounged by the pool. And many a night, fishermen at the local pub speculated over the size of the staterooms and the crew required for the upkeep of such a floating mansion. For surely anyone working on such a vessel was living the good life.

If this were the opening scene of a film, the camera might zoom in on one of those glamorous staterooms, giving the audience a voyeur's view through the porthole, and allowing a glimpse of the famous Margot Browne preparing for dinner on her last night aboard the *Calypso Facto*. A second camera might pick up where the first left off, offering a close-up on Margot's face as she lined her eyes and lips and powdered her famous nose, expertly creating an illusion of youth where youth had long since fled.

The scriptwriter might then allow us into the thoughts of the celebrated actress, in a musing sort of voice-over, and what might be overheard would be a woman's voice, in a deep, thrilling contralto, telling the audience as she prepared for the evening ahead: "Life is so unfair." Also, "I think the sodding cleaners have shrunk my clothes again."

It seemed to Margot Browne as if you were handed a certain amount of luck at birth. Sometimes, it was a huge lump sum, up-front payment. You got all the money, all the looks, all the luck, and then, because you didn't have the sense to appreciate it, to know it was not an endlessly renewable resource, it all ran out. Down the drain like bathtub water. For some people—for the really lucky—the luck got spooned out in periodic doses, like an annuity. Just enough, just in time to save you from disaster, just enough to lift you to the next level. Over and up, and ending in a big splashy funeral with the world's luminaries attending. Grace Kelly had had that sort of luck—apart from the car accident, of course. But even then, she had died driving a British Rover to her palace in Monaco: glamour had clung to her to the very end. It was the same with Gwyneth Paltrow. Even with a magazine named *goop*, her luck seemed endless.

But everybody in the world got the same amount of luck. No exceptions, no overages or overruns allowed.

This was the sort of somber reflection running through the mind of Margot Browne, actress, aged fifty-eight years, give or take; red of hair and blue of eye, and still a rare beauty, even if she did say so herself. We catch Margot on the evening before her death in an uncommon moment of philosophical reflection, because generally her thoughts ran to her more immediate needs.

Her thoughts this evening on the unfairness of life may have sprung from the fact she would soon have to wrestle her spandex body shaper in what had become a daily face-off. This might in turn make her late for the party aboard the *Calypso Facto*, as the shaper seemed to be shrinking along with the rest of her wardrobe. Her new dress, the one she had been holding in reserve to blow the socks off Romero Farnier, was never going to fit over her hips without some artificial assistance from the evil masterminds at Spanx.

It didn't seem fair that just as you needed it most your metabolism slowed to a crawl. She hadn't weighed this much since her twenties, when she had seemed to carry half her weight in her chest, anyway. Her movie stills from the time were making a comeback as dorm room posters, so she had heard, in much the way Farrah Fawcett's had taken colleges by storm. They had become collectibles "in an ironic sort of way," according to her publicist, whatever that meant.

She emitted a yelp more of exasperation than pain as she lost her grip on the body shaper and felt the stinging snap of elastic against her waist. She surveyed herself in the tiny mirror over the bathroom sink and literally growled her frustration: She saw in the unflattering overhead row of lights that her face was shiny and her carefully applied mascara smudged from the exertion. Furthermore, one false eyelash was clinging only precariously to her left eye. *Damn it.*

She thought of calling on Maurice two cabins down—dear Maurice; he'd been her stylist for years, and he was a genius—but something like pride prevented it. She had been as unblemished and wrinkle-free as a baby when last the renowned Maurice Brandon had been her official stylist. She had been a Superstar—that's Superstar with a capital *S*—back then. Before the word had even been invented, before it had become cheapened and degraded, she, Margot Browne, had been a SUPERSTAR. She even had her palm prints on the sidewalk in front of Grauman's Chinese Theatre, right next to Marilyn's. Well, very near to Marilyn's. Practically right on *top* of Marilyn's surprisingly small prints. Her own prints were larger, as she expected her legacy would be, as well.

So she really didn't want Maurice or anyone to see the extra magic that went into pulling Margot Browne together these days.

Sometimes she wondered if poor Marilyn had had the right idea. She was immortal now, frozen for all time in her heart-stopping beauty.

Quickly Margot shook her head, as if literally to shake out the nonsense. *Too morbid.* That sort of gloomy thinking went against her Kansas grain, for her difficult upbringing, if nothing else, had instilled a survivor's spunky, can-do attitude into her mental makeup. She would do a lot of things and she had already done more than could be dreamt of, but she was basically an optimist, and checking out before her time was up was not gonna happen to little Margot-from-Kansas.

By the same token, not a lot of realism had been allowed to seep into the cracks in her psyche, for she had never stopped wondering why the directors and studio heads refused to see she was still able to play the part of a thirty-year-old. Their stubbornness on this score was just beyond her. Well, maybe thirty-five years, but still. It just took a little magic with the lighting and makeup, and magic was their job, after all. A little extra effort on their part was all that was required, the lazy bastards. All she was asking for was a chance to show what she could still do.

She did *her* bit, that much was certain. The neck-and-face exercises, the yoga, the small-weight lifting, the barre classes, the hair coloring with expert highlighting, the Botox, the waxing, the surgery, the veneers, the—actually, it exhausted her just thinking about it. She had been at this game so long, this game of chasing after youth, she began to wonder how much of the original little Margot-from-Kansas was left. The young woman who had left "home"—meaning, the place where she had been raised to adulthood, and having no other place, that word would have to do—left "home" to seek her fortune, knowing it meant a final cutting of family ties. But that cutting was a relief. She was ridding herself of people who had never loved her, people who had actively harmed her, people who had turned against her. She, Margot Browne, had taken herself off to safety, with only the meager savings from her part-time, after-school job to sustain her as she went after the fame she knew was out there, waiting for her. She still regarded it as one of the major acts of bravery in her life. For like many actresses, she was massively insecure, and to fling herself out into the world to be judged, weighed, and measured had taken every ounce of courage she had ever had. Maybe that was where she had used up too much of her luck, she thought now.

Her stride impeded by the body shaper, she delicately toed it over to look out the room's small porthole. Hers was one of the cabins that didn't have even a suggestion of a balcony, and she had spent much of the sea journey in the iron grip of claustrophobia, when she was not busy fighting down seasickness. She could see the lights of the seaside resort of Monkslip-super-Mare starting to twinkle out of the distant gloaming. The beacon of a lighthouse on the end tip of land swept back and forth monotonously. Thank God they'd dropped anchor for the night—she'd had enough of the high seas, thanks very much, and she was looking forward to solid meals on solid land again.

She turned at the sound of a door opening—Jake returning from his "little stroll around the deck." Quickly, she hid the glass of bourbon from which she had been sipping as she did her makeup, tucking it behind a photo of herself as she had appeared in *Circus Girl*. She could still recite word-for-word one of her better reviews for that one: "Margot Browne, playing for some reason a trapeze artist, struggles valiantly to keep this turkey aloft through the sheer force of her beauty. She almost succeeds."

Jake seemed to need a stroll more often than the average person, she thought, and considering the low evening temperatures, his sudden passion for fresh air was hard to understand. She had suggested one night he should get a dog if he liked walking so much. No response to that, except for the little Brad Pitt smirk he went in for, the smirk that really only worked on Brad Pitt.

She wondered not for the first time if Jake had not found a female interest on board. Well, good for him, if so. She couldn't be all things to all men, after all. He was a youngish man, *slightly* younger than she, and frankly he was becoming a bit of a burden. He looked the part as she needed the part played—fit and darkly handsome, well-mannered, but with a devilish twinkle in his eye. Arm candy for the mature woman. Still, it might be time to shove junior out of the nest—time to make room for Mr. Right, who Margot still believed, in her heart of hearts, was out there somewhere, waiting for her, in the same way fame had waited for her. According to *AARP* magazine (which she would rather die than be caught reading in public, but she had smuggled out a copy from her plastic surgeon's office), it was not only possible but probable that people would find their true match later in life. Once the children and other sources of worry and strife were gone, and gasoline poured on the early marriages, and the hopeless liaisons laid to rest—that was when the knight in shining armor was most likely to appear. He might be a bit wobbly in the saddle and he might have to sling his holster a little further down his hips to accommodate his belly, but still.

"Margot, are you about ready? Romero said to be there at seven for some announcement or other. Remember?"

"Of course I remember," she snapped. "I'm not senile." One of Jake's little games was to highlight the difference in their ages by pretending her memory was faulty. Her memory was *per*fect. Years of memorizing lines of dialogue had seen to that. "Besides," she added, "Romero can wait. It'll do him good." Like Elizabeth Taylor, Margot made a point of being late whenever she thought she could get away with it, and even when she couldn't. It built anticipation. It made people understand you were *some*body. These new stars just didn't get how it worked. Well, apart from Lindsay Lohan and a few others.

Margot repaired to the bathroom to renew her struggles with the spandex and the eyelashes. She emerged victorious ten minutes later, flinging wide the little door, ready to take her rightful place at the center of attention.

Even Jake, who liked to pretend he was impressed by no one and nothing, emitted a satisfying wolf whistle.

"You look great," he said.

"Better than Delphine?" she asked, before she could stop herself. Delphine was the yacht's "stewardess" or cruise director or whatever it was she called herself. Margot had seen her flirting with Jake that morning by the pool.

But Jake wasn't taking the bait.

Again with the Brad Pitt smirk.

"You look great," he repeated. "Come on. Let's go."

Chapter 2

EVERYTHING'S JAKE

It was true, thought Jake. Margot was a stunner and no mistake. Even now, even despite. The dim lighting in their cabin helped.

But she'd been drinking again, already. Or rather, she'd redoubled her drinking efforts from earlier in the day. Why did she *do* that? Why would someone who looked like she did, someone who'd achieved what she had, feel the need to prop herself up in that way?

His grandmother, a knee-bending churchgoer, used to say that one day to the Lord was a thousand years, but one day with Margot knocking it back was becoming like two thousand, and Jake couldn't wait to wish her adios. As soon as they got off this freaking ship. If not before.

He supposed there was no explaining addiction. It was in the blood, or it wasn't. His parents both drank, his father in particular, but he had dodged the genetic bullet so far; he didn't really like the taste of booze, anyway. There was that to be thankful for. Otherwise, hanging around Margot all day . . . Well, you could say she drove people to drink. He had seen it happen a lot, out in Hollywood.

Now, apparently made giddy by his flattery, she was pirouetting her way out the door of the cabin, showing off for his benefit, and demanding to know if she looked all right. Which he had told her ten times now. She looked like she couldn't breathe in that dress, but he supposed breathing wasn't the point, and it certainly wasn't worth the bitter recrimination he would face for pointing out that she looked like she was trying out for the Mae West role in *Diamond Lil*.

Convincing Romero to put her in his next movie was the actual point, and a dull point it was—worn smooth by repeated use. Jake knew the parts in *Attilius* quite well—hell, he'd slept with the screenwriter—and he did not recall a part in the script for a woman of Margot's abilities. Actually, unlike most of the dreck Romero churned out, this movie had some decent dialogue, and Margot was not exactly known for being able to wring the best out of a line. In her prime, her looks had kept people from noticing she couldn't act her way out of a burning theater. Nowadays, her lack of talent was the only thing people *did* notice.

The movie in question was set in the time of the Roman Empire, when there were fewer women of fifty-eight, anyway, he supposed. Wouldn't they all have died in childbirth well before then? Margot's argument was not that there were lots of noblewomen of a certain age running about the Palatine Hill, but that she could easily play the part of an actress thirty years younger. It was ludicrous.

Jake, watching as she resumed her primping in a compact mirror, already touching up her makeup—come *on*, already; now they really were going to be late—thought how this night marked a new beginning for him, a possible reboot to his own career. For Jake was keeping a secret, and an explosive one it was bound to be: Romero had offered him the part of a young gladiator. A youngish gladiator, anyway. A *seasoned* gladiator looking forward to retirement from the arena. A speaking part, no less. "*Fratres*! With me!" *Fratres* meant brothers; he'd looked it up. The script was in English, of course, but with some Latin phrases sprinkled throughout for verisimilitude. He had been practicing his lines—words—out on the deck throughout most of the voyage from France. Romero had told him his decision not long after they'd cast off, headed for the coast of England.

"I wouldn't," Romero had said, "say anything to Margot about this just yet." A pause, as he plainly weighed how much more he should say. Then he finished with a lame, "If I were you."

This had been Jake's first clue that Margot probably wasn't getting a part in the film, although there had never been a big chance of that. Not for the first time, Jake wondered what he and Margot were doing on board the ship, anyway, as guests of the famous director. It wasn't as if people weren't standing in line to get on board—it was a world-class yacht, nearly new, with everything to offer in the way of luxurious accommodation. Emboldened by the legendary director's trust in him, and by his remarkable generosity in offering him the part, Jake had said with suitable humility, "I really would like to thank you for including me on this trip. I promise, I won't let you down."

The director had looked at him with something like compassion. Or perhaps it had been closer to weary resignation. He had had a lifetime, after all, of dealing with hopeful stars, young and old. It probably got tiresome. All those little egos, all made of glass.

The two men had been sitting side by side in deck chairs watching the sun set, trying to capture the last of the weak May sunlight. Jake had been drinking a club soda and Romero sipping a double whiskey. Both of them were wrapped in blankets and fleece, but still, it was one of the nicest days they'd had at sea. The women, made of sterner stuff than the men, had spent part of the day by the pool, flaunting the smallest bikinis the law allowed. Jake felt sure it wasn't modesty that prevented them from ditching the tops, but necessity. It was much too cold to go completely topless.

That Delphine, who led the yoga classes, was really something, he thought. (Too bad Margot had picked up on that; he'd have to be more careful.) So was the baroness, but that lady was too much an icy Hitchcockian blonde for his taste. Besides, she was married, and that came with its own drama. Little Tina was hot, but she was spoken for by Romero, so hands off. Definitely, hands off, if for that reason alone.

And of course the hottest number of them all was pregnant. He couldn't remember her name—was it Belinda? She had some unspecified role to play in keeping the ship afloat. But, so much for that game. Who's your daddy? Not me.

"It's only one line," said Romero. "If you screw it up, we'll dub someone else's voice in."

"Oh." That had taken some of the stuffing out of him. "I mean, well, thanks. I know you and Margot go way back, so inviting me was . . . a special concession, like."

Romero had sighed. "We go way back, all right, but I'll tell you the truth: you were invited along to keep her out of my hair. She's pestered me to death about getting a part in *Attilius*. I knew that probably wasn't going to happen, but I thought a free trip on a yacht might pacify her. That was stupid of me. It just encouraged her lunacy."

"I'm afraid you're right about that," said Jake. "It did."

"So, you understand, there will be a teary storm if she knows you've got a part, however small."

"There are no small parts," said Jake, stubbornly. *Great*. Now he sounded like Norma Desmond: *I am big. It's the pictures that got small.*

Worse, he sounded like Margot.

"Whatever," said Romero. "Just, if you know what's good for you, and what's good for everyone on board, just keep quiet about the sodding movie, okay? I'll probably officially announce some of the casting in a few days, just to get ahead of the media, but until then . . ."

"Mum's the word. Got it."

Chapter 3

TAKE TWO

Romero Farnier, the director who had brought so many historical dramas into the world, had a poor sense of his own personal history. Years of "work" with a psychiatrist—if you can call lying on a couch and talking about your earliest memories work, which he did not— had made clear to him only that he seemed to have very few lasting memories. His life had sped by, unobserved and unrecorded, leaving no imprint on his brain. It was like a tape that once used had been erased, or written over with the next episode. He wasn't sure this was a problem but the shrink seemed to think it might be. Of course, the woman billed $350 an hour; she had to find *something* wrong to justify her existence. It was like taking a perfectly good car to a mechanic— they would find something to fix if you claimed it was "making a funny noise."

He stared out over the water, remembering. Some days as he drove to the doctor's stark, modern building overlooking Rodeo Drive he felt he should just make something up to keep her happy. A play-date in kindergarten gone wrong—something involving matches or plastic knives, perhaps. Being accidently locked in a closet as a child and left to die. A dramatic bout with measles or whooping cough. But the fact was, he'd had a perfectly happy childhood, at least the parts of it he could remember, and he didn't want to besmirch his parents' memories, they should rest in peace, by pretending otherwise.

So his sessions with the shrink, you had to wonder: Why did he even bother? Well, his last wife seemed to think he needed help. All his wives had suggested something along those lines, come to think of it. He was an egomaniac; he couldn't see beyond his own nose; his happy childhood had to be a lie—why else would he go into show business but because of some deeply buried secret he wanted to explore on film? People, including reviewers, seemed to regard his movies as offering insight into his subconscious, but they were wrong. His films were entertainment for the masses, pure and simple. Scratch the surface, you'd only get more surface.

But all his friends had been seeing a psychiatrist for years, so Romero thought he'd give it a shot. Only his daughter seemed to think he was okay. But she was making some bad choices on her own these days, so what did she know? Forty and mostly still living at home, and the guy she was seeing now was another loser. Frances had her mother's good looks, so why she would choose this guy was inexplicable to him. A lot of the men she took up with were no-talent actors just using her to get to her father. Why Frances couldn't see through them from the start was a mystery. She was just so damned vulnerable. Romero thought maybe if he got his head shrunk it would help shrink hers, too. Or something.

The thought of ambitious actors led him round to thinking of Jake Larsson. It seemed to Romero that he had ended up promising Jake a role in *Attilius*, although he hadn't intended to. He supposed it wouldn't hurt, although Jake was getting a bit long in the tooth to play a gladiator. Maybe he could play one of the younger senators striding around Palatine Hill in a toga. He had the legs for it.

Yes, some kind of reward seemed to be in order for keeping Margot out of his hair. Margot, and he remembered this well—oh, did he remember it!—was one of those women who had constantly to be entertained, and if anything showed signs of slowing, well, she'd create her own drama. Lovely she was, or lovely she once had been, but a man soon came to the realization that having her in the house was like adopting a cougar and hoping to tame it. He had mentioned her once to the shrink, trying to explain that this particular breakup had not been his fault, but Dr. Nancy wanted to go on and on about why he had chosen someone as unstable as Margot to begin with. What was she, crazy? Had the good doctor *seen* the photos of Margot in her prime? A man would have to be insane *not* to have wanted Margot.

She'd been about the same age as he—well, she was still about the same age as he—but back then, it had meant he'd practically have jumped off a cliff if she'd asked him to. He was just a kid, basically, and stupid when it came to women, but he knew from the start she was going to be something. He was honest enough with himself that he knew he saw her as a way up and out, which was why he'd stuck with her longer than he should have. If from the outside it looked as if he'd dumped her once she'd given him a leg up, well—too bad. *You* try living with Margot Browne.

Funny, though, how the clock could spin round and it was midnight all over again. His current romance with Tina Calvert was showing much the same signs of wear as that long-ago daily tango with Margot. Oddly enough, Tina even reminded him a bit of Margot, and not in a good way. Not physically, of course—Tina was a small thing, a tiny dancer of a girl, and Margot had always been voluptuous. Not big, except where it counted. No, it was a matter of personality, for want of a better word. The business attracted the look-at-me types, of course it did. But these two put the rest in the shade. Twenty-four-seven, *Look at ME*.

It was probably time to find a part for Tina in a movie filming on location somewhere "in a galaxy far, far away." He had always found Thailand or Australia to be ideal for the purpose, and he knew lots of casting people happy to trade in a favor or two. He'd found over the years that was much the safest way to ease himself out of a relationship, and he only wished it had been available to him when Margot was busy making his life a misery. Make them think it was *their* idea to split up—that was always best. It saved face all round, because everyone knew you'd have to be crazy to want to break up with Romero Farnier.

Dr. Nancy called it part of his passive-aggressive nature, and it was one of those things she seemed to think was a problem. But Romero? He thought it was the smart way to get through life.

He'd had nowhere near the clout to get rid of a troublesome actress, not back then.

Now? Now he could hire whomever he wanted, to do whatever he wanted. He had the power.

It was rather a thrilling thought.

Chapter 4

TINY DANCER

The trouble with being on a yacht, Tina Calvert had decided, was that the salt air made you hungry all the time and jogging wasn't really practical—there wasn't quite enough space to run around freely. Besides, the deck was slippy half the time.

So after days of binge-scarfing out of pure boredom, you were in danger of having to be forklifted off the effing ship once it finally docked somewhere. She had weighed less than one hundred pounds since she was in her late teens and she was determined to keep it that way. Of course, what's-her-name—Delphine, the fitness guru or whatever—held daily yoga sessions but it wasn't the same, was it? Tina would choose Pilates any day—less B.S., more workout.

Considering it was a ship that had everything else, including a wine cellar and even a teensy movie theater, it was downright odd there was no fitness center, not even so much as a treadmill.

Generally, Tina liked to burn up extra calories with vigorous sessions of sex but Romero was about a thousand years older than she was and it really wasn't working out—so to speak. She would never tell anyone that, of course, because just being in the company of such a famous guy was fan*ta*stic for her career, but, like, on a personal level? *Meh*. She might as well adopt a cat or something for all the affection or anything else she got from Romero. She didn't even have a diamond necklace or something, like, *tan*gible to show for her trouble. And here he was reputed to be such a ladies' man. Well, back in the day, maybe.

She was at her dressing table in the cabin she shared with him, looking down at her hands and pondering her fate. The nail polish—wasn't it just a little too peachy-orangey to go with her coloring? Redheads had to be so careful about that sort of thing. With a sigh, she twisted the top off a bottle of polish remover, pulled a cotton ball from her makeup kit, and went to work. She would just have time to apply the tomato-red polish and have it dry before for dinner. Romero was on deck, doing something vaguely nautical, giving her room to get dressed. It was easier for men, wasn't it? He just threw on a cravat and a jacket and announced he was ready to party. While she—

Dammit. The red wasn't working, either, not with the violet-blue dress. It needed something more purplish, but this was all she had. The minute they landed or docked or whatever it was you called it in Podunk Village, she would see if they had something like a manicurist. Probably in one of the big hotels—you could just see those huge old buildings, ranged above the harbor—they would have a salon. Her hair could use a trim, too, and some dark gold highlights, but she would die rather than entrust her hair to anyone outside of New York. Just, like, *die*. With the screen test coming up back home—no way could she risk it. It would be nothing less than career suicide. There was a reason Phillipe could get away with the insane amounts he charged.

However—and she was stilled for a moment by the thought—there was Maurice. Technically, he was quasi-retired and it would be a sort of busman's holiday for him but certainly, as he was right here on board with nothing to do, and she was so famous, or soon to be—well, surely, this would not be an imposition. Not that she cared overmuch if it was an imposition. It was, looked at the right way, like doing him a favor. Maurice was close in age to Romero, and certainly, she was doing Romero a favor to be seen hanging on his arm. It would be sort of the same deal with Maurice.

Good old Maurice. He was not exactly a has-been but he had been a stylist for Margot Browne, for God's sake, and if that didn't date a person, what would? Margot had to be edging close to sixty, and it was sort of a wonder she could still *breathe*, much less tag along on this trip pestering the hell out of Romero and generally getting in the way. She, Tina, would never understand why Romero had not just put his foot down in the first place, but Romero could be such a softie.

The unintended pun made her smile, and, catching a glimpse of herself in the mirror, Tina was struck again by her own loveliness. She stopped to gaze raptly at the almond-shaped eyes, the polished arch of brow, the adorably clefted chin. Yes, why pretend? She was spectacular and she knew it. *And* she knew how to work it to her advantage. Her confidence in her looks had carried her this far and it would carry her over the top, yes it would.

As to talent, well, look how far Margot Browne, the old has-been, had got without having any talent to speak of. Tina knew she needed a few acting lessons, but really, the money might be better spent on an orthodontist for invisible braces to wear when she was not on camera. That one tooth in the front crossed just a bit. Romero claimed it was part of her appeal—that winsome, crooked smile—but really, perfection, when it was just within reach, was so much better. So why not go for it?

She waited for her nails to dry, thinking how much more pleasant this voyage would have been without Margot. She was always *there* somehow, trailing her scarves and shawls, hanging about the deck and then lunging at Romero the second she spotted him. She wanted so desperately to be in this film of his and anybody—*anybody*—could have told her that was never going to happen. At least she had the sense not to wear a bathing suit, so everyone was spared the sight.

She'd sit by the pool wrapped to the eyeballs, claiming she was allergic to sunlight, which fooled absolutely no one.

That boyfriend of hers, or whatever he was. That Jake person. Her boy toy? It really was hard to say what was going on there. They acted more like mother and son. Looked it, too. Anyway, there was potential there, if it was true that sexuality was something that existed on, like, a scale. He was amazing, with his dark, smoldering looks, just as amazing as she was, and if Romero didn't shape up, well, Jake would do nicely as a place to land while she thought through her next move. Jake didn't have anything like Romero's stature, of course, but the only thing that mattered was that she not be photographed alone at the Oscars or somewhere like that, only to appear later in *People* or *Us*, mooching around the edges of the red carpet like some *loo*-ser who couldn't get a date. Stars sometimes brought along some old geezer from their family—the fans ate that stuff up, particularly when men brought their moms—but no one had ever seen Tina's family and that was not about to change now. She had shaken the dust of Texas off her boots a long time ago, and there was no going back.

Oh no. The light had changed, and now she could see the dark blue eye shadow was all wrong. Way too sparkly and trailer-trashy. She dipped a small brush in makeup remover and dabbed it along the crease of her eyes, erasing the excess. It was a trick she'd picked up from Maurice—well, from watching one of his videos on YouTube. There. Now she didn't look so much like her sister.

She hadn't thought of Peggy in years. Stuck back there on some ranch in Texas with three kids, each one more homely than the last, trapped in a trailer with that doofus she'd dated in high school. Peggy liked to send photos by text message, as if Tina could somehow be persuaded to show a sisterly interest in that no-talent brood. Beyond thinking how much Peggy owed her, all familial ties were about non-existent. She, Tina, had single-handedly kept their creepy stepfather away from her baby sister so she could have something approaching a normal life. And there the family debt ended, as far as Tina was concerned. Reminders were certainly not welcome.

She sat back in her chair, critically surveying the emerging perfection in the mirror. There was one other male possibility on board, that Baron Whatsit, but he and his baroness looked to be pretty tight. Still, if Tina put her mind to it, the baroness would be packing her bags before she knew what hit her, and headed back to . . . wherever it was she came from. They were both a bit vague about that—she'd asked him when they'd first boarded, and he'd murmured something that sounded vaguely German. Romero had told her he'd met the pair in a casino in Monte Carlo. They'd hit it off, so he'd invited them to join him on the cruise. They were freeloaders, in Tina's estimation, but Romero was such a sucker for the nobility.

The baron might do for her needs in a pinch, Tina decided. He had the looks, *and* a title. Wowzer. And he was about the right age— she was getting a bit tired of this geriatric gig. Romero was sixty, for God's sake. Yes, the baron was definitely something to keep in mind. Maybe the baroness would fall overboard. That would be nice.

Or Margot would. That would be equally nice, and more likely to happen, since she was in the bag half the time, anyway.

There was the sound of a knock followed by a door opening—it was probably Romero, come to collect her for the party. She turned in her chair, kilowatt smile at the ready. Keep him happy, for now.

But it was only Delphine, the cruise maven or whatever. Apart from leading yoga classes each day, it was difficult to say what Delphine did. From the look of her, all long legs and blond ponytail, she might think she was in the running for Romero's affections. *Fat chance.* Tina Calvert alone would decide who her replacement would be.

"I'm just dropping this off," Delphine said, placing a small shopping bag on the floor by the vanity. It had a logo on it, a big red *L.* "As promised. Dinner's in ten minutes."

"I know. I'm just waiting for Romero. It's funny he's not here. He's always on time." She decided it wouldn't hurt to remind this little yoga person that long legs or no long legs, Romero was miles out of her league. "For me, anyway, he's *always* on time. He can't stand to be away from me for a minute. It's endearing, really." Here, a conspiratorial wink: the women were close in age, both in their early thirties. "Older men can be so *needy*."

"Actually, I wouldn't wait if I were you," said Delphine. "I just saw him talking with the chef. They seemed to be in—well, they were having quite a heart-to-heart." Actually, they looked like they were about to come to blows. The chef was temperamental—artistic, sure, but not in a good way. Sometimes a beautiful creation offset all the chaos from which it emerged, but not in Zaki's case. He was a highly strung scoundrel, unable to keep his mouth shut—just to name the biggest things wrong with him. Delphine had learned to tiptoe very carefully around Zaki, and to leave him out of the loop wherever possible. "Anyway, Maurice is in the lounge already, having a cocktail. So you'll have company while you wait. It might be a while."

Tina was thinking she was always her own best company. She stared at Delphine with distaste, for Tina didn't like being upstaged in the "I Know Romero Best" competition. It was a narrow look that would quell most people living at the yoga-instructor level—a look Tina had perfected at the start of her career. "Feisty" was the word reviewers most often used to describe Tina. One treasured review had called her a petite virago—she'd had to look it up, but decided that overall, it had been a compliment.

Delphine stared straight back, calm and unfazed, smoothing her ponytail over one shoulder. She could have told Tina she'd soon be on her way out of Romero's revolving door—Delphine had been around long enough to spot the signs. He'd had nearly enough of Tina's fatuous self-absorption. He'd find a role for Tina and she'd be gone before she knew it.

But Delphine decided to leave all that to Romero. He was so good at it—so experienced.

Hiding a smile, Delphine closed the cabin door behind her with a solid *click*.

Chapter 5

WARRIOR POSE

Delphine moved through the narrow corridor with a ballerina's grace, shoulders loose, arms floating at her sides like a woman treading water, swanlike as she limbered up the lean muscles of her long frame. Her conversation with Tina was already forgotten; Delphine had much bigger things to occupy her mind than that decorative nincompoop. She wondered if she'd have time for a few yoga poses before dinner. It wouldn't matter if she were a bit late to the party; she was a strange hybrid of guest and employee, only there to make sure everyone had a good time, maybe flirt a bit with the male guests. Get them talking about their jobs and accomplishments, and most men were putty in her hands. The problem was she rarely drank—she had an athlete's fear of taking on anything that might affect her focus, form, and concentration—and that made the cocktail chatter a bit of a chore. Certainly she didn't do drugs, either, although she couldn't say the same for everyone on board. Some of her early upbringing had stuck with her and she knew that people who got sucked into using drugs were lost souls, sometimes lost for good, and she wasn't about to join their ranks. If they were dumb enough to use, that was their lookout.

Now she lifted her arms over her head and twisted her upper torso from side to side, working off the tensions of the day. If the narrow passage had allowed for it she would have done a few sidekicks or spun like a whirling dervish—she had spent some time in Turkey two years before and had studied this form of active meditation. Oddly, she had come to believe the frenzied practice had something in common with the quieter discipline of yoga.

Delphine was a woman constantly in motion, never still; she loved stretching her long torso and limbs into poses that would defeat even some of the masters of the art. She was competitive by nature and saw no irony in wanting to be the best at yoga as she once had been the best in dance at her New Hampshire high school. She had grown too tall for the career in ballet she'd been aiming for, but with yoga there were no limits except the limits the mind imposed.

Delphine had been feeling lately that life really was good. This "cruise director" job aboard the *Calypso Facto* was more like a permanent holiday, and the minor irritants of putting up with people like Tina and Zaki were offset by the financial rewards. Besides, she had already decided she would not work with Zaki again; he would just have to go. She would figure out a way, but she had to be careful that Zaki not suspect she was behind his downfall. For Zaki was all about revenge. Such bad karma, that.

As for Tina, that was surely just a matter of waiting. She was yesterday's news and too thick to notice her boredom with Romero was mutual.

When Romero had first offered Delphine the job she had thought it would be a matter of weeks, a temporary gig that allowed her to see a bit more of the world. But it had been many months now; she was in no rush to leave, and Romero seemed reluctant for her to go. She knew he had a hidden agenda in asking her aboard but she had soon put him straight on that score. She had told him her heart belonged to Dennis back home and as soon as she'd seen some of the world and built up her nest egg she would go home and marry him. A bit to her surprise, the famously temperamental Lothario had backed off and was now as tame as a housecat with her. He'd told her she reminded him of his daughter back in California, and he'd now adopted this sort of fatherly attitude toward her. She had quickly seen the advantages of the job and was set to exploit the situation to the full.

The sail up the French Atlantic coast had offered some of the most stunning views she'd ever seen in her life. The rocky coast of Brittany and the cliffs of Normandy had rendered her speechless. Her grandfather had taken part in the famous invasion, and while his war stories used to bore her silly, seeing those cliffs she'd felt a thrill of pride and kinship. Her grandfather had been brave, physically and mentally fearless. The mission had been crazy but he'd not backed down; he had not run away. He'd been reckless and bold, ignoring the risks. Just like his granddaughter. Later on, when he'd returned home . . . well, he might have taken a few shortcuts then, and he'd had one or two run-ins with the law, but risk-taking was just part of his nature. Go big or go home—for sure, that is what life was about. Her parents in contrast had been all about playing it safe. That was not Delphine's style at all.

It was funny how people, once they knew you were into yoga, assumed you were all about world peace and mindfulness. But the sheer physicality of it is what she loved; the mindfulness part was a bonus. Another word for it was simply "focus," and that she'd begun to perfect in ballet. That razor-sharp focus that did not allow for mistakes.

She turned the key in the lock of her cabin. The simplicity of life aboard ship also appealed to her: there was no room for excess baggage, physical or mental. She opened her closet and began sorting through the few dresses she had brought with her. She was dying to wear the new green sequined number, but it would be too much for tonight. Besides, she was saving that for the party to be held at the hotel where they would soon be docking—some sort of film premiere celebration. She took a basic black dress off its hanger instead, and took out the pearls and matching earrings that had been her grand-mother's. Dennis said the outfit made her look like the proverbial pint of Guinness—a tall blonde in a black dress.

Dennis was so sweet. But Delphine wasn't sure Dennis was for the long term. She had made him sound more important in her life than he was: just a little white lie she'd told Romero, with a few embellishments.

Delphine was in complete control of her destiny, pulling all the strings. A free agent.

Talk about mindfulness. She could beat anyone at that game.

Chapter 6

MAURICE

The lounge of the yacht, like everything else about the floating palace that was the *Calypso Facto*, called to mind something Cleopatra might have designed. Or perhaps Imelda Marcos was a better, modern-day comparison, for Romero Farnier's yacht was the equivalent of—what was it, over a thousand pairs of shoes? Whatever. Too many shoes.

Maurice Brandon looked about him, drinking in the golden splendor along with his single-malt scotch, for Romero was a generous host, and no expense was being spared to keep his guests happy. The room was padded and gilded and tufted to within an inch of its life, and had about it the general air of a room in a French bordello cast adrift on the high seas.

It was also a bit like the Titanic, now he came to think of it, a ship that was a floating temptation to the gods if ever one there were. They were miles from any icebergs but the English Channel was sort of like the high seas as far as Maurice was concerned. He was not a sailor and never would adapt to life lived at a rolling pitch. Still, he could only wonder at the star that had led him, little Maurie Baumgarten, out of Central Los Angeles to Hollywood to where he stood now, inured to the ceaseless glamour of his surroundings. If anything, he was finding incessant glamour and glitz to be the norm—absurdly, he found himself fussing if someone forgot to bring him the right sort of fish fork.

It was a very long way from the walkup apartment he'd shared with his mother and younger brother decades earlier. The place had overlooked an alleyway behind a diner, its red brick growing blacker with the years, its trash cans more pungent, and the fights in its alley more lethal as they became more drug-fueled. The first thing he'd done when he'd started to earn serious money was move his mother out of there to a decent little place in Encino with a front yard and a patch of garden in the back. Over her protests, as it turned out. After a year she announced she missed the noisy old tenement, smells and dealers and all. Go figure. She'd died a month after making this late-night confession to him, before he'd had time to do anything about it. She'd been found in her garden among the plants she kept forgetting to water, managing to make him feel he'd hastened her death by organizing for her this sudden, shocking brush with the bourgeoisie.

It was yet another item to chuck under the "no good deed goes unpunished" category, he thought now. Maurice was a meddler and he knew it, but his intentions always were the best. Moving his mother had resulted in much the same emotional snarl as he'd created trying to help Margot, back in the days when they were both young and salad green. He was one of those people who never seemed to learn. His diary entries could attest to that.

He looked out the curved window spanning the front of the ship. That village in the distance, Monkslip-super-Mare, looked so spooky in the gloom of the fading light. There was, he decided, a rather eerie element shrouding this entire trip. That he and Margot should once again be thrust into close proximity, where he could observe her making the same old mistakes she'd always made, most of them involving men. Correction: all of them involving men.

Maurice adjusted his dark-framed glasses, and out of habit his hand went up to smooth back his hair. He kept forgetting that his head was now as bald as an ostrich egg: he shaved it each morning, the same as his chin whiskers. As he'd gotten balder, shaving was the only way to avoid succumbing to the temptations of the dreaded comb-over, but fortunately the naked egg look was all the rage now among many men of a certain age. Among fashionable men at any age, he assured himself.

He twisted the wedding ring on his left hand, missing his partner. Perhaps the new hairstyle, a bow to the inevitable, had brought him luck in love at last. He wished himself at home, bustling about, preparing healthy gourmet meals, instead of here dancing to Romero Farnier's tune and eating far too much rich food, far too many desserts, and allowing himself just that one extra glass of wine at dinner. The on-board chef, Zaki, had too heavy a hand with the butter knife and cream pitcher to suit Maurice's taste. But the job as stylist on Romero's next film meant an influx of serious cash, which was just what was needed to keep the newlyweds afloat. He'd been tempted out of retirement because he'd paid too much for the new house in Nichols Canyon—showing off for his partner, wanting to spoil him rotten. Frank deserved it.

He walked over to refresh his glass at the drinks table set out in anticipation of the dinner party. Really more of a heavy–hors d'oeuvres cocktail party: Romero had decided he wanted the guests to mingle and get to know one another better at last, and a sit-down dinner precluded that. If they didn't know each other by now, Maurice reflected, after being confined to the ship for so long, they never would. Maurice never drank to excess, although right about now seemed a good time to start.

He had a feeling about the evening. He would say this later only to Frank, because anyone else would write it off as after-the-fact self-aggrandizement ("See? I *told* you I was psychic!"). From the standpoint of officialdom, it would come across as foreknowledge of a crime, of premeditation; it would be impossible to explain that his feelings were just and only that—feelings. And to the best of his knowledge, unless he was completely losing his mind, he wasn't planning any crimes at the moment.

But the atmosphere was there, dark, dank, and menacing, and as difficult as his sense of dread and foreboding would be to explain to logical, practical, literal-minded people (which, it was to be hoped, policemen were), it was as real and enveloping as the fog that was creeping its way onto the deck of the yacht, muffling footsteps and masking faces and hiding intentions. Maurice, usually imperturbable, felt disturbed, uneasy in his skin, on edge with a free-floating anxiety he had come to recognize as a precursor of doom—or at the least, of a *very* bad day. He had felt the same way the day his mother died. Too late, he had gone to visit her, not calling ahead as he normally would have done. There was a *sense* propelling him, a sense that told him a phone call would be pointless, as she could not answer.

How he had known that with such certainty he never could explain, even to himself. He had found her murdered in the back garden, the victim of a failed robbery or home invasion in the safe little sanctuary he'd bought for her. If she'd stayed in her slummy walkup, she'd be alive today.

He often wondered if he'd inherited his sixth sense from her. She didn't like her new home, but she'd never really been able to explain why. Had she simply been reacting subconsciously to the danger she could feel coming?

Now the same dread he'd been feeling had to do with Margot's presence on this luxury floating tub, and that was as close as he could get to pinning down the source of his mood. Margot was always trouble, she had always brought trouble with her; trouble was like something she carried in a bottle in her makeup bag, alongside her perfumes and eyelash curler.

He decided to go and have a talk with her. If nothing else, he could warn her to be careful. Not that she would listen, but at least he would have tried. He had failed to save his mother because he hadn't acted quickly on his premonition. Might he not now be given a second chance to make things right?

Chapter 7

NOBLESSE OBLIGE

"I suppose we have to go," said the Baroness Sieben-Kuchen-Bäcker.

"If we want to have any dinner, yes," said her husband. "It's not as if we can send out for pizza."

She sighed extravagantly. The baroness did most things extravagantly. "It's the singing for one's supper part that does get one down."

"Yes, dear," said the baron. "But we must play the hand we've been dealt awhile longer. It would be rather ungrateful of us not to acknowledge how lucky we've been."

Early for the party, they stood waiting on the deck for the others to gather. She turned from checking her makeup in her purse mirror and looked at her husband. Such philosophical sentiment was unlike him. He read an awful lot of rubbish lately, it seemed to her. Alongside self-help books, he liked reading memoirs by obscure members of the royal family, the sort of people it was easy to forget had ever been born. He also liked biographies of Churchill and books about the Third Reich. It was amazing how many of those there were in the world. She supposed he could have chosen worse things to read, but the thing with history, it seemed to her, was that you only had to read it once. Reading a dozen books about World War II was not going to change the outcome, was it?

She suspected it all had something to do with his family's fallen fortunes. Perhaps he was hoping for a book where the aristocracy was restored and landed gentry again roamed the countryside, horsewhipping its servants. If so he should switch to science fiction.

"Luck had a lot to do with bringing us here," she admitted grudgingly.

"You mean, running into Romero in Monte? Yes, although we'd have come across him eventually; he does tend to frequent our sort of place when he's in Europe. And of course simply everyone was there for the Grand Prix de Monaco. But that was a spot of luck."

"Yes. And it was so easy to wangle an invitation," she said. "He's besotted with the upper classes—quite pathetic, really. But I was in the mood for a private cruise, anyway. Public transport is *so* distasteful. Even the *Queen Mary* is full of nothing but parvenus these days."

Recalled to the memory of their last voyage aboard the luxury cruise liner, her husband allowed himself a delicate shudder. They had been guests of the von Rother-Magnums, who would meet them when they docked in Hamburg, but through some sort of confused misunderstanding he and the baroness had been forced on the first night to share a table with three couples from Liverpool. The men had been something in the building trades; the women had spent the whole time complaining that "their dogs were barking," whatever that meant. After such a shocking experience—really, it had been quite intolerable—he and the baroness had ordered their meals brought to their cabin for the remainder of the voyage. The von Rother-Magnums could jolly well afford it. "Yes, but darling, having met that group of electricians or whatever they were we can thank our lucky stars we don't have actually to *work* for a living."

"I think if people knew what it took to keep up the façade, they might call it work. Which reminds me, I will need a new frock or two soon. Everyone's seen simply everything in my wardrobe several times over now."

She wore a tight-fitting sheath dress and an Italian chiffon scarf wrapped about her head, the ends crossed at the front of her neck and tied at the back. It was the way film stars of the fifties had worn their scarves as they tootled around Rome in sports cars with Gregory Peck. She supposed she was being subtly influenced by the Hollywood-style company she was keeping on this trip. The scarf was a good look on her—Audrey Hepburn was such a paragon—but right now, it was practical as well. It was windy on deck, and sometimes when they hit a wave head on water splashed about like they were in the middle of a monsoon. Why didn't the captain watch where he was going? They were lucky not to have run into serious trouble with the weather. It was too early in the season for this sort of carry-on.

Although they were sailing in the lap of luxury, the baroness felt she would be glad to walk on dry land again. Or rather, to let her horse carry her over fields and fences, and then back to the manor for a nice hot drink before a raging fire, rounding off the stirrup cup of port that would have begun the day. That was her true milieu. She longed for the sound of gravel crunching underfoot, and dreaded another day of wobbling about the watery deck pining for entertainment with her own kind. For while she liked lounging about the beaches of the Riviera as well as the next person, she avoided the water, mostly. She didn't like thinking about what was in there. What monsters lay beneath. What fights to the bitter death were hidden under those dark blue waves. Her instincts were those of the huntress—her middle name was Diana, after all—but in addition to the thrill of the chase, there was something *noble*, she thought, in the traditions of the sport. And then there were the lovely dinners and dances afterward, when people of her class gathered to relive the day's hunt. How she longed to enjoy it all again.

She and the baron stood beneath an overhanging balcony, out of the wind for the most part. But her blond hair was so shellacked the wind couldn't much ruffle it, anyway, with or without the scarf. And very little else ruffled her composure, a composure that came from years of being invincible, above it all, above *them* all. It was how she had been raised; it was how her own parents had been raised, and their parents before them. Her husband was likewise smooth and dapper to the point of oiliness. It was a façade he cultivated, and it had served them both well. People expected certain things of aristocracy—even minor aristocracy. It would be wrong to disappoint. Selfish, really.

It was all, if she stopped to think about it, not unlike being in show business. The show must go on and all that. She wondered briefly how the Duchess of Cambridge coped, with everyone scrutinizing every new frock she wore, and every snip of the hairdresser's shears calling forth rapture from even the staidest publications. Those babies of hers had better turn out to be flawless human beings, too. The baroness could almost sympathize—the constant pressure!—but at the same time she wouldn't mind trading places. After all, she was much the same age as Kate, and she had traveled in much the same circles as the now-duke, back in the day when he was single and the world's most eligible polo-playing prince. There had been a time when she had been in the running for his favor, right alongside Kate. Everyone said, Oh, that Kate: she was so nice to him, and that is how she won the heart of a prince.

Nice. Bugger *nice.* Not a drop of royal blood ran in Kate's veins, unless you count that tenuous connection to the 1st Marquess of Lansdowne. Really, it was enough to make one sick. *She* was nice, too, and a born blueblood, and it had only landed her Axelrod. Some people had all the ruddy luck.

"I know, darling," her husband said now. "We won't have to stay with the ship once it's docked in Weymouth. That's Monkslip-super-Mare in the distance, so we've not far to go now. I believe the ship is headed for Amsterdam after Weymouth, and I really can't abide Amsterdam. All those people riding their bicycles in such a suicidal manner, medicated out of their minds. It's irresponsible, that sort of thing."

"The king of the Netherlands is rather dashing, I've always thought," she murmured. "I wonder if he rides?"

"A bicycle? Oh, to hounds, you mean. I've no idea, darling. Anyway, I've mentioned our leaving to Romero and he's fine with it, of course. Soon we'll be free to go."

"Fine," she said. "Just do please keep the Margot person away from me. Keep them all away from me, for that matter."

"Not much longer now, darling. Do be patient."

"*Ya-a-as,*" she drawled, bored. One couldn't smoke out here on deck, the wind just blew everything about and back in one's face, and the captain went mental if he caught people at it. They'd planned to drop into the lounge and have a quick drink and a smoke, but they'd seen Maurice through the etched glass and decided not to engage. Maurice was all right but well and truly, she'd had enough of show business types for now.

The pair stood staring at the lights twinkling in the distance; they exerted a hypnotic, soothing effect. After a moment the baron, finishing off his drink, said, "I can't imagine what our little author Addison could find to write about her that wouldn't be actionable, can you?"

"About Margot? No. No, that's hard to imagine. Much better to drop the whole project."

"Perhaps his real problem will be to find something that hasn't already been written. I mean, the woman has lived her life on the public stage, everything exposed for the world to see, in a manner of speaking."

"I think Addison's going on the theory that she can't last much longer, if you want my opinion. And that will allow him to write what he likes. He told me a biography has a short shelf life, but if it's going to sell, it will sell quickest in the month of the person's death."

Her husband looked at her, astonished. "I say. How perfectly ghoulish of him to think of it. And she's not so very old as all that."

She shrugged. "Perhaps he was joking. But I told you: show busi-

ness types are simply the worst. So grubby, so tacky. I can't wait to
get to the country, back to the hounds and horses. Back to real life,
and real people."

"Here, here," said her husband. "There are few things more civi-
lized than a well-run fox hunt."

Chapter 8

IN SO MANY WORDS

Addison Phelps was at work on his laptop in his stateroom. Actually, he was playing with his new scriptwriting software, Block Begone, in lieu of writing.

He knew he should be working on his book about Margot Browne, the book he had told all and sundry he was writing: a sort of fictionalized tell-all, a nonfiction novel like Capote's *In Cold Blood*. But he'd stalled in mid-chapter and wasn't sure he could pick up the thread again. He'd just spent an hour or so rereading what he'd written, in case there was some nugget, some kernel he could repurpose, perhaps into another art form. He was a great believer in recycling, in hanging on to every word he'd ever written. He called it his inventory. This hoarder's practice had saved him more than once when a script deadline loomed too large.

But it was no good, this nonfiction thing; he'd done a ton of research but now he felt it was all for nothing. It was as if he couldn't work outside the cocoon of make-believe. God knew that trying to get the truth down on paper was always hard—the truth in whatever form. But he was finding it impossible to write even tangentially about a real, living person. He had tried to keep going, to plow on, writing gibberish until inspiration arrived. But he'd found he could not.

And now the script he'd switched to writing as a momentary diversion, a sort of palate cleanser, would not take off for him, either. It had been inspired by a wedding he'd attended—his best friend's wedding, in fact. He had done his best to dissuade Roger from marrying a social-climbing she-wolf, to no avail. So that angry conversation, held practically on the porch of the church, had been the end of a beautiful friendship, and Addy, who had few friends to begin with, had been plunged into despair. As always, a real-life experience got buried for a while, only to turn up months or years later as a script or a book, or even a scrap of bad poetry. The poetry in particular tended to be fermented, like kimchi. The novels were unpublishable. But the screenplays had paid the rent for many years. For whatever reason, he had a facility that allowed him to finish a script in a matter of days. Writing scripts was how Addy had clung to his sanity, ever since he was in grade school.

Now he scrolled back to the top of the page, and read:

FADE IN:

EXT-ITALIAN VILLA-DAY

A wedding scene. A large crowd APPLAUDS as it surrounds the newly united GROOM ONE and the blond, voluptuous bride PIPPA.

INT-CHURCH (SANTA FE)-DAY

Another large, upscale wedding. This time, a New Mexico theme, with bride Pippa, a tanned brunette, wearing Spanish-style white ruffles. The service over, she walks down the aisle with GROOM TWO.

EXT-HAWAIIAN BEACH-DAY

Another wedding, this time smaller, more intimate.

MINISTER

I now pronounce you man and wife. You may kiss the bride.

EXT-RESTAURANT-PATIO-DAY

Pippa's wedding reception. Kate's date BRIAN can't take his eyes off the bride. Kate notices.

BRIAN

Sorry.

KATE

S'alright. I'm used to it.

BRIAN

No, really. Come on. Let's dance.

KATE

Guys go for my sister. They always have. All those looks going for her, plus she's rich now.

The story was a black-widow tale of a woman who marries up (and up) the ladder, attracting increasingly wealthier men as she goes, and discarding the men who had served as her springboards to the top. The working title was, in fact, *Springboard*. It was a stark warning, spelling out what his friend—his former friend—Roger still refused to see. Addy was deciding whether or not to have all the springboards found murdered. Yes. That would make for a really fun plot, he decided. His last thriller had done well.

But the Pippa of the tale was too thinly disguised. If the script made it out of his computer and onto the desktop of a Hollywood producer, he'd have to cover his tracks completely. For one thing, Roger's new bride was named Philippa, which Addy supposed was a dead giveaway right there. He thought a moment, did a quick search and replace, and Pippa was transformed to Rochelle. Okay. Good.

Now the next scene he had in mind involved Kate and her sister

Pippa-now-Rochelle. Perhaps a catfight between the two women, wherein Kate spelled out everything that was wrong with Rochelle, going back to their childhoods together. Or maybe a scene with their parents. He'd met Philippa's parents at the wedding and really, you didn't have to wonder how she had turned out the way she had. What a feral-looking bunch—they looked like they'd just climbed down out of the trees. They belonged to some back-country religion that was practically a cult. In her shoes, he supposed he would have done anything to escape that fate, too.

Including murder? Well, maybe. Probably not. But maybe. Who knew what they were capable of until something came at them head-on—something really bad?

But he knew this was why the story was stalling. Pippa and the whole thing, it was too soon, too close to real life—he couldn't perform the alchemy until a few more months had passed.

Fighting back the rising sense of despair, he reopened the computer file on Margot Browne. Why had he thought writing a nonfic-tionish book would be any easier? Maybe he should just stick to what he knew best: making stuff up. "Useless wool-gathering," as his mother called it.

Anna Phelps came from a long line of financial experts, men without a shred of soul to short-sell among them. All they read were stock market figures in the *Wall Street Journal*. And after a while, their brains soaked in scotch whiskey and their initiative eroded by inher-ited wealth, they couldn't be bothered to read even that much. His uncle Robby solemnly believed the stock market was run by a secret cabal of descendants of the Romanovs who had escaped execution during the revolution—a complicated theory he insisted on explain-ing at great length each and every goddamn Thanksgiving. Why they kept inviting him no one could say. And Robby was the sanest of his mother's seven brothers. On his father's mother's side were the Derby-Whitsuns, a tribe of certifiable Class A lunatics.

Addy began reading aloud from his Margot pages (working title, *Margot!*) hoping to get a jumpstart on his quota for the day. Four pages a day, no matter what. Each page containing roughly two hundred and seventy-five words, for a total of a little over a thousand words. Eleven hundred words, merely. Easy. And at the end of the year, he'd have written the equivalent of four books.

Scripts were easier. Just one hundred pages. Twenty-five days to write, max.

It seemed so simple to do, put that way. It was one of the mental tricks he had to use to get himself going each day. There was also that whole business of writing a book being like driving a car at night: E. L. Doctorow had said you could look ahead only as far as your headlamps showed the way, but that was how you arrived at your destination.

Addy sighed. *Margot!* What he had so far was one hundred pages of largely random notes and jottings, here and there strung together into a narrative paragraph. To complicate matters, Margot had come out of obscurity, and had been adopted into an even more obscure branch of her dead mother's family. This was a family in Kansas, with no show business background, and—judging by what few photos he'd been able to dig up—no great fund of beauty to draw from, either. She had been one of those miraculous children who, coming from pudding-plain parents, encouraged questions as to her true paternity. Questions that for obvious reasons had to be couched in the most circuitous manner possible.

It was a creepy family, Addy thought, with odd offshoots of weirdness to rival his own. Addy had managed to unearth one of Margot's distant relatives for a direct quote, and for the first time, he had felt a crushing wave of pity for his subject, the necessary biographer's objectivity melting even against his will and best interests. He had wanted to know the worst of Margot, and—if he was being honest—he had been hoping to unearth more of it. Dirt sells, after all. But the uncle, or whatever he was, seemed to think Margot owed him something, and he had used the most salacious terms possible to describe her—his own flesh and blood. It made Addy's skin crawl, and for the first time he began to doubt the course on which he had embarked. But he'd come so far, and put in so much work. What was that quote? "I am in blood stepp'd in so far."

How did Shakespeare know? How did he always know? For that was exactly what it felt like: he was in so deep it was just as easy to keep going forward as to go back.

Although every nerve in Addy's body was telling him that was exactly what he should do. Go back.

PART II

Ashore

Chapter 9

FAME

Drownings off the coast of Southwest England are not unusual. Tragic, of course, for all concerned, but hardly rare. The usual safety warnings about fog and tides and winds and waves generated by low pressure systems go unheeded, and people sally forth, thinking the dramatic storms are so beautiful, and the surges are such a lark, and the warnings don't apply to them because they've lived near the sea all their lives and they know what they're doing.

In winter, the danger is more obvious, with blustery El Niño–spawned winds and waves that breach the crumbling sea walls of quaint old resorts like Monkslip-super-Mare. The freezing wind alone keeps most sensible souls indoors, warming their hands by the fireplace as they wait out the worst of it. Cliff falls are not uncommon as nearby bluffs endure a ruthless daily pummeling, and water-soaked headlands erode under the relentless pounding of waves. The damp permeates every aspect of life and death: even funerals are postponed as the ground becomes too soggy for gravediggers to dig. Those people sitting by their fires start to talk about moving to the center of England, where surely they would be spared all this.

Even in the spring, when Monkslip-super-Marians start to emerge from their candy-colored cottages, the warm air can be deceiving, for the water still is freezing, and deadly.

Still, the death of Margot Browne was something, well, special. That it received the sort of international media attention it did was due partly to the fame of its victim, and partly to the glamorous party of people surrounding the victim just before her death, all of them feasting and laughing and also, it would appear, plotting and feuding. The victim, fifty-eight at the time she died, was an actress, once a goodish if flamboyant one, now more famous for having once been famous than actually being famous. And now really, *really* famous for having been found floating dead in the harbor of Monkslip-super-Mare under mysterious circumstances.

If only she could have seen the headlines, mused her former paramour as he sipped his morning coffee. Himself renowned as a director of blockbuster movies that even he found appalling, Romero Farnier as a young man had dreamed of fame, but fame of the immortal kind, fame such as the Coen brothers or David Lynch or Alfred Hitchcock could claim. Or François Truffaut, his idol. He even allowed himself to dream of directing a Shakespearean play. Why not, now? He and Branagh were good friends.

But, no. Instead he found himself directing tiresome actors in imbecilic movies that were more about special effects than about good old-fashioned storytelling, and fending off requests from the studios to do more of the same. He had long since gotten used to the riches his potboiler movies brought in; he was well off, if a bit overextended. Now he hungered for the real thing: FAME.

For Romero Farnier wanted to live forever. He was sixty, and he figured he had twenty-five good years left to him. But when was his ship finally going to come in?

He turned to where the news report of Margot's demise continued on page five, but his mind wandered. He was bored, and anyone of his acquaintance could tell you that Romero Farnier when bored was a force to be reckoned with, if avoiding him altogether were not possible. He was at heart an excitement junkie and he knew it, so the death of Margot Browne should at the very least have livened things up for him. It probably would have done so, had he not found himself, his crew, and all the guests aboard his yacht on the night in question grounded until further notice while the police conducted their inquiries into Margot's death.

Even though they were grounded in luxurious accommodations in the Grand Imperial, one of the legendary Victorian hotels fronting the coast, Romero had things to do and people to meet. The delay was just galling. He could have kicked up a fuss, and if too many days passed he would do just that, but for now it was best to put on a face of amiable good will and heartfelt desire to cooperate to the fullest with the authorities, and so he had advised his crew and passengers.

Margot always did have a gift for complicating his life. It looked to be a gift that carried over into the grave, from beyond the grave. Damn her.

Damn Margot Browne and all her petty little problems and her screwed-up life to hell.

She had always been like this, even as an effervescent, sparkly, up-and-coming young actress of stunning beauty. In life, and now in death, Margot was just a pain.

Chapter 10

MAX TUDOR,
FRONT AND CENTER

Even the Reverend Maxen "Max" Tudor, also reading the paper over his own morning coffee, recognized many of the names mentioned in the story. There were only one or two unfamiliar ones: Maurice Brandon, identified as a stylist, whatever that was. Something to do with interior design, was it? And a passenger named Belinda Bower, who was identified only as a crew member. It was implied she was some sort of witness to the drowning or accident.

But of course he recognized the name of his friend and sometime colleague DCI Cotton of the local constabulary, who was heading up the investigation.

The others mentioned in the story Max knew or knew of vaguely because he was a great fan of the cinema. There was a screenwriter named Addison Phelps whose name Max thought he recognized from the credits of a recent spy thriller, for example. And an actress named Tina Calvert. Although she was clearly a minor character in this particular real-life drama, photos of her must have been readily available, as most of the papers featured her or, more precisely, her plunging neckline, which some enterprising photographer or other had managed to capture at a high angle from above. Her face, while beautiful, seemed incidental. Then there was an actor named Jake Larsson—no photo or further information or credits provided. For an actor, how that omission must have stung. And there had been a "yoga instructress" on board the luxury yacht, but she went unnamed.

Also there had been a Baron and Baroness Sieben-Kuchen-Bäcker—there could only be one couple of that name in all the world, although it was not a baronetcy with which Max was familiar. So many of these little baronetcies came and went, and so many were extinct, dormant, or forfeit.

The death of Margot Browne, while immensely sad, was of no immediate concern to Max, nor were the bold-faced names of those who had accompanied her on her final voyage. Her death seemed merely an occasion for the tabloids to unearth their files on the woman they had deemed a bombshell not long ago, and to tsk-tsk over her fate. Comparisons were made to other "celebrity drownings." The whole was illustrated with an unflattering photo of Margot taken in recent years. She was shown leaving a Los Angeles nightspot, caught in the glare of the camera's flash, looking pale and haggard, one bony, veined hand raised as if to shield her eyes or fend off the photographer.

Max vowed to remember Margot in his prayers that morning, to thank her for the many hours of vicarious pleasure she had given her viewing public. (She had been, truth be told, a frightful actress with a tendency to overplay every part, but still she'd possessed great beauty and a sort of *presence*, and she had excelled at offering the innocent escapism that to Max was the entire reason for the existence of film.) And then he folded the paper, kissed his wife Awena and baby son Owen good-bye, and walked to St. Edwold's Church to conduct the morning service in Nether Monkslip.

He stopped into the vicarage that evening to find on his desk a hastily scribbled note from Mrs. Hooser, the housekeeper. It was then Max began to understand there would be no escape from this particular production.

Chapter 11

GEORGE GREENHOUSE

The trip to London wasn't difficult—the Harry Potterish change of trains in Staincross Minster was the only tricky part—but then Max had made the journey many times before. In his briefcase he carried a sermon that was in the middle of a good polish; he felt it was going rather well. The weather eased his journey by ignoring that morning's forecast of rain.

Max hailed a taxi at the London station and was quickly deposited at a hotel near Thames House. From the anonymous hotel he walked to MI5 headquarters, by force of habit keeping a lookout for anyone who might be tailing him. It was a slight risk in his case, but the first rule was always to assume you were being followed and to act accordingly. Old habits from MI5 never died.

A quick pass through security before he arrived at the familiar, rather anonymous office to which he had been summoned.

"Good to see you again, Max," said George Greenhouse, shaking Max's hand before pointing him to a worn, comfortable seat in front of his desk. It was a dark leather chair Max recognized from years before, a chair in which he'd received his marching orders on many occasions. It was also the chair from which he'd tendered his resignation from MI5, on a black day so long ago when he'd felt he could take no more, and could only think of turning swords into plowshares. He'd recently come full circle when, in trying to escape the violence of his past, he'd inadvertently put his beloved Awena's life at risk. It was at that moment he'd realized there was, for him, no escape.

"And I'm sure you're wondering why I got in touch," George continued.

"I did, rather," said Max. "I got the message from your man Melville arranging the appointment, but he didn't give any indication what it might be about. He said you wanted to meet for lunch, but for that you would have rung me yourself. The word 'lunch' coming from anyone connected with your office often meant, in my day, 'death-defying exploit involving guns and knives.' Am I right?"

"Quite right, Max. Although hopefully, there's nothing that risky involved this time, and the stakes aren't quite as high as what you're used to: a smuggling operation, we think, but we can't get to the bottom of who or exactly what—although almost certainly drugs are involved. Stuff turning up everywhere in London and beyond but MI6 can't figure out the source nor the courier. Where we want to send you in is only our best guess, you understand. But in a situation where subtlety and an ability to mingle with all sorts is required, I can't help but think of you."

Like John le Carré, Max had been recruited while still an undergraduate at Oxford, dreaming amidst the spires, the pealing bells, the golden buildings of Cotswold stone. He'd been chosen not only for his obvious intelligence and self-possession but for a certain quality of awareness—a cognizance hard to define, but once seen, not forgotten: a quality essential for a spy. Today they would call it mindfulness and despite the word's New Agey associations, it came closest to describing Max, thought George. Max let nothing slip past him for long.

This, thought Max, was laying it on rather thick, and immediately all his defenses against flattery went up. Max was used to being courted and sought after, and being told that he and only he could do such and such. In his duties as the Anglican priest for his tiny parish, the things that only he could do were endless, and ranged from quelling insurrections of the Nether Monkslip Book Club to convincing Miss Pitchford that Suzanna Winship had not meant to give offense at the last meeting of the Women's Institute, although Suzanna almost certainly had intended to do so. In the case of MI5, George was surrounded by men and women every bit as capable, Max felt, as himself. This was in fact not true, and George knew precisely what he was about, for Max had been a uniquely intelligent, brave, and stalwart operative—their undercover superstar.

Max's saving grace was his humility.

"Certainly it's not a matter I could go into on the phone," George continued. "I think we all have learned to our sorrow that phone calls and text messages and probably even carrier pigeons can be intercepted too easily these days. Much better to have a trusted human intermediary, wherever possible, and a face-to-face chat."

In an office routinely swept for bugs, thought Max—an unmarked office nearly as illusory as the rooms of 221B Baker Street. If one didn't know better, the outer door to George's inner sanctum might lead to a broom closet. Max waited, remaining quite still, the expression on his handsome face open, attentive, and alert to nuance. George launched into one of his little preambles. Max was used to this, and knew that George was simply gauging the mood of his audience before he got round to the point. As for Max, he had been expecting this day when he would be called back into the field, although perhaps not quite so soon as it had come.

"You've seen the papers?" George said at last, winding down after a foray into the weather and who might win the FA Cup. He'd asked Max about life in the village and laughed appreciatively at Max's description of the fallout from the water balloon–firing catapult on the village green for the last Harvest Fayre, which had demolished the Women's Institute's edible flowers demonstration. George further was to gather that the struggles for supremacy over the Bring-and-Buy table were becoming the stuff of legend.

But George's animated, bushy eyebrows settled down as the topic took a serious turn, finally lowering over the piercing black eyes that had earned him a raft of nicknames over the years. Max's own favorite was "The Demon Fielder," although he still had only the vaguest idea what that meant. Perhaps some holdover from George's days on the cricket fields. "I'm referring to the news concerning a drowning in your neck of the woods—to mix my metaphors."

"You don't mean the actress who drowned off a yacht anchored near Monkslip-super-Mare? Margot Browne? Why, yes. Yes, I did see the news of that."

"I do mean Margot Browne—one and the same. As far as the outside world is concerned at the moment, she simply fell off a yacht and drowned. Got a bit tipsy, the winds were a bit stronger than normal for the time of year. By some of the more dramatic accounts she might almost have been blown overboard, caught by a rogue wave. It's a common enough ending in those waters, however. Of course the nearer you get to Cornwall the more these incidents seem to occur."

"Yes. Quite. The waters can be terribly hazardous, even in summer."

Max was assembling in his mind everything he could remember of the news story. He'd not paid that much attention at the time: It had been one more tragedy in a newspaper that more and more seemed to compete for space over which terrible story to highlight that day. As he recalled, the actress had last been seen at a dinner party on board the yacht of famed film director Romero Farnier. Romero, it was noted, liked playing the host; he collected people, surrounding himself with all sorts who interested him, generally show-business types plus, for added sparkle, whatever minor nobs he could manage to scrape together. According to later reports, Margot's complete absence from the ship wasn't noticed until the next morning—noticed by her "traveling companion" Jake Larsson, identified further only as "an actor." Margot had in fact been swept nearly out to sea at some point during the night, only to be washed up with the seaweed on the incoming tide in the harbor of Monkslip-super-Mare.

Max relayed this summary, adding: "But she didn't fall?"

"Not according to the preliminaries, and not according to our agent, who was traveling aboard the yacht—traveling undercover as a guest of the director, moving under the name Belinda Bower. Her real name is Patrice Logan. I think you may know Patrice?" George's deliberately bland expression revealed what he knew full well: Max had once known Patrice, and very well indeed.

Oh, God. Max had not seen this coming. A long-ago memory surfaced of full soft breasts pressed against his back as he slept in his old London flat. Sometimes he would wake in the morning with his arm numb where her weight had rested on it all night; he'd not wanted to wake her by attempting to disentangle himself. Then there was that shampoo she always used that smelled of green apples, a scent that could still catch him unawares if he smelled it on another woman. Next to Awena, she had the most beautiful long hair he'd ever seen.

There had been those nights when the two of them staggered in, already barely existing on just a few hours of sleep, but still with more than enough energy to make love. The closer their jobs had brought them to danger on any given day, it seemed, the more fuel was added to their desire for each other. The greatest aphrodisiac was the certain knowledge that every day might be the last. But now—he had not in fact thought of Patrice in some years, certainly not since he'd met Awena, but immediately his memories of Patrice and her remarkable beauty flooded in. It was just like watching an old black-and-white film, something with a suitable backdrop of one of the world wars, grainy footage of longing good-byes, of star-crossed lovers clinging together at deserted train stations.

"Yes," said Max. "Yes, I knew Patrice from when I was in Five. *Actively* in Five, I mean."

George cleared his throat. He didn't like putting Max on the spot, but it was necessary to clarify the relationship right away so as not to compromise the mission. If Max's current personal situation might be affected, confounding the investigation, he, George, might have to think again. This was Max, after all, a good man and true, but Max was only human. And his wife Awena, presumably, was only human as well. Empath, clairvoyant, New Agey healer, or no.

Max meanwhile was deciding how far discretion might be confused with deliberate muddying of the waters, when George saved him the trouble, saying, "You were an item once?"

Max nodded. "A bit more than that, sir." The "sir" was a holdover from former days but calling the head of MI5 "George" was something he couldn't often bring himself to do. "We were in fact quite close; we lived together for a time." The truth was they two had collided like meteors glancing off each other before spinning off onto different paths in space. The impact of Patrice on his life had been immense, intense—perhaps too much so. Definitely, too much so. "Too hot, not to cool down," as the Cole Porter song went.

But Max thought he would spare George these little amorous details. Instead he said, "You know how it is: You forge a very strong bond with a person who understands what it is you do for a living, because they are in the same business you are, taking all the same risks. And there is no one else for miles round who could possibly understand. Certainly there is no one to confide in on the outside, living in that bubble as we did." This was as nice a way as he could find to say, "There is less lying involved that way," because George was married to a civilian, and presumably could never share exactly how he spent his time. The people in his life who meant the most to him—his wife and family—were necessarily in the dark about much of what he did all day. Max doubted he could entirely hide his doings from Awena, even to protect her from the evil he well knew was out there. She had that preternatural ability to see through lies and subterfuge, which was unusual in a woman of such integrity. Generally, in Max's experience, it took one to know one.

The need to lie was the downside to working in Five. The struggle to cling to honor in the face of an existence grounded in subterfuge. Many had failed to adapt to such dual existences, and many a marriage had come unstuck because of it.

"So, yes," Max continued. "Once we were close. But there's a lot of water under that bridge."

George nodded sagely. "I thought so, but I wanted to be sure. She asked for you specifically to be brought in."

Max had in fact been the subject of intense discussion between the two of them. Patrice was especially caught up by the fact that Max had joined the priesthood, in a reaction to the death of his friend and colleague Paul. He had decided on the priesthood long years after he and Patrice had split up, so she knew it was nothing to do with her. But she, who knew Max so well, or thought she had, found the whole thing rather unbelievable.

"Why didn't he just join the circus?" had been her scoffing comment. "Or the foreign legion?" Making George think how little she had understood the many layers that went into the makeup of Max Tudor.

"How very flattering," Max murmured now, astonished by the news of Patrice's request. "I don't see how I can help, but of course I'm willing to try. She was a top-notch agent, and if the case puzzles her—well, I must admit I'm intrigued. I mean, if *she's* not bothered by the old association."

"I think you'll find that won't be a problem," said George.

Chapter 12

TEAM PLAYERS

The Monkslip-super-Mare police department had requisitioned one of the smaller rooms of the Grand Imperial Hotel for its investigation into the death of the actress Margot Browne. For no particular reason, DCI Cotton had nicknamed it Camp X, after the secret World War II commando training station. Like the hotel's plush pink lobby and all its public spaces, the room was done up in a style that might best be described as "Early Kensington Palace," all embroidered pillows and tufted silk, fraying a bit at the edges. While it retained its elegant proportions, rather like an aging Victorian lady stuffed into a whalebone corset, it was the sort of place that had radiators clinging like barnacles to the walls, radiators that would intermittently clang and vibrate throughout the night, radiators with ominous-sounding signs attached asking that guests call for assistance before attempting to adjust the climate of their rooms.

Cotton rose from where he had been seated at a rosewood desk to greet Max as he entered, first taking a moment to hand marching orders to two uniforms in the room. Once Cotton had made sure they were quite alone, the two men, detective and priest, settled themselves before a gas fireplace that took up most of the length of a windowless wall. Even in May, and even with the radiators clanking away, a small fire was needed to take the chill off the high-ceilinged room.

Max sat back to observe his partner in solving so many crimes. Cotton was physically unchanged from their last successful investigation, apart from an incremental upward creep of the hairline of his thick blond hair, which accentuated the heart shape of his face. The pale, gray-blue eyes remained clear and ever sharp, the figure trim, the sartorial style flawless. Today Cotton wore a slim two-piece blue suit with a red silk tie and matching pocket handkerchief. He looked like he had just stepped off a runway to assume the role of lead investigator into the death of Margot Browne, not stopping to change into anything less formal. Max doubted Cotton owned anything less formal.

He never seemed to mind Max's butting in on any of his investigations. Quite the contrary. He clearly believed that having Max on board would make the solve a slam dunk, and there was never the slightest trace of resentment of that fact.

"So," said Max. "What have you got?" He rearranged the pile of fringed pillows at his back, preparing to listen. "What are we dealing with here?"

"Well, brace yourself. There is even more drama than you might expect, given the players in this one."

"All right," said Max. "I did gather from the news that you are probably being treated to more media scrutiny than if, say, a casual tourist had been found floating in the water. So what's the story?"

"The initial and still-official story is that Margot Browne, once-legendary actress, somehow fell off the yacht on which she had been sailing with friends and acquaintances. Those friends and acquaintances included what is assumed to be her current lover and an ex-lover. It's already your basic nightmare when it comes to motive, you'll notice."

And if Cotton was talking motive, he was already also talking murder. Max zoomed in on the practicalities. "It's a large yacht, then."

"Yes, it's one of those big-job yachts you could live on for decades and never have to set foot on shore if you didn't feel like it. Well, you might have to pull into port somewhere for suntan lotion and food once in a while. Even then—you should see the supplies on this thing. Anyway, we'll have to come clean with the press soon about the falling-off part of our story. The rumors are already flying that she was pushed off the side, or off the back."

"I think you'll find that's called the stern," put in Max. "The back of a ship is the stern."

"The stern. Okay. I'm learning so much already. Now if I could just learn who killed Margot and why. And that's where you come in, Max."

"So it was murder, no question?"

"Signs of strangulation as well as drugs in her system. Someone really wanted her dead. We could perhaps explain away the drugs as a factor in her going overboard, but not the marks on her throat. Too bad they couldn't raise prints from her neck in this case, or we'd be further ahead."

"Not a suicide." At Cotton's certain nod, Max continued: "All right, I'll do what I can, you know that, but really—this Hollywood and West End crowd is entirely outside my usual remit."

Cotton knew that was true. Max's time these days was largely taken up with supervising skirmishes over the Bring-and-Buy at St. Edwold's Church and acting as peacemaker on the parish council. He also had the more serious duties of pastoral caretaker to a large and growing congregation which was more and more in touch with the influences, for good and ill, of the broader outside world. And of course, there was Max's most recent incarnation as Awena's doting husband and Owen's besotted father, a full-time job in and of itself.

But in traces of Max's early life as an undercover operative for MI5—that was where Max's gifts shone through as far as Cotton was concerned, even in a backwater like Nether Monkslip. Cotton had not met Max until he'd arrived in the village as the new padre, and all he knew of Max's former life in MI5 had been what the Nether

Monkslippers knew, which was a hodgepodge of speculation, exaggeration, and wild rumor. Still, from knowing the man now, Cotton would not be surprised to learn most of the stories that swirled around Max were true. He was an extraordinary man of seemingly endless patience, knowledge, integrity, and bravery. Everything you could hope for in a fellow investigator, in short, and more. Cotton's view of Max bordered on hero worship, and he had never yet been disappointed.

Today Max was not wearing his clerical collar, a choice Cotton had anticipated. Max would consider it to be a misuse of his authority, somehow dishonest, to wear the collar in these circumstances. Wearing it also might boomerang, depending on the suspect. A lot of people wanted nothing to do with a clergyman, especially one asking questions about a suspicious death.

"And mine—it's outside my experience, as well," said Cotton now. "Unless you count my mother—who never quite made it to the big time in the West End, but not for lack of trying." Cotton's mother had been an actress. Or a "performance artist" of some sort, when times were lean and legitimate acting parts thin on the ground. The exact definition of her job title had been left vague during rare family get-togethers—or deliberately avoided as a topic, it seemed to Cotton now. She had, he gathered, been designated the black sheep of her baffled family. Cotton himself had only trace memories of her, having seen her infrequently as he was growing up in the care of whichever relative was willing to take on a small and unobtrusive boy that year, while his mother pursued her "career." His education had been sporadic and varied but miraculously well-rounded, and he could still quote the lines and lyrics of many plays by heart. His memories of his mother consisted largely of being clutched briefly in her powdery embrace as she gave him a distracted hug good-bye, smothering him in feather boas and the scent of perfume and Aqua Net Extra Hold, a fragrance that to this day filled him with an overwhelming sense of sadness and loss.

Max nodded, knowing the subject of Cotton's mother was fraught, and not surprised when he quickly moved the subject back to the investigation.

"Does Five have any particular theories?" Cotton asked. By prior agreement with George, Max was to downplay Five's role in the investigation, not mentioning it to the suspects. Certainly, the fact that the case had reached the highest echelons of the security services could not be penned into the official record—not now, perhaps not ever.

"Not that I'm aware," Max replied. "But I'm guessing the murderer was hoping the body would be washed out to sea, or would be so compromised that forensics couldn't discover much about how she'd met her end."

Cotton nodded his agreement. "That's a good guess. If someone had done the slightest amount of research, they'd have learned they were offloading her body at the worst possible time as far as the tides were concerned. The body was discovered the next morning, quite intact and little the worse for wear, floating in the harbor not far from this hotel. She was discovered by early birds taking their morning constitutional on the boardwalk. The Emersons. Lovely elderly couple who did the right thing and left her undisturbed until my men and women could get there. Quite composed, they were, as if this were an everyday happening, but Mr. Emerson had lived around the sea most of his life and for him perhaps it was nothing new. Anyway, we think what happened was someone ignorant of tides and sterns and things had a hand in it."

"That rather rules out the captain and crew, who would certainly be aware of the tides. Unless of course the killer—or killers—simply felt they had no choice as to timing. You can't leave a body lying about on deck and the most obvious way to dispose of a body on a ship is to tip it overboard. How difficult would that have been, by the way? From photos, she was voluptuous, but I wouldn't say she was a large woman."

"Dead weight is always tricky, but she was a small-boned five-foot-seven and slightly underweight for her height. Rumor has it she got most of her nourishment from alcohol, and the coroner found early signs of liver disease. And as I say, she was drugged."

"Yes—with what, exactly, was she drugged?"

"The tox scan showed GHB, lots of it. GHB wears off quickly, which is why testing for it is tricky on a live subject—ruddy hard to prove in court. But in Margot's case, she died so quickly after ingesting the drug, the evidence of it was still there, plain for the experts to see."

Gamma-hydroxybutyric acid. The date rape drug. "How bizarre," said Max.

"In this context, it certainly is. Forgive me for putting it this way, but in Margot's case the use of a drug for that sort of nefarious purpose would be in most cases unnecessary. You will probably gain a clearer understanding of what I mean by that if you talk with her stylist Maurice. But I would say it was administered so as to incapacitate her—for other purposes."

"So she could more easily be subdued and murdered. How awful. The poor woman didn't stand a chance." Max didn't like this at all. Murder was horrible by definition. The murder of a victim rendered helpless and unable to fight back offended his very British sense of fair play. "It's unlikely in the extreme she would willingly dose herself with such a drug," he added.

"Right you are. Also, there were no defensive wounds that the coroner could attribute as such. No wounds at all that couldn't be explained away by her body's being knocked about the ocean for a while."

"This is your new coroner, is it?"

"Dr. Winterbottom. Yes. Sound man."

"He has a good reputation; I would tend to rely on his judgment. I understand GHB requires high levels to detect postmortem; I'd be interested to know exactly what levels were found. But let's assume, as we are doing, that the drug was administered by someone with no interest in its uses in a date-rape situation. What does that suggest to you?"

"It suggests for one thing that a woman might be the killer," replied Cotton promptly. "Believe me, we are considering that—that it was someone who needed the drug to subdue Margot, because they couldn't be sure who would come out the winner in a fair fight." Cotton paused. "The female guests on board are in every case petite, short, or tall and quite thin—there would be no guarantee they would prevail in hand-to-hand combat without outside help."

"There was no attempt to weigh down the body?"

"None that we could see. If someone had tied an anchor or something to her and it came off, there probably would have been traces: rope burns or some such. No, someone just relied on the sea and the creatures of the sea to do all the dirty work of concealment for him. Or her."

"She was dead before she went in?"

"Yes," said Cotton. "Small mercies, I guess, to be thankful for. No water in the lungs."

"I think," said Max, slowly, considering, "that we have to consider that the death might have been accidental. Meaning, someone didn't actually intend killing her, but then found himself with a dead body to dispose of. An accidental overdose of GHB is not unheard of. Again, sending her overboard is the obvious way to dispose of an inconvenient body at sea."

"It's just possible," Cotton agreed. "The thing is, mixing GHB with alcohol is almost certain to lead to disaster. And finding Margot sober even on a good day would have been the tricky part, according to all and sundry. So maybe the person who administered the drug simply didn't realize how deadly it might prove to be, particularly in her case."

"The worrisome thing is that it's a drug so readily available, isn't it?"

"These days, absolutely. And a lot of people without a clue have started taking it to enhance their fitness, if that doesn't sound too crazy, which it is. It helps build lean muscle—using the parlance, they are trying to 'lean out' their body mass. Which really doesn't help your appearance much when you're dead. We've seen a rise in the use of the stuff, especially among young people, but pretty much across the board age-wise. It enhances sexual prowess, makes the user feel superhuman. Playing with fire, it is."

Max had a few parishioners who were struggling with all the usual addictions, even in the remote outposts in which he served. He hoped GHB wouldn't soon be added to the list. "It comes in liquid form most often, am I right?"

"Right. Nothing easier than to pour it into someone's drink. Since Margot was seldom seen without a glass in hand, as I say—nothing could have been simpler than to tip in a few drops. Again, the goal may have been to incapacitate her, not to kill her, but it's anyone's guess why they felt they needed to knock her out in the first place. It's not as if they were planning to steal her purse or pick her pocket, although that is another of the street uses for GHB."

They both turned at the sound of a knock on the door. It was a sound Max had unconsciously been bracing himself for. Patrice Logan was scheduled to join them for this conference. Uncharacteristically, she was a few moments late.

Cotton went to open the door.

"Ms. Logan, welcome. We've been waiting."

"I didn't keep you waiting too long, I hope. I'm afraid I had to make an emergency stop to powder my nose."

"Not at all, not at all. I think you know Max Tudor?"

Patrice emerged from behind the open door and stood just inside the room. She looked much the same as before, strikingly beautiful, with shiny brunette hair curling to accent her high cheekbones before falling about her shoulders. The same as before, except: Max could see that his former lover was heavily pregnant, and by the look of things, perhaps a month away from her delivery date. Max's mind immediately flew to the childbirth classes he'd endured when Awena had been carrying Owen, those instructional hospital films of bloodshed and carnage resembling footage of one of the world wars. Even though it had been a home birth, Max had wanted to be prepared for any eventuality. To this day, he did not quite understand how either Awena or Owen had survived it.

He shot a look at Cotton—*Why didn't you tell me?*

Cotton shrugged. But then Cotton wouldn't necessarily have known Max's history with Patrice, unless she'd mentioned it—highly unlikely. George Greenhouse certainly knew her condition, and Max thought he might ask him about his silence when next they met. Discretion could be carried too far.

Max collected himself and walked toward Patrice, hands out to clasp hers. Anything more than a sideways hug was out of the question.

"Patrice!" he exclaimed. "You're looking . . . so well!"

"For an inflatable dinghy, you mean? Which is how I feel. Good to see you, Max." Her smile was warm, unconcerned, unfazed; she looked genuinely delighted to see him—nothing more. They might have been people who'd met on a cruise ship years before and happily parted ways, with no hope of meeting again. But his last hours with Patrice could at best be described as icily cordial.

Pointing at her stomach, she said, "You've arrived just in time, as you can see. I'll be handing over this investigation to you, and to DCI Cotton, any day now."

Chapter 13

DROWNING

Patrice did not so much sit as collapse into a chair, flailing about to find a fulcrum to balance the weight she carried in front. Max remembered the same awkward maneuver from Awena's last months of carrying Owen, when she would stretch one arm back, reaching blindly for a chair or sofa arm, simultaneously grasping her stomach. Awena reported that standing up was no easier and that a hoist would have been welcome in the ninth month.

Once Patrice was settled, holding her middle with two hands as if a beach ball rested on her lap, Max placed a pillow behind her back.

"When is your due date?" he asked.

"Not until next month," Patrice replied. "They were getting ready to send in a substitute player anyway when Margot Browne had her 'accident,' and we had to make a last-minute change in the game plan, sending in reinforcements. That would be you. Thanks ever so for answering the call, and so quickly. I've filled DCI Cotton in on what I know, but it's too bad—I was really just getting close to figuring out what was up and now . . ." She trailed off.

"Another duty calls. Got it. But it's helpful to have a neutral party and witness like you to fill me in—someone who had a chance to get to know the victim while she was alive. And to observe her interactions with the others. What was your cover, by the way?"

"We kept it vague," Patrice answered. "I gave out that I was a troublesome ex-girlfriend of some high-profile actor and that Romero Farnier had taken me on board for a free vacay as sort of a gesture of pity. Or to take me off the hands of his high-profile friend, while keeping me from talking to the tabloids. Also that I simply needed something to do to keep my mind off things. Obviously, I wasn't going to be much use as some sort of deckhand, although I did volunteer to help out in the galley, chopping vegetables and so on, where I was not much wanted. Rumors were started that Romero and I were ex-lovers, too, although I quickly scotched that. It was complicated enough without that nitwit girlfriend of his fuming about, suspecting the worst and short-sheeting my bed or something. Tina's the jealous type, even when the object of her jealousy is hauling around several extra stone, is wearing a honking great maternity smock, and has to bolt for the ladies' room every ten minutes."

"He was in on the cover, was Romero?"

"God, no—not in the way you mean. If anyone was a person of interest in this investigation, it was Romero. He's rather a mandarin figure—a puller of strings, a maker of magic. King of all he surveys. Certainly that is the case when he directs his films, where he is said to rule with an iron fist. Well, that's his job, of course, and that's how he chooses to do it. But what we suspected him of doing also was drug smuggling—using the yacht and his status to get past the port authorities somehow. What we hadn't worked out is how. To get me inserted into the situation, Romero was hauled in by the California FBI—scared him witless, by all accounts. But then he was given some soft soap about how they were on the trail of a notorious art thief and only he could save the day. Played to his ego, you know. Dead easy, that. He was only told to allow me on board and pretend I was, as I say, some sort of Hollywood hanger-on who'd fallen for some doe-eyed movie star and was determined to have his child. Having failed at convincing said movie star that he should be hearing wedding bells, I was to be shipped to Europe as a consolation prize for my trouble. Initially, the plan was to have Belinda Bower—that's my cover name—to have her be a crew member of some sort, but once it became evident I could barely make it down the stairs into the hold, the FBI decided it would be better for me to mingle in my now-elephantine way among the guests, where I was sure to learn more, anyway. Sadly, that didn't prove to be true. I learned a lot, but none of it relevant that I could see. They mostly went in, night and day, for shop talk: who was starring in what film, who was bedding whom. Then the cry went up that Margot was missing. You know the rest."

"Do you know if Margot was a strong swimmer?" Max asked.

"No," said Patrice, firmly shaking her head. "No, she was absolutely terrified of the water. She told me so but I could see it for myself. She wouldn't even dip her toes in the little pool onboard, in case someone brushed by and accidentally pushed her in. You couldn't drown a fly in that tiny pool if you tried, though. The best I could do, anyway, was to sort of paddle around like a hippo doing the breaststroke. I watched her—she always took a chair in the shade as far from the water as she could get. Part of that was to protect her skin from the sun—she was a redhead and she really had to lather on the sunscreen; she always looked like an oil slick when she wasn't wrapped head to foot in blankets—but mostly it was to avoid the off chance that someone would pick her up and heave her into the water, perhaps as a joke. It's funny . . ." Patrice had her hands on her stomach and was rubbing the sides in a circular motion, like a fortune teller with a crystal ball. She wasn't wearing a wedding ring, Max noted, but that may have been part of her discarded-girlfriend cover.

"What's funny?"

"Not funny, of course, but now that I think about it, that's exactly what someone did. Picked her up like a doll and heaved her overboard. Despite her larger-than-life reputation, she was on the small side, shrinking a bit with age, too. Not more than five foot seven?" She turned to Cotton for confirmation; he nodded. "It would take no strength at all, really, for someone with a bit of muscle. How cruel . . . to think she went that way, after all—the way she most feared." Patrice gave a little shudder, adding in an absent way: "My mother was always afraid of dying in a fire but thank God, I suppose, she died of natural causes. It was a genuine fear—every time we set out on a trip we'd have to return home to make sure she'd turned the iron and the cooker off, stuff like that. We might be miles away, but she couldn't relax until we'd gone back to make sure. God knows where phobias like that come from."

Max guessed from Patrice's wistful look she might be thinking it was a shame her mother wouldn't be around to see her grandchild. He remembered Mrs. Logan, having met her once—she was a firebrand, to coin a phrase. She'd been an infant-school teacher of keen intellect, a known figure in the education reform movement, whose own three children had been her lasting joy. He supposed she'd died believing Patrice was some generic brand of government employee working behind a desk in tech or finance or some other safe occupation. Most of Patrice's work for Five had been so deep undercover even her closest relatives could not be told what she was really up to, or why she had a tendency to disappear for long stretches of time. He supposed the father of her child might know the truth but even that was not a given.

"I'm sorry to hear she's gone," said Max quietly. "She was irreplaceable. One of a kind."

He and Patrice exchanged small smiles of mutual understanding. Her relationship with the firebrand, while steeped in love, had been tempestuous at times.

Turning to Cotton, Patrice said, "We now are quite sure Margot was not alive when she went into the water?"

"According to the coroner, no, she could not have been breathing. There was no water in her lungs, so she was dead before she went in. To be precise, before she was dropped or pushed in. Possibly in addition to the GHB overdose there was manual strangulation as well, and *possibly* by a left-hander."

"There does seem to be a bit of overkill," said Max.

"Frenzy?" Cotton wondered. "Or just someone methodically making doubly sure she wouldn't survive? The hyoid bone wasn't fractured, says the coroner—'There was an absence of this finding'—you know how they talk; God forbid anyone should be able to understand what they're saying or be able to pin them down to anything. But as you probably are aware, that sort of fracture only happens in about a third of all homicides by strangulation. So the 'absence' means nothing. A tox scan did show loads of alcohol and of course the GHB that remained in her system, so it may not have needed much to kill her. It's a wonder she could stand, really, given the amounts that must have been in her bloodstream."

"She may have been too out of it to put up a struggle."

"Precisely. Candy from a baby, or words to that effect."

"I wonder what she was doing out there on deck, anyway," said Max. "It's still frigid at night this time of year."

"I wondered the same thing," said Patrice. "Was she meeting someone? Taking a constitutional in the middle of the night, without Jake? To get away from Jake? Had she and Jake quarreled? Because strolling about that time of night, it doesn't make sense, especially not given the weather. You'd only do that if you were storming off in a huff, too angry to think about grabbing a warm coat or to really notice the cold. Or, as I say, if she were meeting up with someone."

"We may never know," said Cotton. "If she was wearing a robe or shawl, it was torn off by the waves. She was found in the tatters of a gown that was inadequate to face the climate, to say the least. Anyway, if she'd been alive when she went in, it would have made no difference to her survival. The waters around here are frigid, even in May, especially at night. Say around sixteen degrees Celsius. She wouldn't have survived long even if she'd gone in still breathing. The body reacts to sudden immersion like that by making the victim gasp uncontrollably, drawing water into the lungs—so says the coroner. What happens on reflex is precisely what you *don't* want to have happen."

Cotton sighed and continued, "We find bodies washed ashore here more often than we'd like, but that's usually a question of a swimmer going too far out, someone who has underestimated the strength of the waves, or who has been caught in a riptide. And they're usually out there in July and August, when it's not so ruddy cold. Cold also makes the limbs useless quite quickly—even strong swimmers don't last long."

"And as I've said," put in Patrice, "she was no manner of swimmer at all. Given the conditions that night, even if she'd gone in alive and someone saw her go overboard, there's no guarantee they could have reached her in time."

"Yes," said Max. He shook his head. "The poor woman." Death might come as a blessing to those nearing the end of a long life, but Margot was someone no doubt with hope for the future, and with many good years in front of her. Miracles can happen: the call from a director who could revive her career might come at any moment. She was working in a profession built on hopes and dreams, a vocation that fueled the longings of those who paid the price of admission for a few hours of escape from their own problems. Someone had robbed Margot Browne of her own hope, and of years of giving hope and respite to others.

And it was his job now to help figure out who did it. He vowed he would succeed if he could.

Chapter 14

PIRATES

Max poured himself a cup of coffee from the urn set up on a sideboard by the hotel's room service staff. Throughout the investigation, that urn never was allowed to run empty.

He had just rung off the phone with Awena, who was leaving to take Owen to the toddler's yoga class led by Tara Raine in the back room of Goddessspell. Owen was a bit young for the group but, not surprisingly, was getting the hang of it already, moving quickly beyond the basic child's and cat poses. It must, thought Max, be genetic. Awena practiced meditation and yoga daily, crediting it with her ability to manage her myriad responsibilities with no apparent effort.

He turned now to his colleagues. "Can you fill me in on who is involved—who is in the cast, so to speak, as a suspect?"

"I can," said Patrice. "We're looking at a closed and rather exclusive circle of suspects. By 'exclusive' I mean exclusive in their own estimation. You'll see. Anyway, it's practically one of those locked-room mysteries you used to love so much, Max."

Max smiled. She had given him a collection of Father Brown stories one Christmas. He still had it on a shelf at the vicarage, next to his collection of Agatha Christies. What a long way he and Father Brown had traveled.

"That much is clear," said Cotton. If Patrice's knowledge of

Max's reading habits struck him as odd, he gave no hint. "Since she was killed on board, the murderer was someone on board. Ipso, as they say, facto. If you rule out pirates coming alongside and boarding over the rail, which I think in fairness we have to do."

"Do we?" murmured Max.

"In all honesty, yes, I think so. The crew may not be up to much but I think they'd notice a pirate ship hoving into view on the horizon. And we're talking about the waters off Monkslip-super-Mare, remember, not Somalia."

Max was thinking that so long as unauthorized persons boarding the yacht remained an option, this was not a proper locked-room mystery. But he said nothing.

"Anyway," Cotton continued, "apart from the crew, there were only a handful of people to be accounted for at the time she disappeared. A handful who could have committed the crime, I mean."

"Which was when? It would help if we knew."

"When she disappeared? Well, I misspoke a bit there. We know when she was last seen alive. And we know when someone realized she was missing. We know when her body was found. So there is a window of time during which she had to have been killed."

"I don't suppose the coroner could help you pinpoint the time. They never can."

"I know," said Cotton. "There is no person on God's earth more useless at pinpointing time of death than a coroner. Or 'the absence of life,' as they'd probably put it. Our man analyzed the stomach contents and we know when she left the party and what was on the menu that night, so that helps, but not much. He can't pinpoint the time of death except to say, basically: 'Not long before she went in.' He's giving it an hour or two either side of midnight as his guesstimate for the time of death."

"You say someone realized she was missing. Who was that?"

Patrice stirred. "As I've indicated, she was traveling with a young man by the name of Jake Larsson. Jake had great hopes of achieving fame and fortune as an actor. You know that old song, of course—I've got it stuck in my head now: 'An actor's life for me.' It was felt by all and sundry that a lack of talent was the only thing standing in his way. As one of them said to me, his hair gave a better performance in the Scottish play than he did. I'll let the others describe the situation for you in detail. But Jake, bless him, seems to have felt Margot was his ticket out of obscurity. This is the equivalent of an actress sleeping with the screenwriter to get ahead but that didn't seem to put a damper on Jake's hopes."

"Anyway," said Cotton, "Jake claims he suffers from insomnia and when he woke at one-fifteen in the morning, Margot was not in the room. He says she snored like a train going off the tracks in a hurricane so it was the absence of noise that woke him. Note the 'absence of' again. If his acting career fails he could try for a job as a coroner."

Cotton, Max again was reminded, was a child of the theater himself, the product of a helter-skelter upbringing by a feckless mother. Given the circumstances, his scorn for theater folk was as understandable as it was predictable.

"Did Jake go and look for her?"

"No. He says he went back to sleep."

"So," said Max. "We have Jake in our sights as a suspect. Meaning, we have only his word for it he went back to sleep. He may have followed her out to see what was up. Or he may be lying about the time he woke, trying to confuse the timeline for reasons of his own. Or he may be trying to insert himself into the drama for reasons of his own—to make himself appear to be more at the center of things. Who else is in the frame?"

"Me, I'd start with the director," said Patrice. "Romero Farnier. I mean, have you ever? Even his name sounds totally made up."

"Have I ever heard of him? As a matter of fact, I have."

"He does those gangbuster movies," said Cotton.

"You mean blockbuster," said Max. "Earthquakes, tidal waves, wars, alien invasions, car chases—"

"And a strict lack of anything like plot, rhyme, or reason," said Patrice. "The public just eats it up. And of course, being the director of that chaotic sort of thing pays well—it paid for the yacht, no doubt, and much besides. But Romero is the tortured-artist type. He wants to go all indie film, and now that he's rich he can bankroll himself— once he screws up his courage to go for it. Maybe he'll cast you as the lead, Max. It would be right up your alley."

"Hmph," said Max. "And who else?"

"Well, there's Romero's fiancée. I mean, that's her title, if she is to be believed; his casual girlfriend, if his version of the relationship is correct. Half his age, the usual thing—you know. Blonde ambition personified—or rather, ginger ambition in this case. She'd be a better match for Jake but Jake, as we've said, has not a lot going for him apart from his youth and his looks. Our little Tina has bigger plans for her adorable self than that."

"Tina—last name?"

"Tina Calvert."

"Would I know her? I mean, from film or something?"

"American," said Patrice briefly. "Stage actress. A few indie films. Ambitious, as I've indicated—to the point of ruthlessness. Mostly to be found off-off-Broadway these days, if she can be found at all. But she's counting on Romero to change all that for her."

"You don't like her," said Max.

"It would take a bigger woman than me to like her." She looked down at her stomach and laughed. "No pun intended. But you decide for yourself. I gather that some men like her, if in small doses."

"Okay. Who else?"

"We have a sprig of the nobility in our lineup," said Cotton. "A minor branch of a gilded family tree. He is descended somehow from the Germanic branch of the Windsors, the branch the family would rather forget about now, you know. They tell me he's possibly two hundredth in position away from the throne, but you never know: the other nobs might succumb to a genetic flaw to which he himself is immune. Anyway, I gather that is the hope from his side. He and his wife, the Baroness Sieben-Kuchen-Bäcker, appear to be skint and are living off their fabled connections. They don't have a permanent address of their own—they just drift around in boundless style from one friend's manor house to another friend's manor house, leaving just before they wear out their welcome. Again, I can't emphasize enough, their connection to the real nobs is vague, to say the least, but some people are easily impressed. Again, a triumph of hope over reality. That seems to be a theme of all the people on board."

"They are actors, most of them," said Patrice. "Or connected in some way to the profession."

"Figures," said Max.

"How so?"

"It would be a much more straightforward case if we weren't surrounded by so many people whose job it is to dazzle and blue the facts and skirt the truth. A murder involving a team of accountants would make a nice change."

"Nicely put," said Patrice. "Although why you think accountants are so blameless is beyond me. The man who does my taxes is a complete rogue. Anyway, that is precisely why you're here."

"By the way, does the baron have a Christian name?" Max asked.

"The baron? Yes. It's Axelrod. She is Emma."

"Nice. The baroness—would you say she was an intelligent person? A thoughtful one?"

"No. But she is full of thoughts," said Patrice. "Most of them silly thoughts. I don't think she ever read an entire newspaper in her life. She seems to have formed her world view by reading *Vogue* and gained her insights into the human condition from ads in *Country Life*. He is the brains of the pair, not that that is saying much."

Turning to face Cotton—no mean feat, as it meant shifting two stone to point vaguely in his direction—she said, "I have seen Max unravel the most tightly wound alibi; whatever Axelrod and the fair Emma may have been up to, Max will suss it."

Cotton nodded. "I know. There was one case he solved with an apple."

"Really? An apple? How did—"

"Please," Max cut in. Time was of the essence, and Cotton would have ample opportunity to regale Patrice with details of his old cases once this one was wrapped up. Max suspected that Cotton had begun making notes on the crimes they had worked on solving together, with an eye to publishing the cases as stories one day. That Cotton might see himself as a sort of Watson in the making. Good luck finding a publisher, thought Max. Most of their cases, while true events, contained elements so bizarre as to qualify them only as potboilers. "Who else do we have?"

"There's Maurice," said Patrice. "'Stylist to the Stars,' as he himself would not blush to tell you. He was quite close to Margot; I've seen for myself he's pretty wrecked by her murder. He's taken to his room here at the hotel and hasn't been seen about by anyone except the room service staff. When I put questions to him, he tried to conduct the interview with blinders on."

"I'm sorry?"

"A sleep mask, you know. He declared that the news of her death had torn his soul from his body and daylight now blinded him. Or something."

"Like a vampire."

"Actually, he seems to be rather sweet and to all appearances, genuinely devoted to Margot, if rather frustrated by her antics. I totally get that. Anyway, I finally convinced him I had to be able to look him in the eyes while I interviewed him. Although, of course, he thought we were just having a chat for old times' sake, not an interview. I didn't tell him the real reason for my involvement in all this. There's no need, since I'll be off the case soon enough, anyway."

"How do you mean, frustrated by her?"

"*Smart Women, Foolish Choices.* You know. Margot was low on survival skills, not to mention common sense."

"I gather," put in Cotton, "that if one of her ex-lovers were on board, he might disagree with that assessment."

"Oh?" said Max. "One lover out of how many?"

"How many stars are there in the night sky?" asked Patrice. "And a few husbands, too. Each one a bigger loser than the last, to hear Maurice tell it. And I will. Let him tell you, I mean."

"What about the crew?" Max asked. "Any connections there to Margot, or to the events surrounding her death?"

"Well, the crew wasn't exactly locked in the hold the whole trip," said Cotton, "but they alibi each other. We've made certain of that, of course, or as certain as can be. There are twelve of them all told, counting the captain, and they include the first mate, a couple of engineers and deckhands, a chef and sous-chef, and a stewardess-slash-yoga instructor. The latter is Delphine Beechum and she's the only one who routinely interacted with the passengers. Upstairs and downstairs, you know. She denies it but she may have had a bit of a flirtation going with Margot's true love Jake. They are closer in age and somehow they managed to give the impression to some of the others that something was going on there. Meaningful, longing glances exchanged before descending into down-dog pose, that sort of thing."

"But personally, I think Delphine flirts just to keep in practice," said Patrice. "I can't see her going for Jake in a big way."

"Was Margot typically part of the yoga practice?" asked Max.

"Good heavens, no," said Patrice. "Yoga at sunrise was not Margot's strong suit, although overall she was rather fit—apart from the drinking, I mean. I would turn up each day just to keep an eye on how things were progressing but in truth with this stomach I could only just about manage corpse pose. Such a dreadful play on words, all things considered now, but that's what it's called."

"So Margot's failure to appear that morning—"

"Meant nothing whatsoever. In fact, it is difficult to say when the alarm might have been raised under normal circumstances—she was fully capable of sleeping 'til after two some days. That's if they were simply standing around wondering when she might appear, which to all appearances they were not. The captain heard about a body washing ashore over the radio and decided to do a room check and a head count. *That* was when the alarm was raised. The crew did a thorough search and realized Margot was nowhere on board. This was well before the noon hour."

"The papers had it slightly wrong, then," said Max. "They had what they rather coyly kept calling her 'companion' noticing her missing."

"Not exactly correct," said Cotton. "Just in the area of correct. Typical."

"You can forget most of what you read about the case in the papers," said Patrice. "The majority of them paid lip service to her demise and then just skipped ahead to rehash old gossip from the movie magazines. And much of that gossip was second-hand rubbish. I would imagine Jake is busy recasting himself as something of the alert hero in this particular film. He's not troubling himself with playing the distraught hero, however. That would be punching well above his weight, anyway."

"Another thing," Cotton put in, opening up his laptop. "If we go by the tide tables, we're figuring she probably went in the water between eleven p.m. and midnight. It's another factor that meshes more or less with what they were able to discern from the stomach contents and with what we were able to wrest from the coroner. Remember, he said an hour or two on either side of midnight."

"I just keep thinking it's unlikely she'd be wandering the ship on her own so late," said Max. "Her companion Jake—he noticed nothing amiss earlier in the evening?" Max asked.

"So he claims," said Cotton. "But I don't honestly think he was paying much attention. And in his favor, he's not pretending he ever doted on her every move. So, where should we start? With him?"

Max shook his head. "Jake can wait. I'd rather start with someone who knew her well and liked her in spite of her flaws. We can work outward from there to her known enemies, if she had any. It sounds as if the someone who liked her was the stylist. Perhaps if nothing else Maurice can explain to me just what it is a stylist does for a living. But I'll also want to see the ship itself. I want to get a feel for the setup there."

"We'll have to go out on a boat tender. Perhaps tomorrow—I'll see what I can arrange and when. The port here isn't deep enough for the *Calypso Facto* to dock."

Patrice spoke from deep within the banks of pillows on her chair. "I'll sit that one out, if you don't mind. From now until this baby arrives, I'm staying on dry land."

Chapter 15

MAURICE, ACT II

Max found Maurice Brandon in room 202 of the hotel. He had, he explained to Max, been "positively horizontal, trying to come to grips with what had happened to poor, dear Margot." The blackout shades in the room were drawn and Max, not asking permission, walked over to pull them open.

He explained his mission to Maurice, eliding over his role for MI5—in fact, failing to mention it entirely. It wouldn't do to get everyone too excited until he knew exactly what he, Patrice, and Cotton were dealing with here. And at the mention of MI5, in his experience, witnesses could become either recalcitrant or overly cooperative, making up stories in a desire to "help" the authorities. He had never completely understood this proclivity but people did so love to be in the limelight, helping to catch the bad guy.

Having coaxed Maurice out of his bed and jolted him into cooperation with a few probing but gently phrased questions, Max found he now had only to sit back and listen. He first persuaded Maurice to splash some water onto his face, throw a jacket on for warmth, and join him in a stroll outside and away from his room. He imagined the hotel maids were anxious to get in there to do their jobs.

The hotel boasted an Italian-style rose garden with a number of quiet pathways that led up to the woods ringing the back of the hotel.

The main garden was reached via a terrace, artfully constructed to look as if it were following the natural contours of the land. Max imagined that in summer the flowerbeds would offer a full riot of color, the blooms nurtured by the mild coastal temperatures. At night the gardens would be illuminated by lights hidden beneath trees and bushes, making them the perfect setting for a midnight tryst. The two men passed tennis courts and an indoor and outdoor swimming pool to their right, finding in the center of the garden an oasis of scented peace in which to talk. No one was about.

Four chairs formed a semicircle at the foot of a marble statue of Neptune; Max took a seat and gestured Maurice into the chair opposite. Max had suspected the change of scene would do much to restore Maurice's equilibrium. He saw he was right. Maurice looked about him, breathing in the exotic scents of foliage.

He now was more than willing to talk; it was, in fact, as if he had waited his whole life for this moment. But after five minutes, Maurice had said little that could pertain to the murder, as far as Max could tell.

"Margot applied makeup like someone who was going blind in one eye," Maurice was saying. "I begged her—I simply *begged* her!— to let me help with her daytime makeup. On the set, I could get some control over her, of course, but in her private life? *Noooo*. No! I could only wait and hope for turquoise eye shadow to come back in style. Which of course it never never *never* will. And—"

"I see. It must have been trying," cut in Max, hoping to stem the flow. "So you—"

"And as for the eyeliner—well, there was no pot of shiny black eyeliner left in any drugstore in the land once Margot had passed through town. The cheaper, the better—she probably bought it in bulk. Appalling taste, she had, like a teenager experimenting with makeup. No sense of style what-so-freaking-ever. Elizabeth Taylor in *Cleopatra* was an exercise in understated nuance by comparison. Poor

Margot, if only she'd lived, I feel I could have brought some influence to bear. Don't get me started on the hair extensions."

"I won't," said Max. "Tell me—please—how long you knew Margot? How did you two meet?"

Maurice settled back into an open, reminiscent posture, crossing one trendily coutured leg over another, and tipping his bald head back to gaze at the sky as he collected his thoughts. He was wearing hip-hugging trousers of a stretchy leatherette fabric in a color Max was sure Maurice would call "eggplant." Max was not entirely certain Maurice was the last word in understated nuance himself, but still Max would trust him to have his finger on the pulse of whatever Paris and Milan had decreed for the fashion world this season.

Maurice took a deep breath, dropped his gaze to meet Max's, and said, "She was just a girl starting out when we met, so this was thirty-five years ago. Thirty-five years! No, I tell a lie, it was more. More like forty years—I can't get over it. We actually shared an apartment for a short while. It didn't last, of course. Too much drama. But one feels one gets to know a person well over that first cup of coffee in the morning and that last drink at night. I am probably one of the few people on earth besides her mother who has seen Margot without her makeup, and wearing a pink chenille bathrobe. That's how much she trusted me, to let me see her at her worst and know I'd never write a tell-all. Of course, in those days she had that perfect alabaster skin, and dark lashes out to there, so she could get away with very little makeup. Some redheads are cursed in the eyelash department, not to mention the freckle aisle. That's when you get that albinoish *Game of Thrones* look if you're not careful." Another deep sigh, this time accompanied by a shake of the head. "She didn't take care of her complexion over the years—I told her and *told* her that hard liquor sucks out the collagen and if you're going to sunbathe you'll end up looking like a roasted turkey—and of course the last little nip-and-tuck left her mouth looking so stretched she could play the terrified ingénue in a fright film without actually having to act. Which of course would have been a *bless*ing by that point, too. I doubt she could even blink for some months after that last surgery. The doctor was later struck off the list, you know. *Quite* the scandal. She—"

"You say, 'It didn't last, of course.' Sharing the apartment with her. 'Too much drama,' you said. Why is that? What was the drama about?" Part of the technique any interrogator kept in his arsenal was simply to repeat back the suspect's own words. It focused their minds wonderfully to realize someone was actually paying attention to what they said.

Maurice returned his gaze to the view of clouds passing overhead as he grappled to frame his answer. Finally he looked at Max and said, "There is no diplomatic way to put this. Margot liked men. Lots of men; the more the merrier. Tall, short, handsome, ugly—it didn't seem to matter. One guy she dated looked like the sort of troll you'd find under a bridge in a fairy tale, I'm not exaggerating. She would come home from a party, three sheets to the wind, with some guy in tow who could have been a professional burglar or drug dealer by the look of him. She liked a bit of rough, in other words. I hope I'm not speaking too frankly, um—what is your name again?"

"Max Tudor. Please just call me Max. I'm not with the police in any official capacity as a detective, you understand. I'm not attached to the force. You're not obliged to talk to me. It just may help catch her killer if you do." He felt he couldn't emphasize his non-status enough, but Maurice seemed to accept his presence without question. He found Max to be agreeable company and he was, as Max had noted, eager to talk, anyway. Max could have added that in his line of work as a vicar he'd been rendered fairly shockproof. The more the years passed, the more he had come to realize how true that was. His work for MI5 was practically a ladies' auxiliary tea party by comparison. One met all sorts of people as a vicar, people who had made all manner of poor choices in their lives and were struggling with the consequences. Or people who had in all their innocence been flattened by random tragedy. Those sorts of people were the reason churches— and temples and synagogues and religion in general—existed in the first place. The rich, complacent, and happy didn't need a lot of consoling, nor did they tend to heed advice, anyway. Not until it was their turn on the wheel of fortune.

"No worries," said Maurice nodding. "You're just here to help—I do see." He seemed to assume Max was some sort of trained psychologist come to calm the traumatized witnesses. Max decided to let him go on believing that for now, batting away the twinge of conscience that whispered how easily he had resumed his deceptive MI5 ways. It was all, he told himself firmly, in the greater cause of justice.

"Of course," Maurice continued. "Well, if any of the men Margot dragged back to the apartment were going to amount to something one day, they hadn't got started yet. A couple of times, things actually went missing from the place. Spare change. My checkbook. One time a frying pan—" and here he held up a hand to ward off questions. "Don't ask, no idea. But the next time something like that happened I told her it had to stop. I wasn't exactly celibate myself but I was choosy who I brought home, who I got involved with. Hollywood is a small town but it's not like a small town in Kansas—that's where she was from, Margot. She simply didn't have those filters that said, 'This man is *cray*-zy. Do *not* go near him. Do *not*, above all, sleep with him.' To her it was all 'Experience, Darling!': Live life to the full, my cup runneth over, my candle burns at both ends, and et cetera and so on. She was a hopeless romantic, Margot. *Hope*less. She seemed to think it was all research for some future movie role. I didn't try to change her or fix her or even advise her to carry mace with her at all times if she was going to date these bozos. I simply had to protect myself. I called a final come-to-Jesus roommate meeting with her after some jerk stole my first edition Jack Kerouac one night. Some screenwriter she'd met along the way. Oh, and by the way, he'd dropped ash on my new living room carpet. I smoke myself but I hate smokers when they're inconsiderate, don't you? Anyway, that really was it for me."

"Last straw," said Max. "I do see. How very odd. A frying pan, you say."

"Yes, perhaps you have a different word for it in the U.K."

"No, we call it a frying pan. I just meant, what an odd thing to steal. But if you're quite sure . . ." Max at least was getting a sense of what Cotton had been hinting at with regard to the date rape drug. It sounded as if rendering the poor woman helpless for such wicked purposes had hardly been necessary.

"Yes, I'm sure," said Maurice. "When you think about it, it's rather difficult to misplace a frying pan. You don't tend to leave it in the living room or propping up books in the bedroom. No, he stole it. I guess he really needed one. Anyway, there were plenty of those last-straw moments when I would swear I'd had enough. I really did like Margot, and I felt protective of her. Talk about a babe in the woods. I loved her in some ways, I suppose, like an older brother. But in the end she was just too dangerous to keep around. I gave her a month's notice—it was my place, my name on the lease—and helped her find a small place of her own." He shook his head. "Later on, she'd sometimes show up in the makeup trailer with a bruise or a shiner. I felt terrible. *Ter*rible. That had never happened when I'd been around the apartment. I'd no idea—my presence alone had protected her some-how. I'd thrown her to the . . . to the *wolves*. To the trolls. To the trolls of Hollywood, the worst kind."

There were tears pooling at the corners of the man's eyes, and his throat had closed over his last few words, rendering them almost in-audible. He fished in his jacket for a tissue as Max waited, knowing those tears to be real. It didn't mean Maurice wasn't the guilty party. Max believed he was close to Margot, at least had been at one time.

But the best of friends quarrel. A best friend can be standing in the way of something the other person wants—and not even know it.

From behind the tissue came a series of thunderous honks, the sound of a hundred geese startled into flight: Maurice blowing his nose. When he had finished he was somewhat more composed but his eyes still were red. He probably hadn't slept since it happened, dark room or no.

"I have asked myself so many times," Maurice said now, "if I couldn't have done more to save Margot from herself. Over many years I've asked myself—not just since she . . . since she died. If I couldn't have got her into therapy or something. Staged an intervention. Locked the booze cabinet. Given her a one-way ticket back to Kansas. I don't know. *Some*thing."

"Would she have listened, do you think?" Max asked.

Maurice smiled at him bleakly. "Of course not."

"There you are." The latest New Agey advice was never to interfere with the difficulties of others. A compassionate man like Max, not to mention a man with the need to see justice done, struggled with this concept all the time, while recognizing its wisdom: there was safety in not getting involved.

"And since there were never any real consequences—her career began to soar, there was always another movie, another man; there was always makeup to hide the bruises—it was difficult to warn her where she was headed. I wasn't sure I knew that myself. A lot of women would have killed to be Margot." He caught himself up. "Oh. Sorry."

"Unfortunately, the story you're telling isn't all that unfamiliar. Some women are attracted to abusive men—in general, to people they think they can fix. It takes a whole lot more than warnings from their friends and family to get them to start trying to fix what really needs fixing, which is their own terrified, lonely selves."

Maurice nodded eagerly, relieved to be understood. "Because

each one of these creeps, you see, was the *one*. Some one-night stand she met at a party that she managed to turn into a month-long stand if she was really unlucky. She thought she'd hit the jackpot if she convinced one of these Neanderthals to actually marry her. She was *such* a little fool. She would tell me all about it as I dabbed concealer under her eyes. A yellow-based pot concealer works best, you know. It neutralizes the blue. It took forever to camouflage the damage but you watch her films—you can't tell it's there. I really blended it in until no one could see. It's different now, with high-def film and all . . . oh, my God. Don't *even* get me started."

Max nodded solemnly, again unwilling to stop the flow of words.

"*Any*way," said Maurice, perhaps realizing that Max was not the ideal audience for makeup tips, "one time it was a swollen lip and there wasn't a lot I could do about that. Everyone assumed she'd gone crazy with the Botox. Anyway, the latest Misunderstood One was so talented, so smart. He just needed a break and she was going to recommend him to her agent, her director. Or she would buy him new clothes, get him a new haircut, whatever it was she thought he needed. It goes without saying she cooked and mended for these guys, and if they were late with a car payment she'd help them out—just this once, you know the kind of thing. It was enough to make you sick. Well, it made me angry, to be honest."

"How many times was she married?" Max asked.

"Do you know, I rather lost count. Seven? She gave up on the big weddings after about the third one and would sort of elope to Las Vegas to cement her subsequent unions. She seemed to realize no one who cared about her wanted to encourage this crazy behavior anymore and besides, once her career started to soar, she didn't need anything. I mean, how many toasters and coasters can you use?"

"No children, I gather."

"None she was aware of. Sorry, that's an old joke." Maurice's voice drifted off, and his gaze traveled to where Neptune listened, uncaring.

"There were rumors of a child, way back in the beginning, maybe back in Kansas. Or was it after she came to Hollywood? Sorry to be so vague. She never ever *ever* talked about it. Not even in her cups." He glanced sideways now and his gaze remained there. He sighed. "She would have sworn me to secrecy, anyway."

Max wondered if that was an admission he knew more than he was owning to.

"The child would have been given up for adoption, presumably?"

"I guess so. Or left with a family member. The only reference she ever made to the whole episode was a sort of Scarlett O'Hara moment when I overheard her telling wardrobe she used to have a nineteen-inch waist or something."

"Then how do . . . Sorry, but how is it you know so much about it if she never spoke about it?"

"Oh. Some gossip columnist got hold of the story, years ago. God alone knows how. The studio paid out to shut them up and the whole thing died down. It couldn't happen now: that's another thing that's changed, along with high-def film. You'd go broke paying hush money to the scandalmongers now, and it probably wouldn't work, besides. The genie has left that bottle."

"Was it a girl? Boy?" asked Max.

Maurice shook his head. "No idea. Sorry. And, mind, I can't confirm there *was* a baby at all. It was gossip, I tell you. I'm sorry I brought it up." He looked straight at Max. "You have a way of getting people to let down their guard, don't you?"

Max made a mental note to get Cotton on the case. Even if the records were sealed, if there had been an adoption, the police might be able to persuade a magistrate to open up the files in a case of murder.

It would take time, however. And so long as they were in the dark about what was going on, time was what they didn't have.

Chapter 16

ROMERO

Romero Farnier was in one of the grander suites of the Grand Imperial Hotel, as only befit a man of his stature. Max knocked and entered as commanded, to find the famous director standing on the balcony, staring out to sea like the captain of a whaling ship. The day was turning cold and windy; the light over the sea had dimmed after a brief squall, shredding plump white clouds into gray smudges. It all made for a dramatic backdrop, and Max wondered if the director hadn't chosen the setting deliberately, almost instinctively. Those who worked in cinema might go through life like that, framing every setting to exploit the maximum beauty and drama from the moment, which was not, when Max thought about it, a bad way to go through life. The Hollywood sort of crowd, however, might also keep rotating to highlight their best angle, to stand where the light was most flattering, and that sort of thing might soon prove exhausting to be around.

The director turned as if startled at Max's approach. Romero might have been in the company of bad actors a bit too long; some of it had started to rub off.

"This is dreadful!" Romero declared. "I can't tell you . . ." *Big sigh, furrowed brow, heaving chest.* "You are Max Tudor. That inspector person—Cotton—told me to expect you. Although what more I can say I just don't know."

"Do you mind if we sit down?" Max asked. "We may as well be comfortable."

Romero scanned the room. They were in the suite's living area, where several chairs were grouped by a carved stone fireplace, the overmantel of which rose nearly to the ceiling. But Romero led Max inside to the bedroom where there was another grouping of chairs and a sofa in one corner—a sort of large Santa's grotto. Romero pointed Max into a chair directly in the path of the sun, and the director took the seat opposite, where an angelic light from behind cast him in shadow. None of this struck Max as accidental. Harmless antics, perhaps—an automatic byproduct of the job at which Romero was reputed to be a master—but signaling a need for control over every transaction, a backlight to every scene whenever possible.

"Margot was always a handful," Romero began, unprompted. Max suspected that opening was rehearsed and unspontaneous, as well. "She was lovely, and everything a star should be. Imperious, you know: *grand*, in the way old-time movie stars were grand. Given to large gestures. Generous. But tempestuous as well. Tempestuous, yes, that is the best word to describe her. She drove producers wild as they watched their investments explode before their very eyes. Of course, now we are left to wonder, who did she rile so much they would want to kill her? It is unimaginable, and yet . . ." Romero's eyes drifted off to scan the walls for answers. His gaze caught on a framed etching of Durdle Door and paused there, as if captured by the cinematic possibilities of the limestone arch.

"And yet it is what happened," Max finished for him.

"Really? I was content to think it was an accident, you know. But knowing her . . ." He shook his head dramatically, a man burdened by the weight of too much reality.

"Do you know," Max added conversationally, to move Romero beyond his rehearsed speech. "I've always wondered. What exactly does a producer do?"

Romero laughed. "Mostly they get on the director's nerves. They are the ones who try to hold me to a budget, for one thing, but at the same time go about talking about their 'vision' for the film and wringing their hands over who should play the lead. Margot drove them into a darker state of crazy, the money guys. Because she simply doesn't care about anything that wasn't circling around Planet Margot. Didn't care, I should say." A pause. "If you believe in that sort of thing, I guess she really is in a place now where she couldn't care less what some producer thinks."

"I am certain that she is. But, I do understand it's a business where every delay counts," said Max.

"Yes." Having been diverted from his prepared notes, Romero's attention was already wandering, his eyes again casting about the room. As he turned his head, Max saw the barely visible wire that emerged from his ear: a high-end hearing aid, unlike the National Health Service aids Max was more accustomed to seeing, which were just a step up from the ear trumpets of old.

"Whoever chose this wallpaper was a lunatic," Romero declared at last. "So turn-of-last-century, or the one before that. If they had wallpaper in the Cheddar Caves this was it. If I have to stay here much longer I'll have people in to tear it down and repaint. Something in a soothing gray violet, to reflect that gorgeous light glancing off the waves."

Max wasn't sure if he was joking, but then Romero smiled. It was a smile of great charm—the term "reckless charm" came to mind—a display of great white teeth beneath a well-tended walrus mustache. He had the thick eyebrows to go with the mustache, well-tended also, but white where the mustache was dark. The shock of thick but receding salt-and-pepper hair came across as a compromise.

He was an exceedingly good-looking man. Max wondered why he'd not appeared in his own films, but some people, he knew, were happiest working the spotlight rather than being in the spotlight. Max himself was one of them.

"Would you mind starting at the beginning?" Max asked, to bring the director back on topic. "How long had you known Margot?"

"Oh! Well, I suppose we must dig up all that ground. Well. I met her in London, as it happens. Decades ago. She was performing in some play—don't ask me the name, it was utterly forgettable. But she was not—my God, she was not. I sent roses backstage. That's the kind of idiotic thing one did back in the day, to win a lady fair."

"I don't think much has changed," said Max with a smile.

"Oh, don't you? Well, that's sweet. But where have you been living?"

"Nether Monkslip, actually. And it is a bit off the beaten path. My wife loves any sort of flower, by the way, especially wildflowers. So tell me, what has changed?"

"Nether . . . oh. Well, these days—I have a daughter living at home, so I know." He waved a hand in the direction of a framed snapshot displayed on a dresser across the room. It showed a smiling young woman standing on a beach holding a surfboard. "They show up on motorcycles and practically drag her out of the house by her hair. And that's just the girls. It's shocking. Gallantry is dead. Anyway, back in the day, it worked, the flowers. Margot let me come backstage—this was before anyone knew who I was. Correction: before I was anybody in London." He actually preened, sitting up straighter, and saying, "Now I can go backstage pretty much anywhere I please."

"So you two began dating."

A minimizing shrug. "We went out to dinner a few times."

"That's all?"

"Pretty much," he answered smoothly. "I gathered she was playing the field and apart from the fact that I stand in line for no one, then as now, that sort of playing about is a bad idea. This was before the AIDS epidemic really started gaining ground, but even so. She needed to keep herself tidier—I think that's how you British put it: guarding the reputation? She needed to guard her reputation better. Margot was no good at keeping herself tidy."

"There is an impression . . . that is, I was given to believe your relationship with Margot was of more moment than that. That you and she were an item, at least for a while?" Max kept it deliberately vague who had said this to him, for indeed, no one had. It was more an impression he got from the director himself, from the type of man he appeared to be, and from the over-insistent tone of his denials.

"Oh, really?" The expressive eyebrows shot up. "And from where did you get that impression? Margot herself?"

"Indirectly, I suppose—yes. There's been talk. Of course I never met Margot, but . . ."

And right there—that was the rub, thought Max. He had never met the victim in this case. And so often, what could be learned from the life could act as a signpost to a hidden murderer. To how the victim came to meet up with his or her killer, and why the meeting turned fatal. To be able to see "in the flesh" the mannerisms, the expressions, even the hairstyles and dress—this showed an investigator so much about the victim's character, background, choices in life. Without that animation of the living being, that spark of life, one was left only with the impressions of other people, impressions often viewed through their own distorting prisms. The stories they might tell about the victim so often were told to benefit only themselves. The truth, ever elusive, became more so at second remove.

Romero sniffed. It was a sniff of great contempt. Of anger, even. He practically growled, "I thought so. God knows what some of the people from the yacht have been repeating as fact, without considering the source. Well, let me tell you, it suited Margot to pretend we had this big, passionate love affair, a love to transcend the ages, yada yada. She wanted me to put her in my new film, and my refusal, if there were one, had to look like an utter betrayal of our timeless love.

It was all bullshit but it was how her mind worked. Frankly, Margot could be a complete pain in the ass." He hesitated, then added: "May she rest in peace."

"You say *if* there were a refusal. Does that mean you were considering her for a role?"

"Oh, sort of. Maybe. There was possibly a part for her as the mother of my hero. A brief scene, the sort of thing where he drops in to say, 'Bye, Mom, I'm off to war.' Kiss, kiss, hug, hug; here, take these homemade brownies with you. You know. Anyway, Margot began pestering me for a part and it occurred to me she could just about handle this scene, so why not? She still has lots of fans who would gather round to make sure she was still breathing. Oh, sorry, I guess that sounds—*any*way. She could just about handle it and I was just about to say the part is yours when she started coming up with all these brilliant ideas for expanding her role. She could be dying of something and the son visits her on her deathbed. Okay, fine. Then she could have this long deathbed speech where she gives him lots of advice as he heads out to war. Not so fine. Then she thought there could be flashbacks to her youth—heavily backlit and shot through heavy gauze, you know, to make her look young. Absolutely not. We had reached the absolutely not stage when she died."

"She was made distraught by this? Upset?"

"Well, yes. I'm afraid she was, to be honest, and there was a tiny little scene with her at the party that final night. I may as well tell you because someone else is bound to. She was mutinous, alternating anger with a sort of manic hysteria. The usual thing. Only she was smashed, more smashed than usual, so it was a bit, well . . ."

"Over the top?" suggested Max.

"Precisely: over the top, even for Margot. Then she started in on Tina—accused me of robbing the cradle, of throwing her, Margot, over for a younger woman. I mean, I ask you. She and I had the tiniest fling decades ago and now I'm throwing her over for a teenaged temptress? I mean, it was ridiculous. Absurd. For one thing, Tina's high school years are long behind her."

Max noted that a couple of dates with Margot had increased in importance to a tiny fling. Overall, he felt they were inching closer to the truth—perhaps. He couldn't quite get the measure of the man. It would not be to Romero's benefit to admit a closer relationship, of course, and Max did not imagine Romero would stop at bending a story to suit his needs. He would not be the first person to want to distance himself from a murder victim.

"So," Max asked, "you and Margot had not resumed your relationship at any point over the years?"

"No."

"You never saw each other?"

Romero looked up from examining his fingernails. They were manicured, Max noted, the backs of his hands soft and white, with a light dusting of dark hair. They were the hands of a man who had never done a day's manual labor, or at least not for many years. He would have people for that.

"Well, of course we saw each other at parties and suchlike. Hollywood is really a small town, at least for those of us in the industry. Which I guess if you count the wannabes, is pretty much everybody. And Margot, while she was starting to slip to B-list status, still wormed her way into A-list parties once in a while."

Where presumably Romero Farnier was always to be found. Only at the A-list parties.

Max thought of asking him again if he and Margot had resumed their relationship at any point but it was just asking for a categorical denial—one that may even have been true. He decided if there had been anything like an affair going on, it would have made its way into the rumor mill, and it would be better to wait to confront Romero when and if he, Max, was on firmer ground. He decided on a slight switch of topic.

"That night at the party," he began.

"The last supper, in a manner of speaking. Margot's last supper. Yes, what about it?"

"I gather a lot of drinking was going on?"

"Well, sure. It was a pleasure cruise, not a pilgrimage. A pleasure cruise combined with a bit of actual location scouting to keep the IRS off my back. But the booze flowed freely. I am," he added modestly, "known as a generous host."

"It sounds wonderful," said Max. "All expenses were paid for your guests, were they, on this cruise?"

"Oh, yes, absolutely. For me that is the whole point—spreading the wealth among the people I find interesting, for one reason or another. I collect people, if you want to put it that way, and there's nothing sinister about that. That young writer, Addy, for example: if I can help him in some way I want to. He's got a real gift that should be encouraged. I grew up poor and I am well aware that luck comes and goes, sometimes quickly, sometimes overnight. I am determined to enjoy it when and as I can, and, as I say, to share my luck. I firmly believe that is how luck is magnified. It gets reflected back."

"I couldn't agree more," said Max. He felt he knew more about Romero's background from news stories than from reading Patrice's dossier on the director, which had served as a light refresher course. The son of immigrants to America, Romero had never finished high school, instead working alongside his father and numerous siblings selling items door-to-door—items that had mostly fallen off the back of a lorry. From such dodgy beginnings the family had earned enough money to start a small neighborhood restaurant, but with so many mouths to feed they often went hungry, surrounded by food they were forbidden to touch. Romero's escape was the movies, and he admitted to stealing from the restaurant till, risking punishment at his father's fists, to fund what he called his "addiction" to film. He also became adept at sneaking past the ushers in theaters. He made his way to Hollywood and later London, achieving commercial success with his first release. He bought a home for his parents—in fact, the entire family profited from the success of what had looked to be a prodigal son. Long divorced from, among others, Nola Lars, the famous Dutch actress who had appeared in one of his early films, Romero had only one child, the surfer daughter whose photo was the room's only personal decoration.

"I am assuming all the guests were at the dinner party," said Max. "Apart from Margot, that would be Maurice, Jake, Tina, Addison, and the baron and baroness."

"I believe the captain popped in for à moment," put in Romero. "And Delphine. She is technically part of the staff, but she's become more like family."

"Ah, yes," said Max. "The yoga instructor."

"She's a bit more than that. She is more like a cruise director, making sure everyone is having a good time. Like Julie on *The Love Boat*, you know? She was doing a fabulous job, up until all this happened." Romero flapped his hand, disdainfully wiping away "all this." "She's a nice kid. People like her. Jake for one and Addison in particular, I believe. But I don't know . . . he wears a man bun."

"Sorry?"

"A man bun. It's a clip-on bun. A hair extension. Ghastly thing. Leo DiCaprio was an early champion of the style. If we can use the words champion and style in the same sentence in this context."

"Um. So, Delphine was included in the dinner party. And there was a bit of a fracas?"

"A verbal squabble, nothing more. Like I said, Margot got it into her head that I'd promised her the moon, or I owed her the moon, or something. And she started taking swipes at Tina, my—well, my friend. I let her get away with it for a bit and then I felt I had to intervene. Margot finally went stomping off."

"Alone?"

"That's right. Boyfriend Jake *not* in tow, although she tried to drag him with her. It seemed to infuriate her even more that he didn't immediately jump up and do as he was told. I've been noticing on this trip some trouble in paradise between those two."

Truth? wondered Max. Or an attempt to point the finger of blame at Jake?

"Was everyone drinking the same thing at dinner?" Max asked. "The same wine?"

"I think I see where this is headed. Yes, we didn't have course pairings. I always think that's just pretentious, don't you? But then, I'm from simple stock. There were no courses to speak of, either. We had a nice table red for all the offerings, which included both meat and seafood. Several bottles of it. We all shared. So if anyone tampered with the drinks—you see, I'm way ahead of you; I have directed more than one movie with that plot—they tampered not with the bottles but with the individual glasses. And before you ask—no idea. It wasn't a proper sit-down dinner, you see. It's a big yacht but it really doesn't run to gigantic long tables for sit-down candlelit meals. This was more like a cocktail party with heavy hors d'oeuvres. People stood, people sat, people leaned against the piano, people lounged about talking. So tampering with Margot's drink, if that's what you're getting at, would be a snap. Assuming that happened. Of course, I've no idea. Just guessing. It's a lot like the plot of my film *Rampage!*—you've seen that one, of course. No? Really? Anyway, she was beyond plastered when she stormed off, but I'm afraid that's nothing new. Actually she didn't storm off so much as vaguely point herself toward the exit and stagger in that direction. She really was in bad shape."

"Margot, I do gather, may have been an alcoholic. And that usually goes along with a certain lack of judgment."

"It seems to go with the entire territory, if you ask me. The whole 'artiste' scene is not for me. As a director, I have to be in control. Yes, I'm an artist, but I don't need alcohol to be creative. A lot of actors and actresses seem to find it essential. It's performance anxiety, I guess. They're the ones in the spotlight, after all, with people staring and gaping, just looking for flaws and tearing them to pieces in some goddamn blog or other. But you know, when you're a director premiering a movie—that's pressure, too. And I know few directors who feel they have to get blotto to get through it. At least, not as a matter of course. There are always exceptions. Margot—well, I never knew her to be sober, I don't think. I also think she got worse at covering it up as time went on. What was she, nearly sixty?"

"Fifty-eight," said Max. "No great age."

"Hah! I can see you aren't in show business. For a woman, she was done at forty or even at thirty-five—her life was *over*. Forget Meryl Streep and the handful still in business at that age or more. Meryl is the exception—lovely woman; I'd give anything to direct her. And Helen Mirren—my God! Margot was nowhere near that level of talent even at her peak. She was worse during the live stage performances. One can see why, I guess. No do-overs, no rewrites. Shame, it is." He shook his head. "It's a real shame."

Max was wondering why, if Margot was so blotto all the time, anyone would bother drugging her on top of everything else. But the problem with alcohol was that one got to a level of tolerance where even a bottle or two of wine might not show one off too badly. That could go on for decades; then one day the body's chemistry simply changed. The liver started to revolt and it was all downhill from there.

"So, Margot stormed—or staggered—off after the meal?"

"Yes. The rest of us stayed on. No one was willing to let her spoil the party. We'd had over a week of that sort of thing by that point. It was boring."

"No one left with her—you're certain of that? No one followed her out, or simply drifted off to their own cabin?"

"Well, I don't know, really. The police asked all the same things, more or less—several times. I wasn't keeping tabs, you see. The room, and it was a smallish room—well, it didn't seem to get *less* crowded, at least not all at once. That's the best I can say. Anyone could have come and gone. And it was a party. *No one* was busy keeping tabs, I don't think. We were too busy enjoying ourselves."

This was not a new situation for Max. While a student at Oxford, he'd investigated the murder of a member of one of the famous drinking clubs. The trouble had been that everyone's memory of events on the night in question had been so hazy. This situation looked to be the same sort of setup. They'd all been drinking; no one could remember what happened when. No one had an eye on the clock.

Except, perhaps, for the murderer.

"Did Tina stay?" he asked Romero.

As if on cue, the sun vanished just then behind a cloud, casting Romero's face in darker shadow. "Tina Calvert? Well, yes. I guess she did. But she may have slipped out to the ladies' room. She never lets a minute go by without touching up her lipstick."

The tone was brutally dismissive. Max could almost swear Romero was talking about an actress in his employ rather than a young woman with whom he was sharing a bed and presumably a life. The tone did not bode well for Tina's future with the director.

"Was Tina angry with Margot? Jealous?"

Romero's answer confirmed Max's sense of the man's indifference. "What, you're asking if Tina was jealous enough of Margot to do away with her? Very unlikely. For one thing, Tina and I were no big deal. *Are* no big deal. Not worth killing over. And for another thing . . ."

"Yes?"

"Well, have you seen Tina?"

"I haven't had the pleasure."

"She's no bigger than a child, really. No way could she hoick Margot overboard. Simply put, there is no way."

Not without help, thought Max.

Chapter 17

JAKE, ACT II

After leaving Romero, Max wanted a word with Margot's companion, Jake Larsson. He decided to ring him rather than turn up at his door. As it was nearing the noon hour, Max hoped he might interview the young actor over a meal. There was no answer at his room, so Max called down to the front desk.

The helpful clerk seemed to be under the impression that Max had an arrangement to meet Jake for lunch, because he began to provide a rundown of the possible places he might have gone for a meal, ending with, "Of course, we're serving lunch now in the Green Room. You could try him there."

Which was where Max found Jake a few minutes later, sitting alone at a table for two by a large picture window overlooking the water. The room had been designed to provide as many ways as possible for as many guests as possible to enjoy the sight of sea and sky—a half-oval space jutted out from the building in a large glass-enclosed balcony. But instead of taking in the view, Jake was staring at the screen of his mobile phone.

Max knew a buffet breakfast was served in this room each day—the traditional British "fry" and more were included in the price of the hotel stay. Right now the room was nearly empty, but in season it would no doubt be crowded, providing a feast for people watchers: A woman buttering her bread with German efficiency. A baby demanding immediate release from its high chair. A teenager plotting escape from its parents.

Max recalled with something like nostalgia what solo diners had done so many years ago, before the invention of the personal phone. There of course had been books if you remembered to carry one with you. Or, if on vacation, postcards to write to send back home. And there had been simply staring at the view.

Max walked over and introduced himself, asking Jake if he could join him. Jake was taken aback at first, having no idea who Max was, but he recovered quickly when Max explained his mission: at the request of DCI Cotton, he wanted to talk to Jake in an unofficial capacity about Margot. Jake lacked the imagination to wonder what "unofficial capacity" meant. Or perhaps he was just eager to talk to anyone willing to listen to his story. Max wasn't certain such a direct approach would have worked with the average British citizen, so famously reticent. In any event, Jake tucked the phone in his jacket pocket and gave every appearance of cooperation, saying, "I can't get over it. It's like a frigging nightmare."

"I can imagine."

"I was just looking at the news online. This was what Margot most wanted in life, this kind of attention, however fleeting it will be. Most people under a certain age won't even know who she was. But that's not fair, is it? I mean, she *used* to be someone."

An elderly waitress came over to their table, handed them menus, and described the specials, all of which involved fresh seafood: scallops, mackerel, Dover sole, and crab. She offered that samphire was on offer, even though it was early in the season—samphire being a sort of salty sea asparagus—and suggested they share it as a side dish. Jake declined but Max said he'd try it. This was apparently the right answer, for she brightened considerably, explaining that it was a favorite of hers from when she was a girl. "Now it's gone all trendy."

She wore a starched apron tied round her thin frame and a cap like a maid from a wayside smuggler's inn; she looked as if she might have been serving food since the hotel was built at the turn of the nineteenth century. Her white lace-up shoes had thick soles such as a hospital ward nurse might wear, the better to sneak up on sleeping patients to administer a three a.m. dose of medicine. A name tag announced her name was Hazel.

She left to get their drink orders—bottled water for Max, white wine for Jake.

"She's still someone, Margot is," said Max. "But may she rest in peace after what seems to have been a rather hectic life. How did you two meet?"

Jake played with the knife of his place setting, turning it over and over on the table. "Oh, you know. The usual. Actually, my agent introduced me to her. She seemed to think it would lead to something, the agent. God knows what. I think she just wanted me out of the country for a while and out of her hair. It led to a murder investigation, but I don't suppose that's the kind of publicity Kara had in mind."

"You know the saying about all publicity being good."

"Do you know, I've never found that to be true? It's the sort of thing Tina Calvert would say but I don't think 'Out of the mouth of babes' applies in this case. She is only a babe in the sense she is just unbelievable in a bikini. Romero bought her those, count on it. The implants, I mean. Anyway, Max—may I call you Max?—anyway, with Margot I soon found myself taken up with more drama than I could handle, but precious little publicity of a useful sort. She drank, you know. Prodigious amounts. My father drank so I thought I could handle it; I thought I knew all about alcoholics. My mother also drank but she wasn't a patch on my father. I went to Al-Anon meetings for years. But this was one for the books. My dad looked as sober as a judge in comparison with Margot. I suppose that's what killed her. The booze, I mean."

Was it possible he didn't know? Max wondered. Jake had said "murder investigation," but even so, it seemed as well to clear up any misapprehensions.

"Her drinking did not cause her death," Max told him. "At least, not directly. The police say she was dead before she—before her body—hit the water."

"You don't say? You mean somebody choked her or something?" *Was that just a lucky guess?*

"It is possible she was strangled, yes." And possibly by someone left-handed like you, thought Max, although he didn't add this tidbit of information. "What *is* certain is she didn't jump. Judging by the height of the safety railing and her own height, she must somehow have been lifted up and sent overboard. A dead weight."

The waitress arrived with their drinks. She was a good waitress with almost preternatural hearing who pretended not to have overheard what she'd just heard. Her shock would be saved for when she was safely back in the hotel kitchen sharing the news, and swearing the staff to secrecy. Remarkably, they were all so well trained in discretion they would abide by their promise until the circumstances of Margot's death were made public.

The waitress took the men's orders—baked cod for Max, shrimp casserole for Jake—and treaded silently away, her narrow legs as they emerged from the big white shoes making her look like a character in a children's cartoon.

"So the murderer was someone strong," said Jake. "I did a few *CSI* shows—*Crime Scene Investigation*. You get that here?"

"Certainly." Max was a fan of the show, which came on in the wee hours in Nether Monkslip. Quite often he had rocked Owen back to sleep to the show's soundtrack of eerie electronic instrumentals, which his son seemed to enjoy.

"They were walk-on parts, sure, but hanging around the sound stage waiting your turn you pick up a lot of good forensic tips. I remember one time I was in this crowd of punks that discovered a body, and it turned out the body had been moved from where it had been killed. Stuff like that."

"Useful knowledge for the future, I'm sure," murmured Max. But the suggestion spurred a thought—after a body had tumbled around the ocean for a bit, wouldn't the normal pooling of blood, had there been any, be affected? Had she lain on the deck for some time before being sent overboard, or was she immediately deposited in the ocean? Could the experts even tell? He wasn't sure it was important but he'd ask Cotton to ask the coroner. He looked at Jake with something approaching, if not a new respect, some gratitude for the bits of potentially useful information that could come from the unlikeliest sources.

Jake seemed to capture the prevailing spirit, for he grinned at Max and said, "I do want to help here. The thing with Margot that nobody got was how endearing she could be. If she liked you, there was nothing she wouldn't do for you, or try to do." That tracked what Maurice had been telling him, only Maurice had put a somewhat darker spin on it: Margot, in his telling, was simply being used by one loser boyfriend after another. Did Jake fall into that camp? The age difference suggested it was so but wasn't it true that people found the missing pieces of their personal puzzles in the most improbable places?

Max saw the waitress approaching with their meal and paused the conversation as she set their plates before them. She had handled the heavy tray with the ease born of years of practice. He had been well aware of her earlier quickening of interest, but that was all the news of the investigation he was willing to leak for now. It was important at this point that the staff realize if they had any information—if they heard or noticed something odd going on among the guests—it was important that they let the authorities in on it. That this was not just a routine investigation of an accident, as the papers had led people to believe.

She trundled off with the tray stand in one hand and the now-empty tray tucked under one arm. Max returned his attention to Jake, asking: "And what exactly was she planning to do for you? Before she was killed, that is."

Jake stabbed a fork about his casserole, taking his time before answering. "Margot knew all the studio heads, the directors, the agents—everybody. These connections went back years but they still held. Let me speak plainly—I suspected she might be holding information over the heads of some of these people. If you follow."

"If you're talking blackmail, I think I do," said Max. He sampled the buttery cod, which was delicious. It came with a side of early spring salad seasoned with olive oil and an unusual combination of herbs that reminded him of meals at home. He wondered if the chef had got hold of Awena's cookbook. It wouldn't surprise him at all. Her book had quickly become the go-to vegetarian bible for the back-to-nature foodie movement. Her homemade yogurt alone was legendary, and it was said the chef at Buckingham Palace was serving her recipe for roasted brussels sprouts with honey-mustard sauce.

"I don't think money changed hands in some arm-twisting way, not really," said Jake, pausing for a sip of wine. Setting down his glass, he added, "At worst, it might have been a matter of, 'Can you spare a dime for an old friend?'—that sort of thing. Keep in mind, all these people we're talking about are loaded. It would have meant little to them to write her a check that might keep her afloat for a month." He paused and, catching himself up, he added, "Oh, God. Sorry, bad choice of word."

"No worries—these old phrases do creep into one's speech, don't they? But I gather the implied threat was that she had some kind of sordid information she might share with the world or the authorities, unless she was given, as you say, enough money to keep her afloat." Max stated the case baldly. It wasn't going to help Margot if he gilded her actions with fairytale interpretations of those actions. Much more likely it was—and helpful—to realize she may have come to the well too often to suit one of her soft touches. The thought led him to: "How was her relationship with Romero?"

Jake put down his fork and took another thoughtful sip of his wine. He shook his head, saying, "I never would have thought the English could get a decent wine to grow in this climate, but they've managed it. Anyway, you've honed in on a perfect example of Margot's technique. If she was putting the squeeze on Romero for money, it was so subtly done as to be unnoticeable, at least from where I stood. But she was really more interested in getting a part in his new upcoming extravaganza epic bio-spectacle. They were—still are, I guess—going to do what was essentially some amped-up redo of *Troy*. The new film was complete nonsense, of course, but the people in the bleachers were sure to love it. And I was in the running for a part. Margot may even have put in a word for me—I'll never be sure now. I just know Romero said I was in."

All this was conveyed with what appeared to be a disarming honesty. Jake was neither Margot's apologist nor was he really her companion in crime, if what she was doing rose to that level, which Max doubted. After all, what actress had not angled for a part in a play or a movie? He imagined that was the norm and not the exception. If she had spared a thought for helping Jake get ahead, that was to her credit.

This was all-in-all a different shading on what he had expected to learn of Jake's relationship with Margot. Pragmatic and self-serving it was, yes. And Jake was clearly ambitious. But none of it came across as particularly sleazy, not by the standards he'd heard were the norm in Hollywood.

"So she may have put in a word for you?" said Max. "That was nice of her."

Jake nodded. "She was a good old girl, she really was that. But

Romero didn't want her in the film, you see, so he wanted me to, you know, soft-pedal my good news. It made life a bit awkward."

"Did you think of the relationship as long-term?" Max pretended an intense interest in buttering his bread as he asked this, not wanting the skepticism in his eyes to guide Jake's answer. But Jake seemed unfazed and not in need of visual cues.

"Lord, no," he said. "She was ages too old for me. I think she knew that, too. Sort of."

"Did you ever talk about it?"

"No. Of course not."

Of course not. The golden goose might go away and lay her eggs elsewhere, to apply what Max acknowledged was an outlandish bit of imagery. But from what he knew of Margot, she would need the illusion this was a forever romance in order to stay. Otherwise, as Maurice had hinted, she was more than capable of folding up her tent and heading off yet again to greener pastures.

"Not to insist," said Max, "but why do you think she may have been aware of the age difference?"

"The references were constant," said Jake. He was rootling through the bread basket, which held an assortment of rolls and slices of fresh-baked bread, looking for the most tempting. "Some song would come on the car radio, and she'd hum along and then say, 'Oh, of course, you're too young to remember this.' Or something would come on TV and she'd go on about the actor, and then say, 'Of course, this was all before your day.'"

"Why do you think she did that?"

"Why? I think it was my cue to rush in and say something along the lines of, 'Oh, darling, don't be silly. You can't be that old—you don't look a day over thirty.' But I wasn't playing that game. She looked her age, a bit older if truth be told. And I wasn't going to gush at her in some gigolo sort of way. We had the relationship we had and I think it worked for both of us, even though it was never destined to last forever. Well, that possibility's gone now, anyway, so why belabor the point? As these things go, it was an honest relationship—possibly the most honest relationship I've ever had." He inspected a slice of bread, its crust golden and embedded with seeds, and reached for the plate of soft butter rosettes.

"Fine," said Max. "Now, on the night she died . . ."

"I was snug asleep. I heard nothing. I did wake up once briefly and she wasn't there. I realize now she may never have returned to the room—I undressed in the light from the porthole and sort of collapsed into my own bed; I didn't notice if she was in the other. I told the police this."

"What time was it?"

"No real idea," said Jake with a shrug. "After midnight."

"One-fifteen? I believe that's what you told the investigators."

Another shrug. The inconsistency didn't seem to concern him. "I tend to wake up about two a.m., sometimes three—a maddening form of insomnia. But that's not proof of the time. In fact, I avoid looking at the clock as it makes me nuts to verify that it's the middle of the goddamn night and here I am yet again, wide awake."

"So, wide awake as you were, you didn't get up for a stroll around the deck? To use the bathroom, to get a drink of water?"

"No. It's a rarity that I fall right back to sleep, but that's what I did. I completely conked out—that is such a novelty I remember that sort of thing for days."

Max wondered if there was a reason for this. Had *he* been drugged? Either by Margot herself, to keep him quiet so she could keep a rendezvous, or by the killer?

"I awoke the next morning, late," Jake continued, "and she was still gone. I thought nothing of it. With Margot, you never quite knew what was up."

"But you weren't worried about her."

"Not in the least."

Chapter 18

THE BARON AND THE BARONESS

Max lingered over an after-meal coffee with Jake. The conversation moved away from the investigation into a wide-ranging discussion of life on a film set. Max didn't leave for another half hour, by which time the dining room was quite deserted. He came away with a greater understanding of the jealousies and insecurities that fueled the film industry, thinking there must be easier ways to earn a living.

As Max said his good-byes and started to rise from his chair, Jake surprised him by saying, "I'll miss Margot, you know. I really will. She wasn't full of gossip and poisonous misinformation like some of these old ducks you see running around, never happier than when they're describing someone else's misfortune. She wasn't like that. Truth be told, her head was mostly full of concern over her new haircut, her wardrobe, things like that. But she wasn't mean-spirited—I guess that's what I'm trying to say. She wasn't mean about people. I liked her for that. It's rare, especially in actors."

Max had nodded, agreeing that it was an exceptional quality to find in anyone, anywhere.

He decided it was time for a word with the Baron and Baroness Sieben-Kuchen-Bäcker, the posh nobs on board the night Margot died. He was a bit puzzled by their presence, as they weren't part of the usual Hollywood crowd. He imagined they'd been included to impart a touch of upper-class polish to the already glamorous proceedings. As he sought out their room in the hotel, he called to mind what he'd gleaned about them from an earlier conversation with Cotton.

"You ran them through the Interpol database, of course," Max had said.

"Well, there's no of course about it—the privacy laws are in a constant state of flux. But yes, we managed to pierce the bureaucratic walls of both Interpol and Europol, and the baron and baroness appear to be who they say they are."

"A dead end?"

"So far, yes."

"That's too bad."

"It's odd, though," Cotton continued. "That business of their having no fixed address. The address they gave out for their passports was the home of a friend they were staying with at the time. That's not *really* illegal, of course, but strictly speaking it is odd, given who they are, or who they pretend to be. I guess I'm saying, for someone of their class and background, it is unexpected. Don't all these people have palaces and mansions to retire to, when they aren't busy frolicking on the open seas?"

"In many cases, Her Majesty's Revenue and Customs got hold of the mansions—back taxes, gambling debts, the usual. Then there's wood rot, legitimate heirs dying out: whatever stream of misfortune befell the families. Often the places were given over to the National Trust or English Heritage when the upkeep got to be too much, throwing tens of butlers out of a job. What address did they give when you interviewed them formally?"

"Another address, another friend."

"It must be nice to be so well-connected."

"Looked at another way, they don't stay in any one place long enough to put the friendship at risk. There's that. Plus, most of the places they stay *are* like palaces. It's not like they're underfoot all the time in some bedsit, leaving the cooker on and setting the curtains on fire, or letting the cat out and forgetting to buy fresh milk. Half the time I'd be willing to bet their hosts have forgotten they're camping there with them."

"It's not a priority right now, but we may want to look at these friends a little more closely if the investigation warrants. Perhaps they are hostages to fortune, people who are being imposed on because the baron and baroness have some strange and interesting hold over them."

"Blackmail, you mean?"

"I doubt people like this would use the term. More like 'calling in a favor,' or 'belonging to the same club'—the usual rubbish that keeps the masses baying for blood outside the palace walls."

It was odd, thought Max, how frequently that concept— blackmail—was coming up in the investigation.

"N.O.K.D. 'Not our kind, dear.'"

"Precisely that sort of thing," said Max. "Blackmail might be too strong a term but I have seen the nobs close ranks over one of their own kind, particularly when it's in their own best interests to do so. Look at what happened with Lord Lucan, or so many think—his own kind helped him escape justice. It's quite expected, when you think about it."

Now Max knocked on the door of the baron and baroness's hotel room and was shortly admitted by the baron himself. He wore a smoking jacket over his shirt and tie—of course he would have a smoking jacket, thought Max—and he carried a cigarette holder in his left hand.

The baron was as tall and elegant as an old-time matinee idol, mustachioed and dark-wavy-haired, and Max thought he must have fit right in after all with the yacht's party of beautiful people. He gestured Max into the room and saw him seated in a chair near the balcony, the door to which stood slightly ajar, admitting a cool after-noon breeze. This particular room overlooked the hotel's outdoor pool rather than the ocean—still a delightful view.

The baron tucked a cigarette into the ebony holder, lit his ciga-rette, and drew smoke deep into his lungs. Max, who had never smoked but once or twice when playing a part undercover, still appreciated the scent of expensive tobacco wafting through the well-ventilated room. The baron, he saw, was studying him closely while pretending not to, standing in a sort of dancer's pose: he cupped one elbow, holding the cigarette away from him and idly watching the smoke unfurl, as if watching smoke unfurl were his entire raison d'être. To Max it was like suddenly finding himself onstage in a Noël Coward play, an im-pression reinforced as the baroness now drifted in from the bedroom, trailing clouds of perfume. Was it Coco Chanel who had said a woman who didn't wear perfume had no future? The baroness had taken the advice to heart. She was tall, possibly an illusion created by her heels and her wafer thinness, as blond and fair as her baron was dark, and insubstantial as a dream. The fine bones of her face were beautifully highlighted by her pale pink rouge, and her eyes were tipped in gold at the lashes. She wore a clingy satin dress in a champagne color ex-actly matching her hair. Max stood politely and shook her hand, which she had languidly held out to him, rather as though expecting him to kiss it.

Were these two for real? Max wondered. So young and beautiful they were. Gatsbyesque, Cotton had called them: "Like Jay Gatsby, no one knows where he's from, or where his fortune came from. Presum-ably, he just inherited it. Like you do—or rather, as one does."

But Max was as strongly reminded of the couple in one film ver-sion of *Murder on the Orient Express*—the elegant count and countess.

"We have to go soon," the baroness informed her husband, who surely knew that already. "The Hugh-Nesbitts are expecting us at the weekend."

The baroness now dipped her impeccable blond head in Max's direction and said, "Mustn't disappoint, you know." Despite the triple-barreled German name, her accent was strictly upper-upper British class, as was her husband's, carrying only a hint—"We haff to go"—of their Germanic ties.

In the pages of background information Patrice had provided him, the baron and baroness were officially squeaky clean, visas and passports all in order. But she had noted that, according to the MI5 grapevine, their arrival on the doorsteps of various of the U.K.'s landed gentry was not greeted with universal rejoicing. And they had left one lord's house in rather more of a hurry than had been expected.

"I almost wonder if they're blackmailing some of these nobs," is how Patrice had put it, in a perfect echo of Max and Cotton's thoughts. But as Max reminded her, the U.K. is still rich in landed gentry and castles to pick and choose from, and as it appeared the baron and baroness made a point of rotating and spacing out the visits on their royal progress, it was possible their stays weren't as burdensome in most cases as might be imagined. Max did gather from Patrice that they never offered to pay room and board, and of course it would have been rather tricky for their titled host to suggest they do so. Although now, after a few minutes in their united company, he was willing to bet one or two lords had been tempted.

Although their Christian names were Emma and Axelrod, Max had only heard them referred to by their titles. "I rather gather they insist on it," Patrice had told him. "And you'll get much further with them if you play along, is my advice. His father, from whom Axelrod inherited the title, was named Alexis, by the way. He was something in shipping."

"The only Alexis I ever knew was a girl," said Max. "I baptized her last year."

"It's trendy right now; it's one of those names that can be masculine or feminine." She had glanced down at her hand, which rested on her stomach. "I'm thinking of it for the baby, actually. Since I don't know yet if it's a boy or a girl—I didn't want to know—it will save time."

Now the baroness ("Her people are something in Nottingham") was playing a variation on the theme of the fleetingness of life— referring if only glancingly to the tragedy that had befallen Margot. Then she got more into the specifics: "She was well-intentioned, I think. In that rather *earnest* way of some actresses. But really, she was the type to be ruled by her emotions. At the *mercy* of her emotions. And if she fell off the ship, well, it was simply her destiny. You *do* see that, of course."

Before she could get too caught up in some aristo riff on the inevitability of it all, Max said, with studied politeness, "If I could take you back to the events of that evening for a moment, would that be all right?" He had decided already that Patrice had been right: the best approach with these two might be to grovel a bit. They seemed to expect it.

A deep sigh and a great heaving of tiny brocaded bosom from the baroness. She held out her right arm and pointedly consulted her diamond-studded watch. The pair exchanged glances and Max was sure he did not imagine a spot of telepathy at work. (*Show him the door? No, he'll just be more trouble later if we don't answer his questions now.*)

"I suppose. If you must," said the baroness. "But please do keep in mind we are keeping people waiting."

"Yes, I know," said Max. "Such bad form. But your friends will understand, given the enormity of the tragedy." This was said in such a way as to graciously if firmly stifle further argument. "Besides, your friends are probably dying to hear all the details."

She seemed at least to understand this concept of increasing her value by carrying insider news of the scandal to the blue-blooded masses. Max was reminded of Jake's comment about old ducks who loved nothing better than discussing other people's troubles, and how Margot had lacked the inclination. It had been, thought Max, a surprisingly perceptive and thoughtful comment on Jake's part, although Max was absolutely certain Margot would have bridled at being called an old duck.

"There was this little party on board," the baroness began. "The trouble started there—rather, it came to a head. We—"

But she got no further before she was interrupted by her husband. "Much better to let it pass, don't you think, old boy?" This was the baron-as-sahib, a creature at large at a time when the sun never set on the British Empire. "Let the fuss die down? I mean, it's such a tawdry event and it involves such a tawdry person."

There was, thought Max, a great deal of acting going on here—perhaps even more so than with the professional actors on the list of suspects. He was offended and struggled mightily to smother the retort that came to his lips. Looking at this privileged pair, alight with carefree youth and beauty, he wanted to say: Margot was once like you two. She was young and beautiful. She also worked for a living when and as she could, rather than sponge off her friends as you do. She grew old and she probably had only a future alone to look forward to, and that is no crime.

"Murder is always tawdry," he said evenly.

"Murder?" they said in unison, exchanging glances.

"Yes. And the process of rooting out the person who is to blame for this crime you will find even more tawdry, Baron Sieben-Kuchen-Bäcker. The police questioning may go on for days, and lead to no end of fuss. Much better, don't you think, to help clear the air as quickly as possible?"

From his acidic expression, the baron did not take to the idea of being held up for days. But deliberately Max had used the man's full title, feeling ridiculous as he did so, even as he watched the baron flower under this sprinkling of flattery. To keep his temper with the man, Max wanted to avoid letting the conversation drift in the direction of whether or not Margot might be considered tawdry. He supposed some people would think she was. But she had been in a profession where age and appearance mattered above all, particularly for a woman, and her diminishing future prospects must have been frightening to contemplate.

Then remembering how terrified she'd been of the water, Max felt a particular repugnance for this crime rise up in him. How closed-in her life seemed to have become, and how sad her ending. Still, up until the end, Margot kept up appearances as best she could. She was not one to go down without a fight.

Which returned him to the subject at hand. Had there been a quarrel on the yacht, a fight that had ended in her death? He asked the baron and baroness (the B & B, as Patrice liked to call them) if they had seen any signs of the trouble ahead that night.

"No," said the baron flatly. "She drank too much at dinner, as she always did, but I saw nothing like an argument with anyone building, if that's what you mean. Anyone apart from Romero, of course. But to be quite honest, we were used to that. She did keep complaining of the cold. Shivering and carrying on. Finally she left, presumably to find a coat or something to throw around her shoulders."

"No one offered her a jacket or their own shawl?"

"No. Why on earth would they? She was just complaining to complain. The room wasn't cold. And besides, she didn't ask."

"So, again, you saw nothing out of the ordinary?"

The baron shook his head.

"Oh, but, darling," said his wife. "Did you not see how her little paramour looked at her? One could tell he felt he was in for rather a long night and he didn't look as if he enjoyed the prospect, not one bit."

"No, my dear, I didn't notice. He is not altogether the sort one does notice."

"*Ya–h–s–s*," she drawled. "A good-looking example of his type, of course, but quite, *quite* vulgar. May I have one of your ciggies?"

Her husband withdrew a packet, retrieved a cigarette, and handed it to his wife. Max observed them as they went through an elaborate ritual of lighting and puffing and smiling at one another and waving the smoke away, mirroring each other in their graceful postures, their bodies tilted slightly back at the waist. The cigarette was unfiltered and the baroness delicately pinched away a shred of tobacco from her tongue. She was eyeing Max appreciatively now, stretching her swan-like neck for a better view.

"Was there anything else? Of course we're too, too anxious to help, but we have these people waiting—so awkward. You do see." How many times was she going to tell him about her waiting friends?

"Was there a particular topic of conversation at that last dinner?"

"Oh, I don't know," said the baroness vaguely. "The weather. Yes, someone—I think it was the captain—started in on the weather. How they'd had these dreadful storms last year and everyone was praying the El Niño or whatever it was that caused it wouldn't return again. Yes, it was the captain, I do recall now. His entire conversation is taken up with naval topics like knots and velocity and so on and so forth. I can barely understand what the man is saying half the time, can you, darling?"

"No, my dear, I cannot."

"If I'm honest, the only one I can even stand is that little writer with the topknot. Addison. He's promised to take a look at mummy's memoirs. He thinks there might be a market for that sort of thing. He says he'll speak to his agent about it."

"I thought he was a scriptwriter," said her husband.

"Playwright, scriptwriter, I don't know, what's the difference? It's all writing—all make-believe, as with all these show-business types we're surround by at the moment. They are make-believers with no work ethic whatsoever. Addy at least does try very hard. Every time you see him, he's got the Moleskine out—scribble, scribble. Or he's banging away at that laptop. At the moment he's writing a novel, I think. Or maybe it's a biography."

"Oh, ye gods, yes. I'd forgotten. A book about The Margot, is it not?"

"Yes, darling. The mind simply *reels*."

"If we could turn our minds for the moment to the night in question," put in Max.

"I say—Mr. Tudor, is it?—I wonder when we'll be allowed to go back onto the yacht to retrieve some more things?" the baron wanted to know. "We're running low on proper clothing, particularly evening wear."

"I even left behind the necklace I always wear with this frock," the baroness added.

Max stifled a splutter of annoyance and willed his expression into even, steady lines, like a man watching a mildly amusing video on the Internet. He had the distinct impression the baron was somehow mistaking him for a member of the hotel staff, or perhaps a constable sent by DCI Cotton to fill them both in on matters of routine. It was again taking an effort for Max to keep his composure around the B & B. Margot was barely pulled out of the water and onto a slab in the morgue and these two were worried whether they had the right shoes and jewelry to go with their evening costumes.

The baroness had dropped one clue, however, for what it was worth: anyone who had lived through the past winter's savage cold weather wouldn't soon forget it or dismiss it so lightly. Max imagined the couple had not been in the area, no doubt having found themselves a nice warm spot in which to ride out the bad times. There was a fading tan line at the baroness's neckline that confirmed his guess that she had lolled about a tropical resort in the not-too-distant past. Possibly one of their many put-upon friends wintered in the Bahamas.

"How did you happen to be invited aboard the yacht?" Max asked.

"We met Romero in Monte, wasn't it, darling?"

The baron looked to his wife for confirmation, and she nodded, adding, "He was quite insistent we come aboard as his guests. It seemed a pleasant way to travel back to England. Little did we know! If we'd known Margot was in his entourage we would probably have refused the invitation."

"We would most certainly have refused," put in her husband. "A famous film director is one thing. That woman was—well, she was trouble from the start. And now look what it's all come to."

"It was purely an accidental meeting, then? You didn't know Romero, or Margot, from before?"

"Really," said the baron, "do we look like we would know people in show business?"

Max had to admit they did not.

"If we do see a film it's a private screening in someone's home," the baroness put in. "I mean, really."

Sorry I asked. "So, the only topic that evening was the weather?"

"I think Romero was going on about his *moo*-vie." Here, from the baron, an exaggeration of Romero's American accent—complete with a surprisingly adept imitation of his macho mannerisms. "His *film*, you know. And Margot started banging on about how she'd be perfect for the part. You could tell, he just did *not* want to have that conversation, not for a moment, but nothing was going to stop The Margot from getting what she wanted. Or from trying until he threw her overb— Oh, wait. I didn't mean that literally, of course. She just fell off the side, of course. We all know that. Murder? Preposterous."

"Did you see her at any time after the dinner? On deck or any-where else?"

The baron hesitated, shrugged, then seemed to realize there was nothing to be gained by a lie.

"We decided at some point to pop up on deck for some fresh air. We saw her there. Weaving about. She collapsed into a deck chair. We pretended not to see her and walked away. It was just embarrassing, you know. For us. I don't think Margot had enough sense to be embarrassed by the state she was always in."

"What time was this?"

They exchanged glances, and the baron said, "Around midnight?" A look passed between him and his baroness that Max could not read. It was done in the sort of shorthand adopted by a long-term couple.

"That's right," she said. "Maybe before?"

"And that was all?" Max asked. "Think hard, please. It could be important."

They looked at each other, and then they both looked at him.

"That was all," they said in unison.

Chapter 19

TINA AND CO.

Tina was aptly named, as she immediately made one think of all variations on the word "tiny." Her given name, Max knew, was Christina, but the nickname fit her perfectly.

Petite, diminutive, waiflike, she couldn't have weighed ninety-five pounds sopping wet and wearing a towel, despite the obvious implants to which Jake had referred: she had the exaggerated sort of bosom seen on mermaid figureheads of old whaling ships. A perfectly formed woman-child in miniature. Max imagined that for an actress her stature might be a drawback, as she would forever be cast as the ingénue, or even the voluptuous teenage daughter. A sort of curse of *The Flying Nun*.

Although Max knew she was thirty-three, she could pass for sixteen. A rather sultry and vixenish sixteen, hair coiled provocatively on her breasts and eyes outlined Cleopatra-style, but still. She had cinched the waist of her blue polka-dot dress with a wide red belt to accentuate her figure; around her short slender neck she wore a nautical-themed blue scarf. He wondered idly if she had to shop in the girls' departments at clothing stores, for while the wearer of the dress was provocative by nature, it seemed the dress itself was rather childish. But she had somehow managed to find ruby red heels to compensate for her short stature, and those surely had not come from the children's department.

There's no place like home, Max thought idly.

There were many such young women in his parish, girls who seemed to have leap-vaulted straight from childhood to middle age, not bothering to stop to enjoy adolescence—if, he acknowledged, "enjoy" and "adolescence" were terms to be used in the same breath. He wondered what his Owen would be like as a teenager. Right now he was the most agreeable baby on the planet, too young to have formed opinions in opposition to those of his clueless parents, or to worry about anything except his next meal. Long may it last, Max prayed.

As for Tina Calvert, she was eyeing Max up and down, not bothering to be subtle in her obvious appreciation. Max was used to it. He smiled genially.

This, her returning smile seemed to say, was more like it. She even put away her emery board to focus on this vision before her. She widened her eyes, saying, "The last person to have questioned me about Margot was some policewoman. She was not half so interesting." Probable meaning: I couldn't manipulate her, and I did try. Max smiled to himself. Sergeant Essex would not have stood for a moment of nonsense from this woman. How very tiresome for Tina. "But I've told all I know, and she wrote it all down. Every word. You could just read her notes. Then we could move on to something more exciting to talk about. I mean, poor old Margot and all that. But it wasn't all that unexpected, was it? Her dying like that, I mean."

"Really?" said Max. "Why do you say that?"

"Don't I know you from somewhere?" she asked. Not, Max felt, because she was being evasive, but because Margot Browne and her murder simply didn't interest Tina as a topic for long. It was difficult to bring Tina into focus as a suspect, in fact. For her to have killed Margot, or to have had anything to do with her death, would have required an outward shift in focus—a turning away from the self of which Max already felt Tina to be incapable.

Of course if her intense self-interest were threatened, Margot might have needed, in Tina's view, to be disposed of. A minor inconvenience, merely: someone to be edited off the playlist.

"Were we in a play together or something?" she wondered aloud. "Although, I don't think I'd have forgotten you." She returned his unwavering smile with a practiced, perky one of her own. Max imagined "perky" was Tina's default setting. It went with the tiny waist and the rather elfin features, the upturned nose. Now she swung one leg over another, jiggling a shoe off the toes of one foot, as if impatient to hear what he had to say—which he very much doubted: after only a few minutes in her company, he imagined any conversation that did not center on Tina and her doings would not be a conversation worth having, in Tina's opinion. He already felt her attention drifting away, her eyes looking at a point over his shoulder. Her face held a vague expression of concern, but he imagined she might only be trying to recall if she'd screwed the top back onto her bottle of nail varnish.

"Well, Ms. Calvert," he began. "Thank you for being willing to take the time to talk with me."

"Don't mention it," she said, returning her gaze to meet his. "Pleasure, I'm sure." She spoke in an American accent, a drawl he was attempting to pinpoint geographically. Finally, he asked, "Houston?"

"Wow," she said. "You're good. Or did the police tell you?"

He shook his head. In fact, the file on Tina only gave her birthplace, which was Kentucky. But he'd spent time in Houston, seconded to follow a case of antiquities fraud: a papyrus for sale that had been stolen from the British Museum—a papyrus that turned out to be fake. The museum had not been as grateful for this discovery as they might have been.

"When I think of what I've paid voice coaches to get rid of that accent," she fussed.

"I do regret the occasion that prompts this conversation, however."

"Huh?"

"Margot. Margot Browne. Her death."

"Oh." *That*.

"As I'm sure you can appreciate, the police are gravely concerned to have had this matter turn up in their bailiwick. I've been asked in an unofficial capacity to talk with the people closest to Margot, to try to get some sense of who she was and how this might have happened to her." This was of course balderdash but no one so far had really questioned it, the possible exception being Maurice. Maurice, Max had decided, was altogether a more inquisitive sort than the others he had spoken with—more perceptive, more other-focused, more *there*.

Tina confirmed his impression of her disinterest by saying, "I don't really see why you'd bother. I mean, someone might have been doing her a favor, you ask me, darlin'. But the chances are huge she simply got trashed and, deciding she was done for, jumped overboard."

"Well, how interesting," said Max, returning her perky smile with one of his own. "Why do you feel that is true?"

A shrug, accompanied by a little grimace that might, on anyone else, have expressed pity. Max thought she was probably an appalling actress, trying to mimic emotions she clearly did not—perhaps could not—feel. The very definition, he recalled, of a psychopath, someone able to don a cloak of normalcy just long enough to get what he or she wanted from someone else. "She was washed up, done for in the business. She was wasted half the time. And going broke, or so I heard."

"From whom did you hear that?"

"Oh, I can't be expected to remember everything, can I? I have enough trouble memorizing my lines."

Max didn't doubt that for a moment. She looked down, examining the ankle emerging from the dangling shoe. She had slender calves that he was clearly being invited to admire. He kept his gaze steadfastly on her face. Annoyed by his obstinate refusal to play along, she shoved the foot back in the shoe and placed both her feet firmly on the ground.

"It was just some gossip at a party in Malibu," she went on sulkily. "Romero was going to cast her in a small part in an upcoming film of his. A pity casting. You know—throwing a dog a bone. The film was all crewed up, ready to go. She turned it down! Got all huffy drama-queenish with him; gave him a bunch of grief that she wasn't being offered the lead. She said she needed the cash. As if *that* was *ever* going to happen—her getting the lead role. The lead was already cast, that's what CDs are for, anyway—that's like, casting directors?" she added helpfully. Max nodded to show he was following. "But that was beside the point." A brief pause here while Tina held out one hand to inspect her blood-red manicure. "Margot was about a hundred *thousand* years too old for the role. There are Egyptian mummies more qualified."

"I imagine that's difficult for a talented actress. The whole age-and-beauty thing. The industry does seem to be skewed in favor of younger women. It's strange that men don't seem to face the same barriers."

Finally he'd arrived at a topic that roused her attention. She leaned forward, one finger tapping her knee for emphasis. "Tell me about it. Robert Redford might be stuffed like a hunting trophy one day and they'll still cast him in favor of an actress the same age. Half his age, even. I'm lucky I look so young . . . or so some people say."

Bat, bat went the eyelashes, the cupid's-bow lips curling into a simper. This was clearly Max's cue to exclaim gallantly over her youthful appearance, but he decided to let that opportunity pass. When he said nothing and began searching his pockets for his notebook, she added crossly, "Besides. Whoever said Margot was a talented actress?"

"A seasoned actress might be a better expression," said Max.

That got a laugh out of her, a shrieking giggle that seemed to ricochet off the sparkling floor-to-ceiling windows of her room. "Seasoned," she said. "That's rich. Like a side of marinated beef, yes she was."

"You didn't like her, did you?"

"You try liking someone who hates you. I'm not trying out for sainthood here."

"Hates? What did she have to hate you for?"

"Oh, puh-*leeze*." He had earned a "what a doofus" stare. "She and Romero were an item once, but not for long. Nothing ever seemed to last for long with Margot, if the gossip is true. Which it is. Either she'd get bored and move on or they would, the men—in most cases, they would."

"I don't follow," said Max, all guileless wonder. He could guess why, but he wanted to hear her spin things out for him. "Why would she hate you?"

She looked down at herself, at the sheer perfection of her tiny body, as if this explained everything. Since Max didn't seem to be taking the bait, she said, very slowly and carefully, explaining the ways of the world to a child, "Because she was *jeal*-ous. Of *course* she was jealous. We were so happy together, Romero and I. So perfect a couple in every way—way more perfect than Brad and Angelina ever were, with all those freaking kids hanging off them all the time. The world could see that we were *so* happy. And here was old, worn-out, schlumpy Margot. The old bag who had missed her chance with Romero long ago and was now too old for it, past it all. Bitter and angry. She probably cried herself to sleep at night, wishing she were in my place."

Jesus wept. That would of course be Tina's view of things but Max was still exasperated to hear this judgment on Margot pronounced like . . . well, like the gospel truth. Besides, this description of endless bliss was rather at odds with what he'd heard from Romero himself.

Max thought he could almost bring himself to pity Tina in her turn, but that was another opportunity he was going to let go by.

"Tell me about that night, the night she disappeared."

"Disappeared, is it now? I mean, clearly, she got rat-faced drunk and jumped or fell off the yacht. I don't see what all the fuss is about. The wonder is she lasted as long as she did—she'd been like that the whole trip. Just draping herself over Romero, trying to make him feel guilty, and drinking like she had a hollow leg. That's what my daddy used to call it. He'd say someone drank like they had a hollow leg. He was so funny, my daddy. I get my acting chops from him."

He tried again to break through the impenetrable mass of ego that was Tina Calvert, feeling like a man in need of a battering ram. "Was there anything special about that particular night? Did anything out of the ordinary happen?"

She considered. After a moment she offered, rather grandly, "There was a big fuss coming from the galley. But that wasn't unusual. The chef is, like, super high maintenance. Carries on when he can't find his favorite paring knife or something. It's a small ship, as these things go. I mean, we were in an enclosed space. So we could always hear the tantrums."

"This was worse than usual?"

"Sort of. Yeah. I guess. Romero had to go have a word with him. Not for the first time. These chef types—they can be so temperamental."

Like actors? "What exactly could you hear him complaining about?"

"I don't know, do I?" She laughed. "I don't speak much French—I never saw the point of foreign languages when the whole world speaks English. But you could tell he was angry. Something about the glasses was wrong."

"The glasses? The drinking glasses?"

"Uh huh. I guess. Any more questions? I have an appointment for a manicure in an hour." Catching herself at last, and perhaps realizing this was a frivolous comment to make given the occasion, she added: "Life must go on. I have to look good for the party. The local film premiere? You never know who might be there. See and be seen. You know." But she ruined even such a lame excuse with that cupid's-bow smirk.

Max's one remaining question, he supposed, was what an obviously intelligent and evidently successful man like Romero was doing hanging about with such a nincompoop as Tina. But that was, he conceded, an unchristian and unworthy thought. It was his job as a vicar to find the good in everyone. It was always there, even if in some cases one had to dig a little deeper. He merely thanked her for her time, pretending she had been wonderfully helpful.

Which in fact she had been, as things later turned out, but without intending to be.

Max found the director lounging by the indoor pool. An opened bottle of champagne was swaddled in a white cloth in a silver cooler at his elbow, alongside a stack of scripts. He was perusing one intently when Max approached.

"The dreck they send me these days," said Romero. "You wouldn't believe it. Albino bank robbers. Two of them—twins, no less. Good grief."

"I thought that had been done already." Max pulled up a chair and went straight to the point. "When we spoke earlier you indicated you had a fling with Margot in London," he said. "A fling that didn't work out because she played the field too much."

"I said I barely knew her," Romero shot back. "We dated."

"I'm not going to parse terms with you. You had a relationship, but Margot was not known for monogamy, except perhaps of the serial kind. Who else was she with, do you know? Who did she leave you for? We're trying to reconstruct as much of her past as we can."

Romero shrugged. "If you're going down the list of paramours, or even husbands, good luck to you." He rolled his eyes in an upward glance, as if straining to remember the old days. Max had the sense he remembered too well. Indeed, Romero quickly caved in and confirmed that impression, for Romero, unlike some of the people he directed, was a terrible actor.

"Some nob," he said. "I've no idea who it was—she wouldn't say. But she dropped me pretty quickly when she spotted greener pastures. I was nobody much—then."

How that must have rankled, thought Max. "So she didn't play the field so much as simply leave you for someone else."

A sullen shrug, and a "Whatever," like a sulky teenager. Romero pulled on his upper lip, scrunching up and smoothing his luxuriant mustaches. "What can I say? She had appalling taste in men. Present company excluded, of course."

"There was some manner of disturbance in the galley the night of the murder," said Max, taking a different tack. "What was that about?"

"God knows," said Romero. "I really don't. The chef is French—Algerian, actually—and even when he's speaking English I have the devil's own time understanding him. He is also volatile in a thoroughly Gallic way. A perfectionist. They all are, the good chefs. So I put up with him. *And* I pay him a small fortune." The director took a sip of champagne, eyeing over the rim of the glass a young woman in a bikini entering the pool area. "If she'd work on her posture she'd be a stunner," he said. "She needs to learn to walk more on the balls of her feet."

"Try to remember," Max said. "It could be important. It's the only thing I've found so far that was a bit out of order that night—out of the usual. Tina said that whatever the chef was talking about, it had to do with a glass or glasses. Possibly a pair of glasses?"

Romero stared at him, his brow furrowed and his head cocked to one side. "Oh!" he said finally, with a laugh. "That's right. He was ranting about some dish that had been spoiled. Something to do with the powdered sugar. Something the sous-chef, I guess, put on a pastry or in a pastry. Or something."

"I don't follow."

"*Glace*," he said. "*Sucre glace*, is what she heard. I guess literally the translation would be sugared glaze. But it's what we Americans call powdered or confectioner's sugar."

"And we Brits call icing sugar," said Max. "Got it."

Chapter 20

O CAPTAIN!

"Good," said Cotton, presenting himself at Max's door early the next morning and casting a glance over his casual wear. "I see you're ready for another adventure, this time on the open seas. 'They that go down to the sea in ships, that do business in great waters.'"

Max wondered if Cotton realized he was quoting from the Bible. He had been after Cotton for years to attend a service at St. Edwold's. So far Cotton had made several generous donations to the church, and had helped capture a villain within its venerable old walls, but the DCI had not otherwise put in an appearance. Still, Max was a fisher of men's souls, and an infinitely patient one.

"'They reel to and fro, and stagger like a drunken man, and are at their wits' end,'" quoted Max back at him.

"I certainly hope not. Come along, they've found a boat tender to take us out to the yacht. The tender is like a bathtub with an awning, but I am told it's safe as houses. I hope you've brought your Omega Seamaster."

Max smiled at the reference to the exploding Bond gadget. Cotton was a fan of the eternally running series. He rather thought that in Cotton, George Greenhouse was missing a chance at an eager new MI5 recruit.

"The captain's out there waiting for us," Cotton continued as the two men headed toward the harbor. "I had Sergeant Essex call ahead to tell him we're on our way. We'll have a chat with him, and then we'll have a look-see at the entire setup, with special attention paid to Margot's room. Jake and Margot's cabin, I should say. We'll see if we can't quickly bury the head of this rattlesnake."

"I beg your pardon?"

"Murder poisons everything. You have to bury the head of a rattlesnake right after you've cut it off," Cotton explained.

"Really? Have you ever even seen a rattlesnake?"

"Well, no. I meant metaphorically, of course. It's something Romero told me. If you don't bury the head another animal might come along and eat the snake head and die. The poison is in the head. So you have to bury it."

"And what does he know about it?"

"He owns a cattle ranch, somewhere in the California foothills. Do you know what else? He owns a Jeep with B6-level security. You know, protection against high-powered rifles and suicide bombs."

"I know what B6-level security means, thank you. But does he really need all that?"

Cotton shrugged. "Rich people can be paranoid."

Max knew from experience how true this was. "Anything else?"

"Cows eat grapes."

"Again, I beg your pardon."

"Cows eat grapes, he tells me. Romero also owns a small vineyard. They once had a broken fence out there and the cows got in. They ate the grapevines down to the nub. He had to start over with new plants."

"It sounds as if you and he had quite the little chat. Did the subject of the murder even come up?"

"Interesting guy," Cotton went on, ignoring him. "It has to be said, most murderers are just boring. People who just want the attention, basically. The families of victims are often struck by how dull killers can be. They're expecting Satan himself to walk into the court-room and what they see instead is just some doltish, underachieving jackass with tattoos and bad skin who *wants* to be evil, perhaps, but doesn't have the brains for it."

"One of Satan's many disguises is ignorance. But we can't dis-count Romero because he's an interesting overachiever."

"Of course not. It's just very difficult to see a man like Romero stooping to murder, particularly a murder like this one. There would have to be rather a good motive."

"On that we can agree."

The two men walked the paved promenade toward the harbor to find the little craft that would convey them the short distance to the yacht. Patrice had reiterated her determination to stay behind. ("I've lived through the sea-sickness and morning-sickness combo enough for one lifetime. How women on the way to the new world managed it I've no idea.")

It was a sunny, brisk day, the sort of day that stirred the blood, lifted the heart, and made a person think the world was spinning along exactly as it should. Max thought he might bring Awena and Owen out for a day at the shore as soon as the temperature warmed. This day he wore a woolen scarf tightly knotted round his neck, and he was wishing he'd thought to bring gloves.

He anticipated what Owen's first encounter with a large body of water might be like, knowing the child would love the shore as much as his parents did. Right now Owen's only experience was with the River Puddmill wending its ponderous way through Nether Monkslip. Max thought he might also look into swimming lessons for Owen, even though it would mean weekly drives to the pool in Staincross Minster.

He and Cotton hurried on, heads down against the cold. Monk-slip-super-Mare's harbor, just deep enough for small fishing boats, was wedged between Dorset and Devon, in an area where the Jurassic cliffs briefly paused before resuming their dramatic sweep up the coast. The village sat majestic and assured, its useful harbor and the voluptuous beauty of its surrounding hills guaranteeing its continued existence. Baffled archeologists could only guess at a time line for its origins. The winding streets had retained their medieval bones, and some relics remained of the area's importance as a gathering place in olden times of chieftains and kings. The gentle overlay of centuries allowed the visitor the illusion that if he stood very still and listened intently, all the sounds and voices from long ago would come rushing past his ears. The scent of clematis was carried on the wind, borne down from hills thick with greenery; hidden by trees were ancient holloways which had carved themselves into the landscape over centuries. Some of these trails cut inland for miles, secret and enticing, never quite deserted by mankind, never deserted by wildlife.

Despite its popularity, the resort had been spared over-development and the worst sorts of seaside entertainment: the shops selling plastic spades and buckets and refrigerator magnets with British flags had been consigned to a single meandering side street; the newest large buildings were the Victorian hotels sunning themselves above the promenade.

Max had taken advantage of the concealing holloways just the night before, stealing away to ring George Greenhouse from within the enfolding, twisting darkness of the ancient path nearest the hotel. It had been a quick call to say only that they had no solid leads, but hoped a closer examination of the ship might yield some clues. The rules of an MI5 engagement were that the operative was on his own with little or no contact with higher-ups, but Max had taken extraordinary measures not to be seen or overheard. Anyone entering the holloway automatically set off nature's alarm system, sending woodland creatures scurrying.

Max and Cotton located the boat tender and boarded with care: the sea this day was choppy, and water sloshed against the little boats at harbor, washing them in a sudsy white foam. The sky seemed to melt into the water ahead of them; in the distance the yacht wobbled like a ghost ship. They were being ferried to the yacht by a weathered man with a neglected beard who looked like an abandoned DIY project, all jutting angles and missing fastens.

"The couples, married or otherwise, pretty much alibi each other," Cotton was saying a few minutes later, shouting to be heard over the noise of the motor. "For what it's worth," he added, "which is not a lot, the baron claims to have been sound asleep on the boat in the arms of his baroness. You've talked with them by now. Your impressions?"

"Yacht," corrected Max absentmindedly. "To be considered a boat it would have to be much smaller. Yes, I spoke with them together yesterday. There is something odd there."

"Yacht—got it. I've no more experience with sailing than I have with the great outdoors. As I think I've mentioned, I feel that the great *in*doors was invented to keep us all safe and out of trouble."

Indeed, he'd confided to Max that as far as he was concerned, all sailing craft had two positions: safely afloat or sunk to the bottom of the sea with all hands lost. He could tell the *Calypso Facto* was a beauty, however: a floating luxury hotel.

"How is it you know so much about boats and yachts, anyway?" he asked Max now.

"I don't, really. I know fore and aft; I know 'port out, starboard home.' I gather I've been living a lie on that subject for many years, however: the POSH acronym is meaningless, as it all rather depends on which direction you're sailing as to whether or not you've got posh accommodations." Max didn't elaborate on the fact that his limited knowledge of sailing came from his time serving undercover on luxury cruise ships, trying to discover, for example, who was smuggling stolen art out of the U.K.: he'd been seconded several times to the Met's Art and Antiques Unit. He might reminisce with Cotton and

Patrice later, once this crime had been solved, but so much of what he had done in days past was covered by the agreement he had signed with the government to keep secrets secret. It was easier in the end never to talk about any of it.

"I see," said Cotton. "Well, I couldn't agree with you more about the baron and his lady: there is something odd there. No one seems to know why those two were aboard, as I've indicated. Even Romero was a bit vague. But he's American, you know, and I gather a bit taken with the idea of being associated with nobility, however tenuously, and however minor they may be. Which is strange, when you recall that his country was founded on the idea of getting the nobs out of their hair—out of their powdered wigs, I should say. In my experience, Americans love them all now. Almost single-handedly they have saved the tourism industry. Ah, here we are."

They clambered aboard the yacht to find the ship's captain waiting for them on the main deck. Cotton, Max noticed, had managed the trip with not a hair out of place nor a splash of water on his clothing. He was wearing lace-up shoes but with rubber soles—clearly an enormous concession to the occasion. It was probably Cotton's idea of resort wear. Max had watched as Cotton boarded the tender and sat down, hitching up his perfectly pressed trousers to preserve the crease.

"Really?" Max had said. Max was wearing jeans and trainers with a wool jumper under his weatherproof jacket. The rather gaudy scarf had been knitted for him by a St. Edwold's volunteer, and its main benefit was that it was warm. Max never had the heart to refuse these spontaneous acts of generosity coming from his parishioners, which made him one of the most colorful priests in the area. Cotton wore his usual suit and tie.

"What?" Cotton asked.

"I mean, was your tuxedo at the dry cleaners?" Cotton had to be the most debonair policeman on the force. Max doubted the urbane detectives of Paris and Rome could hold a candle to him and his wardrobe. Max wasn't sure if Cotton was dressing for success and aiming for the next rung on the ladder, or if he simply liked clothes and dressing up for every occasion, choosing each tie and pocket handkerchief with care. Perhaps a bit of both.

The captain proved to be just under six feet tall and roundly built. He sported a Captain Ahab beard—a reddish chin curtain that contrasted with the graying brown hair springing from his forehead. His eyes were pale blue and sunk into a permanent network of squint lines.

"Captain Smith, at your service," he said, offering a gnarly hand to both men. "I understand you'd like the cook's tour. Nasty business, this. It does a ship's reputation no good to have an unsolved murder attached to its name. Crews can be superstitious, and so can passengers. There'll be talk of a ghostly woman in white before you know it, mark my words."

"We're doing what we can to solve this murder," Cotton told him. "That may put the stories to rest."

The captain shook his head. "The last time I heard of the like happening it were two passengers that had quarreled over a woman. One claimed self-defense but there's no way that could happen here or on any modern ship, not unless the victim were eight feet tall— you'll see that for yourselves. Folk don't just fall off a ship like this: it were custom built for extra safety so things like this couldn't happen. Where would you like to start?"

Max said, with a glance at Cotton, "I don't think we have a set agenda, but at some point I'd like to concentrate on the guest cabins."

"Fine. There are twelve of those. Also there are smaller cabins for the crew members, of course."

"What sorts of amenities do you have on board?" He'd been filled in by Patrice and Cotton but it never hurt to hear from the man who presumably knew the yacht better than anyone.

"What don't we have is the better question. All the usual, plus a putting green, saunas, pool, hot tub—all that. Wine storage and enormous freezers. A game room. A safe room and storage vaults for valuables. A laundry station. And of course for this lot there's a private theater so they can study themselves on film. We have a large crew as these things go but we're stretched thin keeping it all running." The captain's face as he listed these creature comforts was not unlike a missionary discussing the religious rites of cannibals he'd been sent to serve—a combination of awe and revulsion. Captain Smith looked to be of the old school, where real men subsisted on hard tack and a pint of fresh water a day if they were lucky. The frivolity of a luxury yacht like the *Calypso Facto* seemed to rub him up the wrong way. He probably was well compensated by Romero to blunt the effect.

"How large is the galley?" Max asked. "How many can it serve, I mean?"

"I take your meaning. How many, that depends on how often we dock for supplies, but I can tell you that area's nearly six hundred and twenty feet in size. That's not including the storage areas for provisions, of course."

"Of course," said Cotton, whose entire, sparsely furnished flat was six hundred square feet. He called it his Zen Den.

"And there's a safe room? How interesting. Like a panic room, is it?"

"We never panic," the captain admonished him. "That's not a word I'll allow on my ship. But yes, that is what some would call it. Of course, we travel nowhere near pirate-infested waters—it's a ship built for mindless pleasure, not a cargo ship—but a safe room is all the latest rage and this yacht has all the latest."

"We'd like to see that, too, if we may," said Cotton.

"Right this way."

The captain took them down in a coffin-like elevator to a room secured with a keypad-style computerized lock. He asked the two men to turn their backs to him as he punched in the four-digit code that would unlatch the metal door.

"In here," he said, swinging it wide to admit them. "It's all bullet-proofed, this lot," he added, with obvious pride, possibly longing for the day when he could foil boarding pirates with this secret failsafe to protect his crew and passengers.

Max and Cotton looked around them at shelves containing rolled bedding and tins and packets of food, and vast canisters of staples like sugar and flour. The area was ringed with bench seating for per-haps a dozen people; at the far end of the room was a bank of com-munications equipment. It would be a very tight fit but it could just about accommodate everyone on board in a temporary emergency. Max would have given a lot to see how the baron and baroness might have adapted to being penned in with the ship's crew. They would probably have rather taken their chances being cast adrift on a lifeboat, using the baroness's diamonds as fish bait.

"You could survive in here for about a week if you had to, as far as the provisions go," the captain told them. "But with the communi-cations equipment—all state of the art, you know—we would signal for help and be rescued long before the food ran out." Clearly, for him, this room was far, far better than the ship's froufrou nonsense like putting greens. This was where the oftentimes hazardous business of running a ship was made manifest.

Max was wondering how easy it would be to sabotage the venti-lation system to the room. Certainly that would be taken care of by whatever ship's architect had designed the space. But what one per-son could design or invent, another person could disrupt.

His eyes roamed over the shelves of canned and boxed provisions.

"Was this area searched before?" he asked Cotton, who nodded.

"Certainly. But only just. It's kept locked, as you saw, and we were focused on the rooms that might be more directly connected to the murder. We only looked in here on the slight chance of finding a stowaway. It was a possibility that had to be eliminated."

"Quite right," said Max. "But send someone out here to look inside these tins and boxes. To search the contents of each and every one." He didn't have to tell Cotton what they were looking for, which was essentially anything that didn't belong.

"I say," put in the captain. "I don't—Is that really necessary? I supervised the loading of the provisions myself. You can't be too careful these days. You have my word; nothing dodgy came aboard."

"No, one can't be too careful," Cotton agreed. "Now we'll have another look at the guest rooms."

Max and Cotton walked away as the captain busied himself securing the door.

"If we knew the spot where Margot went overboard, it might help us pinpoint what happened when," said Max.

"Oh, but we do know now. Or we are fairly certain we do. Come along; I'll show you."

Chapter 21

A ROOM OF ONE'S OWN

"You see these marks?" Cotton asked. "My team found them during the initial search but weren't sure if they were significant. They took photos, as Sergeant Essex thought it might be important. She's usually right."

"That were never there before the murder," said the captain. "That lot will need to be sanded and polished back and painted over."

"Not just yet," Cotton told him.

What they were looking at were scratches: one deep gouge in the wood railing and similar, smaller marks about a foot away from the main injury to the wood.

"We're thinking that whoever hefted Margot overboard had a bit of struggle. These marks were likely made by the high-heeled shoes she had on that night—she often wore heels to compensate for her moderate height. And because they were the fashion, I suppose. Anyway, the lab confirms that these marks were made by a rubberized tip or tips scraping against the wood. The sort of rubber heel tips you'd find on a woman's shoes. There's also a trace of red shoe paint, probably rubbed off one of the heels. The boyfriend says her red shoes are missing from the room they shared."

"The cabin. We don't have the shoes themselves?" said Max.

"No, undoubtedly they came off as the body was pulled about in the water. The coroner found marks of heel straps where they'd abraded the skin after death, presumably in being torn from the feet. Still, it's all indicative: this is likely the spot where she went overboard."

The ship bristled with spikes and hooks and ropes and poles that clearly served some specific nautical purpose. Max, carefully side-stepping a hook that seemed to point at him with murderous intent, said, "Not jumped over." It was not a question.

"No way. She went in with the help of someone on board this ship that night."

"Could the coroner say anything about the height or weight of the assailant?"

Cotton shook his head. "Not really, no. He can only guess that whoever it was had a struggle with what was effectively dead weight. They none of them are large people, the suspects. Not the sort of heavy-weight champion who could simply have hefted her over, clear of the rail. There's one lad in the boiler room or whatever you'd call it—"

"There's no—" the captain began.

"Some sort of engineer. He's the right size for the job, but there's nothing to connect him with the victim. Whoever it was had to shove and maneuver the body over, leaving these scratches on top of the rail."

"It is an argument for only one killer. Or to be precise, only one disposer of the body."

Cotton shrugged, nodded. "Perhaps," he said. "Or two not-very-strong people. Perhaps with so much wine sloshing about the party that night, gathering the strength needed for body disposal was an issue. What are you thinking, Max?"

"Honestly, I'm not sure; I'm not there yet. My hunches won't do us much good without facts to back them up."

They took their leave of the captain at this point and began a search of the cabins, first doing a cursory examination of the crew cabins. The guest cabins had been left undisturbed except that most of the personal objects of the occupants had been removed—once their rooms had been searched by the police, they had all been allowed to pack whatever belongings they would need for several days' stay at the hotel. In the case of the baron and baroness, Max reflected, that included some but not all of the necessary accoutrements.

"Anything good turn up in your searches?" Max asked.

Cotton shook his head. "Nothing. Delphine left behind a pen with the Grand Imperial Hotel's logo on it. But she claimed she'd never been to the hotel before."

"So how did she come by the pen?" Max mused.

"She said she had no idea—it could have come into her possession in a lot of ways."

Only Margot and Jake's cabin, when they got to it, retained the imprint of its former occupants. Jake had not been allowed to remove so much as a toothbrush, a fact over which he had complained at length.

Max and Cotton looked about them. As in all the guest cabins intended for two occupants, the twin beds were separated by a nightstand, and the room was decorated in a nautical style with blue wallpaper in a pattern of ocean waves and white furniture of a clean, modern design. Much of the furniture, as on any ship, was bolted to the floor for safety.

This particular cabin bore Margot's imprint much more so than Jake's, and gave every appearance of being a dressing room backstage at a theater. There were traces of powder everywhere, seemingly on every item—light powder in addition to the darker fingerprint powder left by forensics. Max raised an eyebrow as he surveyed the makeup table; Cotton correctly intuited the unspoken question.

"Not the kind of powder you may be thinking," he told him. "No drugs of any kind were found in the room, apart from some sleeping tablets, over-the-counter cough remedies, and the like. The hardest-core powder found in here so far, according to the forensics team, is that made by Max Factor. Of course they're still testing the contents of all these bottles and things but I was told not to get my hopes up. Everything passed the sniff-and-taste test when forensics initially went through the room."

"Surely this cabin is messier than the norm?" In addition to bits of clothing strewn wildly across the floor—giving the place the appearance of a room once occupied by teenagers—lipsticks, pots of eye shadow, wands of mascara, colored pencils, brushes, and bottles of perfume were scattered everywhere on the small dressing table. Max thought it was interesting what was *not* there: there were no family or holiday-style photos, no personal snapshots of any kind, but several professional headshots of the actress were ranged across one narrow shelf over the tabletop. She was posed almost identically in each, head thrown back, her face in three-quarter profile. As the years progressed, the photos got progressively blurrier, as if she'd been photographed through a lens smeared with petroleum jelly, as perhaps she had been.

"It may be a bit messier than usual," said Cotton. "I did gather she and Jake, not entirely a match made in heaven, quarreled at times. Items were thrown, regrettable things were said. Someone commented they were less like lovers and more like a pair of old roommates squabbling over who forgot to buy the bread and washing-up liquid. Perhaps she threw a big powder puff at him and it scattered."

"Who was it who said that?"

"I'd have to search my notes, but I think it was Addy—Addison Phelps."

"I shouldn't wonder. Screenwriters and writers in general can be sharp-eyed when it comes to other people's relationships. I suppose it's in the job description."

"What's this?" Cotton was holding up a fuzzy strand that might have fallen out of a wig.

"It's a hair extension."

"A what?"

"You weave it into your hair to make it look longer." Max knew this from finding such an item in his mother's bathroom one time while he was visiting. Alarmed that she was losing her hair to treatment for some dreadful disease, he'd confronted her with it. She was still regaling her bridge partners with the story as she sailed round the world on yet another cruise, hair extensions in place.

"Oh," said Cotton. "Is there a reason anyone would want to do that?"

Max thought. "No compelling reason I can think of offhand. But it operates more or less on the same principle as the toupee. It's a sort of vanity item."

"There's no shortage of that here."

"No, I agree. No expense spared on cosmetics and so on—it all looks like fairly high end stuff to me. Much of it French in origin. But there's nothing that looks suspicious, either." Max surveyed the landscape of the room, his eyes alert to any incongruity. The cabin was necessarily small but like all ships it had been cunningly designed to maximize the space. "It's a wonder Jake had room for his shaving kit," he said.

Cotton nodded: shawls and feather boas and scarves were draped everywhere, including over every lamp shade, perhaps serving the same purpose as they did in *A Streetcar Named Desire*—to conceal and soften the trace of years across the actress's face. Cotton vividly recalled his mother's using the same old hat trick.

As for Max, the plethora of makeup and hairpieces and artful whatnot in this room, the place where the victim last had lived, all confirmed his impressions of Margot: She had not been one to go gentle into that good night. She would fight the inevitable with every potion known to science. If the thought she had committed suicide ever had been considered, the state of this room put the lie to that. Margot would not have given in to despair. She would have lived to fight another day—given the chance.

Had she fought the night of her death? Probably not. Probably she had been too incapacitated by her killer.

And that struck him as the saddest thing of all.

"Come on. Let's go have a talk with the crew."

Unsurprisingly, of the skeleton crew left behind to man the ship, no one knew anything, no one had heard anything, no one had seen anything or wanted to see anything, ever again. To a man, what they wanted was to go home.

"I had a half-dozen people on board here interviewing each one of them, right after it happened," Cotton told Max. "The notes are voluminous and you are welcome to see them all. But overall, the impression is of a terrified bunch of people who think we're going to pin this on them because they're 'not nobs,' like the guests are. A couple of them have shady backgrounds, but nothing that rises to the level of murder. Petty crime, juvenile stuff, nothing more violent than a shoving match at a rugby game."

"I guess if you stretch the definition of 'nob' I understand the fear. The guests are going to point to the crew, either directly or by innuendo."

"It's happened already. The baron and baroness were quite quick to point out that the 'servants' must be behind it. Don't you just love that? The 'servants'? Where do they think they are? Downton Abbey?"

Max could just hear them saying it, waving their cigarettes about. "Why am I not surprised? Anyway, where did the chef go to?"

"He's staying in the hotel, doubling up in a room with the sous-chef. I hear they do not particularly get along but since the boss, Romero, is footing the bill they are forced into proximity. As an employer, I'd say Romero is generous. Luckily the knives remain on board— although I do hear that the high-level chefs travel with their own set."

"Ring ahead to the hotel, will you? Tell someone on your team to let those two know we want to talk with them—and to make sure they stay put until we get there."

"The two of them together, do you mean?"

"Yes. I want to see what happens when we bounce them off each other. Maybe they'll give more away that way."

The executive chef of the *Calypso Facto*, Zaki Zafour, had a comically mournful face with the long upper lip of a camel, a toothy, winsome smile, and thick lashes framing enormous brown eyes. He wore mismatched resort wear, a madras shirt and pinstriped slacks, in place of what was undoubtedly his daily standard gear of toque and chef's jacket. The mismatching was perhaps a result of years in that uniform. In the same way do former military members make some strange sartorial choices, thought Max.

While the yacht was flagged to the Cook Islands, it was crewed by people of all nations. The chef's underling, sous-chef Angel Torres, was a less imposing figure, nearly half the height of the chef, with a compact, muscular build and a fighter's stance. Max suspected that even on such a comparatively small yacht the man worked extra duty—that essentially he *was* the galley staff. His job title might encompass responsibility for provisions as well as slicing, dicing, and preparing food. Despite his short stature he appeared to be the brawn of the outfit; the chef, the brains.

Zaki confirmed as much with his opening remarks.

"When might I be allowed back into my own galley? I cannot be expected to plan meals when I don't know when or even if we will be allowed on board. I need to buy fresh provisions while we are ashore but there is no point if everything will just be allowed to sit on a dock and spoil. Of course, I am aware of the sad occasion which causes this inconvenience. But even so I—"

"We will be releasing the yacht soon," Cotton told him. "As to when you may board again, that is up to your employer."

"There may also be a question as to who else will be joining you," put in Max.

"How so?"

"When we determine who committed this crime, we will be able to release everyone not responsible for it. But will they be rejoining you on the *Calypso Facto*? I imagine some of them will prefer to leave the memories and the ship behind. And of course, Margot Browne will never be joining you again. Nor will her killer."

"Yes, poor lady." The man's large eyes were glazed with tears. It was an apparently authentic reaction, Max thought. So why did it strike him as superficial? Some people could cry on command. Most of them were actors.

"You were fond of Margot, were you?"

"Not particularly, no. I didn't know her. But her death diminishes me, of course it does. Her death had nothing to do with the food, thank God, and so nothing to do with me."

Angel, standing beside him, nodded his head in woeful unison. Max turned to study him. Angel was a good-looking man, with the broad, flat nose of a tiger and the tiger's wise, watchful eyes.

Max could not help but think the somewhat stagey reaction was rehearsed between the pair of them. It was a bit too perfect. When, he wondered, had he become such a cynic? Perhaps Margot had endeared herself in some way, in spite of being a stranger to them. Bought them a little present or simply praised their cooking.

"I understand there was a bit of a fuss the night Miss Browne died," Max said.

"Well, but naturally," said the chef.

"I meant before that. A ruckus of some kind was heard, coming from the galley."

"Ruckus?" Zaki stared straight ahead but Angel, less able to hide his reaction, allowed his eyes to slide sideways toward his boss. It was a telling glance, with a tinge of "I told you so" around the edges. Then Angel returned his gaze to Max, and then to Cotton, and back to Max, with the innocent expression of a choir boy. Max, with some experience of the lies choir boys sometimes told, knew that the more innocent the expression the larger the crime might be, although it would always amount to petty crime—telling the parents they were at rehearsal, for example, when they were actually in Staincross Minster for the matinee showing of *Star Wars*. Or of one of Romero's blockbuster films.

Thus Max met the look of celestial innocence and wonder with one of hardened episcopal steel. Angel let his gaze drift, until it finally settled onto the pattern of the room's carpet. His colleague stepped into the silence, filling it with his soothing, melodious voice.

"Ruckus?" he repeated. "I don't know what you mean. Angel and I, we are a team. A well-oiled machine. It all goes smoothly. I create the recipes. He helps me fulfill my vision. I have won awards! Yes, I, a humble man from poor beginnings, I have become world renowned. I do not merely cook or bake, I create the masterpiece. Not the ruckus."

Max, who did not doubt they were a team—but a team of what?—now adopted what Cotton thought of as his saintly expression, the St. Max of Tudor face of endless patience and bounty. Cotton saw it coming and took a metaphorical step back to allow Max room to maneuver.

"We have signed statements from witnesses that you were—how did they put it, DCI Cotton? Yelling and screaming at the top of your lungs?"

Cotton, who had no idea, really, what statements Max was talking about, nodded sagely, letting his own features harden into an expression that could be used to mold a warrior mask. When it came to working as a team, he thought, he and Max could teach Zaki and Angel a thing or two.

Angel lifted his gaze from the carpet. He seemed to have settled on Max as his confidant.

"It was nothing, really. One of the items on the menu was spoilt and it had to be done over—my fault entirely." Max doubted that but realized the politic wisdom of Angel's adopting the role of sin eater.

"What item was that?"

"I don't remember, really. The sugar?"

Angel turned to Zaki, as if he felt he had carried more than his share of the load now. Zaki gave him a brief glare, a zing of hatred that could almost be seen shooting across the space between the two men. He said, "It was a simple mistake. A mistake quickly rectified. As I said, we work as a team. And when mistakes are made—well, that is where my genius for improvisation is most allowed to shine."

It was a wonder, thought Max, that the ship had not sunk to the bottom of the sea with the weight of so many egos aboard.

At an imperceptible sign from Max, Cotton took back the reins. "Fine, thank you," he said. "We'll have a word with Angel privately now."

It appeared all this was not going according to Zaki's plan. The big brown eyes widened, the expressive eyebrows drooping with exaggerated dismay.

"I must be present at all interviews involving my subordinate. It is . . ." Anxiously, absurdly, he drew on his genius for improvisation. "It is the law of the sea."

"You're on dry land now," said Cotton. "And this land is my land, in a manner of speaking. Thank you again, sir. We'll talk with Angel alone now." As Zaki still did not make a move to go, Cotton added sternly, "Good day to you, sir. We will be sure to commend you to Mr. Romero, and to the captain, for your cooperation today."

The soft soap worked where nothing else would, apart from using bodily force to evict him. Grudgingly, Zaki took his leave, allowing himself a final, warning glower at his sous-chef.

When the door was firmly shut behind him, the two men turned to Angel Torres. Max said, "All right, then. Let's have the truth now."

Chapter 22

NO ANGEL

"I'm glad it's all coming out," Angel Torres began. "I'm sick of living like this."

They heard a shuffling movement coming from outside the door to the hallway. Cotton held up a cautioning finger to silence the sous-chef. Then he crept toward the door and flung it open. Zaki Zafour stumbled into the room.

"I think we'll have to ask you to leave, sir," Cotton told him. He pulled up his sleeve and to all appearances spoke into his wrist, instructing a member of his team in the incident room to come retrieve Zaki and escort him to the hotel lobby, where he was to remain for the duration of the interview.

Max, captivated by Cotton's new foray into high tech, made a mental note to give him grief about the smart watch at a later time.

"You can't do that," said Zaki. "I know my rights."

"Actually, I think you'll find I know your rights better than you do," Cotton replied cordially. "It's my job to know, after all."

Once Zaki had been extracted from the scene, Cotton returned to his place in front of Angel, who seemed pleased with these developments.

"The man is a bully," he told them. "It's nice to see him put in his place." Angel spoke good English with a soft accent. In answer to

Cotton's opening questions, he told them he was from Barcelona and had attended cooking school in Seville. He named a world-renowned establishment, adding, "They probably saved my life." Max, via Awena's knowledge of all things culinary, was well aware of the school's history and fame. It had been started fifty years before by a priest with the aim of giving children from poor homes marketable skills, to help lift them from poverty and away from drugs. What had begun as a vocational school to employ street kids in low-level kitchen jobs had grown into a world-class establishment, turning out some of the finest gourmet chefs in Europe.

"I've heard of the school," Max told him. "It's very well-known. Is that how Romero found you?"

"It was actually Zaki who hired me. I think he had in mind someone who was desperate for the job and willing to—what is your expression?—turn a blind eye. He got both things wrong, as it happens. The man is an idiot in addition to being a bully."

"Your situation was not desperate, or you were not willing to ignore what you saw?" asked Cotton. He was busy taking notes.

"Both," Angel replied. "You do understand, if I tell you what I suspect—what I know in my heart, to be honest—I am out of a job. And I am only willing to say anything because I was planning to move on, anyway—come what may. Now with the murder . . . It is just so not worth it to remain."

"Understandable," said Max. "Why did you answer, 'both'?"

"I come from a solid middle-class family. Most of the students these days at La Cocina de Santos come from such a background. It is years since students were recruited from off the streets by Father Mateo. Now people stand on line to get in. I would not be destitute. I would just disappoint my father. But Zaki, he plays the card—am I saying that right?"

"Yes, I understand," said Max. "Threats and intimidation to keep you in line."

Angel nodded eagerly. This man understood. He was reminded very much of the priest in his church back home, and for a moment he stopped to wonder why.

"And the other side of 'both'?" Max prodded.

"I didn't see anything. You have to understand that. I had suspicions only. But the more I got to know Zaki, the more I watched his manner, the more I understood that he was up to something, and that if something went down, he would try to toss me inside it. The man is a liar, completely without honor. And you can take my word for it or not. He will try to blame it on me—including this murder if it helps him in some way. Especially since that woman went overboard, I've been waiting, just waiting for him to try to, how you say, throw me under the bus. At the very least, if I tried to leave, he could give me a terrible reference. I know him. He would try to make it so I never got another job." He shook his head, angry and frustrated. This weapon had been hanging over his head too long. "He is crazy," he said with great finality. "A monster. Do not be fooled by the nice manners he puts on for you."

"And? Go on, please."

Angel drew a deep sigh, the sigh of a man who had fought the good fight and was giving up. "Just because I grew up in what is called a nice family doesn't mean I don't know drug use when I see it. Zaki is using for sure. So many of these guys are. And I also think maybe he does something more."

"Dealing. Smuggling."

Angel nodded. "But he had help. From someone else on board."

"Do you have anyone in particular in mind?"

"Yes. Yes, I'm afraid I do. Delphine."

Some time later, Max and Cotton walked away from the room Angel had been sharing with Zaki. They decided to talk over coffee in one of the trendy cafés in Monkslip-super-Mare as they waited for the call from the police team searching the ship. This time, the searchers had a better idea exactly where and what to search for.

As Max and Cotton left him, Angel was already busy packing—given leave to depart the premises, with the condition he keep himself available for further questioning.

"I know what Angel means," said Cotton as he and Max neared the busy quay. "About so many of these guys using. The kitchen of a high-end restaurant is a pressure cooker—no pun intended. A lot of them, taking themselves far too seriously, think they have to get high to get through the night."

"I know," said Max. "As if the fate of the world hung on whether the soufflé collapsed or was a 'masterpiece.' But to do essentially the same job night after night, with variations . . . I suppose there is pressure in that. And some boredom."

A waitress seated them at a window table and took their orders. Next to them a couple sat having coffee. Max soon noticed the woman had a habit of thumping her fingers on the table for emphasis as she talked, like someone playing chords on a piano. She seemed to be angry about something. The body language of the man with her, his head turned away, said clearly that whatever it was about, he didn't want to listen.

"But Zaki had a nice cushy little job, if you ask me," said Cotton. "He got to travel the world, and he never had more than—what, a dozen people to prepare his gourmet meals for? I'm sure the crew ate whatever leftovers he told them they would eat on any given night."

"If anything, boredom might be the bigger issue."

"What? Unlike most of the crew, he had a private cabin, as well. I could try doing that for a living, if only for a while."

"That's what I mean. It's not for everyone. The same routine day after day, at least until the ship pulls into the next port. Maybe that's why . . ."

"Why he got into drugs? Perhaps. Or he just got hooked from

the get-go. Some addictions are like that. And that would explain why—"

He broke off as his phone vibrated. "That was fast," he said. He answered, then looked over at Max and said, "Essex." He listened closely, asking only a well-aimed question or two. Just before ringing off, he added, "And put a rush on those financials, would you?"

Tucking the mobile back inside his jacket, he told Max, "Angel's hunch was right." He put a five-pound note on the table and led the way outside to where they couldn't be overheard. There he said, "The safe room is stuffed to the ceiling with drugs. They're estimating so far about fifty kilograms of cocaine alone."

"Some of it in the tins of icing sugar," said Max. "I did wonder why there was so much sugar in a safe room . . . It got me to thinking: they'd all have been bouncing off the walls like toddlers if they'd been stuck in there in a real emergency."

"Yes. We're quite sure it was a hunch, are we? That Angel didn't just know all about it because he put the stuff there himself?"

"I believed him," Max said simply.

"So did I."

"It was either a preemptive double-bluff, telling us about the drugs before we got suspicious of him, or he was what he appeared to be—a man caught in a net not of his own making. With Zaki for a boss, Angel could see for a long time where this was leading. Zaki would throw him in the soup, if you'll pardon the expression, at the first sign of trouble. And how could he ever prove his innocence?"

"So, what do we have now?" Cotton stood with his back to the harbor, the breeze blowing his hair into a halo framing his face. Passersby were taken with the sight of two striking men, one fair, one dark. They might have been mistaken for tourists but for Cotton's immaculate suit. Perhaps they were actors connected with that director's yacht in the harbor? Several people smoothed their hair and adjusted their clothing on the off-chance a film camera was in range.

"The night of the murder we know there was a disturbance of some sort. Angel, running out of the icing sugar he needed for the pastry, had gone to the safe room; he knew Zaki kept the combination written on a card in his chef's jacket, which was hanging on a nearby hook. Zaki had actually left for the night, knowing everything was in capable hands. He seems to have done very little of the actual cooking and baking. Anyway, Angel retrieved the 'sugar' from the safe room and used it to make icing for that night's pudding. Angel didn't taste or test it—why would he? But Zaki came in to do a last-minute check and saw the tin of 'sugar' sitting on the counter. He saw the misidentifying label, and realized what must have happened. He was angry not just because Angel had gone into the safe room—he'd been told not to do so—but, of course, because his mistake could have got them both in serious trouble. The passengers might have been taken deathly ill when they ingested the drug, but at a minimum, they were going to notice the weird taste of what should have been sugar. And that would affect Zaki's reputation for creating nonstop masterpieces. He ordered Angel to throw the pudding away. The guests had tinned apricots that night instead."

"That might be the part that sent him off the edge right there. The master chef sending such a poor excuse for a pudding out of his galley."

"But where does it get us?" Cotton asked. "Did Margot get caught up in this scene somehow? She went storming out of the party, remember. Did she see something? Did she suspect drug use and drug smuggling were going on? Was Zaki dealing to the passengers? Did she use drugs herself? I suppose once you allow in drugs as a factor there are all manner of ways she could innocently have put herself in harm's way."

"Yes. If she found out about the drugs, if she caught Zaki redhanded somehow, would she be allowed to live to tell the tale?"

"I doubt that very much," said Cotton.

"So do I," said Max.

Cotton sighed. "What we need is a confession."

"That would be most helpful. But whoever did this is looking at charges of murder, perverting the course of justice, preventing the burial of a corpse—just for starters," said Max. "The chances anyone will break down and confess given the gravity of the situation are small."

"Actually, it has to be premeditated murder, given the drugs. She didn't dope herself with all that lot. There was nothing spur-of-the-moment about any of this."

Much later that same day, Cotton and Max shared an after-dinner drink in the situation room.

"The guesstimate was about right," Cotton told Max, ringing off another conversation on his mobile phone. "So far my team has found more than fifty kilograms of cocaine—well over a hundred pounds. It's not a huge bust, not what they're used to in London."

"But it's quite a nice haul for Monkslip-super-Mare," said Max. "That'll be many millions in street value if it's high grade. You're sure to be mentioned in dispatches."

Cotton looked pleased at the idea, and Max was amused to see a faint blush spread across his friend's face. At the least there would be an official commendation added to his file. It would all help when his super's job fell open. "The question is, did the captain know? Did Romero?"

"I doubt the captain knew exactly what was going on," Max replied. "Romero—maybe he knew, maybe not. But there's no earthly reason for him to be involved, that we're aware. He certainly didn't need the cash; your team looking into his finances seems to feel the lavish lifestyle was well funded. He might overreach his limits one day but so far, so good. Still . . . some people get into this kind of thing solely because they think it's a lark. They're in it for the thrill of pulling one off against the authorities. For those addicted to excitement, the thrill is all."

"I've met the type before," said Cotton. "Nothing they do makes sense, on the surface." He paused, thinking, then said, "The captain at least had to have suspected something, don't you agree? Still, lack of clear knowledge is no defense against guilt."

"There's a legal concept I've always had trouble grasping—how do you condemn someone who had no clue? All right, he was in charge of the ship, but even so . . ."

"The buck has to stop somewhere," said Cotton.

Max smiled at him. "These Americanisms. That was Truman, wasn't it? Anyway, I wonder how long it's been going on, the smuggling."

"It's hard to say. The safe room was built into the ship a year ago, replacing the small gym that had been there before. So at least we know the time frame of when the safe room could have been used to conceal the drugs. The regular storage areas may have been in use before that time for the same purpose, of course, but it's a dicey proposition. What if the sous-chef went to bread the chicken with flour and accidentally used cocaine? He could have wiped out everyone on board. With the safe room, it was a safer bet, so to speak. So long as only the chef and captain knew the combination. And the captain had no need to go in there as a matter of routine."

"And then one night the sous-chef ran out of the icing sugar he needed to decorate his pastries. And unknowingly, he used cocaine powder from the stores in the safe room."

"Right."

"No doubt, as Angel said, it helped the chef to have someone like Delphine Beechum flitting about, acting as go-between. We noted before her usefulness in bridging the crew and the guests. Her ability to penetrate those social barriers at will. And it helps explain that blue hotel pen found in her cabin, the one with the fish logo. There are other explanations for her having it, of course—it's not conclusive. But if she is lying about having been at the hotel before, perhaps passing drugs to and from the ship, we have a good indicator she's lying about other things. She's a memorable person and someone on the staff here will remember seeing her—"

"She was dealing," said Cotton. "Had to be. I wonder how big a part she played. As a courier, or in procuring the stuff in the first place. She will need a good explanation for the large amounts of money we're finding in her numerous savings accounts, which can't be accounted for by her paychecks alone."

"I think we can rely on what Angel told us—he suspected from the first she was the conduit. She and the chef had too many hushed conversations for there not to have been something going on. What earthly use is a cruise director on such a small yacht? The chef will spill the beans soon enough—sorry, what an appalling play on words. But remember, his style is to cast the blame, and with Angel out of the picture I doubt he'll hesitate to implicate his actual accomplice. If you're asking for the most likely scenario, she found buyers, passed the stuff along, and took a cut for doing so. Her financials don't add up otherwise; there isn't that much money in teaching yoga."

"But there's certainly better karma there than in drug smuggling."

A pause, as Max sat thinking back over what they had learned. He watched the play of light in the amber liquid of his drink. "Tina," he said, musingly. "What was her given first name again?"

Cotton rustled through some papers. "I think it's short for—yes, here we go. It's short for Christina."

"It's also a street name for crystal meth, as I'm sure you're aware."

"Are you thinking there's a connection?" Cotton asked.

"Not really. What's in a name, after all?"

"Quite a lot," said Cotton. "There is quite a lot to a name."

Max looked at him. He had never before asked. It simply had not come up in all the time he'd known Cotton. "Do you have a first name?"

Cotton looked at the ceiling, at the floor, out the window—everywhere but at Max before saying, "It's Prospero. Yes, you heard right. Prospero Cotton. I was presumably named after the character played by my father. Whoever that was."

"Oh, sorry, man. That's tough. I mean it must have been hard. In school and everything. Prospero, eh?"

Cotton shrugged. "Most people were pretty decent about it."

Max had to wonder. Life couldn't have been easy for a boy named Prospero. It certainly helped explain why Cotton was so well read up on the plays of Shakespeare. But Max wasn't going to pretend it wasn't an unusual choice of name for a baby.

"I think my mother was crazy, actually," Cotton said. "Or she thought I'd have a career in the theater. Which was never going to happen, after my having seen the life they all led. Chaos was reserved for the good days. The rest of the time it was pure ruddy mayhem."

"If nothing else," said Max mildly, "it's helped give you the advantage in this case. I think you see the psychology of many of the suspects quite well." It might assist him in other ways, too, Max thought. Perhaps the ability to tell when a suspect was lying was enhanced by a childhood of being surrounded by people playacting a part.

Or did it hinder? Could Cotton always spot the truth, given that background?

But Max was still grappling with "Prospero." On reports, he'd only seen Cotton use his initials: P. C. Cotton. No wonder. He was afraid to ask him what *C* stood for. Probably Caliban.

Max made a deliberate attempt to excise the knowledge from his mind, to tuck it away in a little cabinet marked "Unimportant Information." Cotton would always be just plain Cotton to him.

Chapter 23

LYRE, LYRE

The next morning, Max interrupted Addison Phelps as he was updating his Web site. He invited Max into his room cordially enough, but asked him to wait a moment while he made sure his files transferred safely.

"The Internet connection in this hotel seems to come and go with the tides," he informed Max. "Or perhaps it's connected with the phases of the moon. Right now, it's a very weak signal—just glacial. I hope you don't mind—I haven't done my updates for days. And now that I finally have the chance to do it, well . . ."

Max nodded amiably and took a seat near the open balcony window, where a cooling breeze lifted the sheer curtains framing each side. He took the opportunity to study the young man as he sat at the hotel desk, focused on his task. Addison, nicknamed Addy, was wholesome looking rather than conventionally handsome, with fair, lightly freckled skin and good clean lines of nose and jaw; he was spidery of build, and of indeterminate years. Max would have placed him at twenty-five and prematurely balding if he hadn't known better from reading Patrice's files. She had made a notation next to his name, a single phrase: "V. bright but sometimes plays the scatterbrain, don't underestimate." He had grown a beard he kept trimmed short and wore his sandy blond hair in a fashionable samurai topknot. His hair frizzed about his hairline, as if pulling it tight each day were breaking it at the roots. He sported a T-shirt that announced he was a fan of some band Max had never heard of, and artfully torn jeans that made him look as if he'd been attacked by ravening dogs.

The laptop he was working on emitted a small ping, indicating it was satisfied, and Addy closed the browser window. A photo of a colony of penguins appeared on the screen. Addy carried his desk chair over to sit near Max, giving him an artlessly sweet, good-natured smile. From what Max could see of the screen before Addy had logged out, he'd also been working on a document in screenplay format, with large white margins and headers indicating character names and strips of dialogue. With so much white space on the page, it looked to Max almost like cheating, like an author could write a full screenplay in no time compared with a manuscript, but Max suspected there might be more to it than that. God knew his sermons, however brief he tried to keep them, took forever to write. The trick, he had discovered, was always to open with a joke. One he had found recently on the Internet was, "What do Winnie the Pooh and John the Baptist have in common?" Answer: "The same middle name." The congregation had loved that one.

"How can I help you—Max Tudor, is it? That detective told me to expect a visit from some sort of consultant on the case."

Max nodded. Even under normal circumstances, he resisted being addressed as "Father Tudor." He liked to think of himself as neither low nor high church, but falling somewhere on a broad continuum where compassion and common sense outweighed dogma. Titles created a distance between people that was difficult to bridge.

"Why do I feel suddenly like the Ghost of Christmas Past?" he asked. "With people being warned of my visit? But yes, and call me Max, please." He hesitated a moment before adding: "In actual fact, I am an Anglican priest from Nether Monkslip, a nearby village. But I am here to talk with you about Margot Browne. The police have asked me to assist in this inquiry, if you've no objections to answering a few of my questions. In any event, I'd appreciate your keeping my— well, my mission to yourself for now." Max wasn't sure why, but he had made a decision on the spot to trust Addy with his actual identity and affiliation, where he had not done so with the others. There was something in Addy's gentle manner that made Max feel he might be more amenable to a chat if it were clear that Max did not represent the full authority of the law. At least, not of earthly law.

"Of course," said Addy. "I mean, I guess it's okay. Her murder is all anyone is talking about here, for sure. I dare not leave my room for fear of being blinded by photographers' camera flashes. What I can't imagine is, why are you here—I mean, really? Are the police that short-staffed in England they have to recruit stand-ins from the local church? Who is minding the altar, in other words?"

Max smiled. "I have an able assistant filling in for me: the Rev. Destiny Chatsworth. I suppose it must look as if the police were desperately underfunded and understaffed. They are, in point of fact. But that doesn't apply, not in this case. It's more that DCI Cotton and I go back a long way." He decided to leave it at that. If it implied Cotton was calling in some sort of favor, or implied nothing at all, that was fine with him. He was abashed to realize his truth telling during an investigation also fell along a continuum. But he certainly couldn't explain to Addison or anyone that he was actually doing the rounds of the investigation at the behest of MI5.

"I see," said Addison. "Or rather, I don't see but I don't imagine you're going to tell me any more than that, are you?" He had a focused, concentrated way of listening for answers, almost as if he were hard of hearing and had deliberately to filter out any background noise.

Spot on, thought Max, who realized he was indeed talking with one of the brighter sparks in the group. After time spent with Tina, who struck him as more cunning than bright, it would come as a relief. "How do you like to be called?" Max asked him. "Is Addy all right?"

"Sure. Everyone calls me Addy. Addison is too pretentious to live up to, don't you think? I'd have to buy a cravat and riding boots and spend all day swapping bon mots with the baron and baroness."

"Perhaps your parents had high aspirations. Or is it a family name?"

"Both. It's a family name. My mother's family. She was an Addison"—and here he lifted his voice into a nasal falsetto—"'you know, the famous makers of Addison's Idaho potato chips and other wholesome snacks.' 'Famous' being a euphemism for richer than God, which they were—are—and never let anyone forget it. I have four siblings, all with names starting with *A*, but with normal names like Abigail."

"I believe I've actually heard of the brand—or of the family, rather."

"It was her grandfather, my great-grandfather, who started the line of products. He was a wily old coot, by all telling, who was buried clutching his Bible, which had his first dollar tucked between the pages—probably somewhere around St. Paul's letter to the Philistines. He renovated an old factory during the depression and started helping to feed the nation's appetite for relatively cheap, deep-fried foods. You can lay North America's current obesity epidemic squarely at his door. I never eat the things, myself."

"I see. So, you're from Idaho, then?"

Addy nodded. "That's right. Beautiful place. Great skiing. You ever been?"

"Not yet," Max replied. "One day I hope to visit. I do know you're a long way from home. What brings you here?"

Addy crossed one leg tightly over the other, lacing his hands together rather primly on top of his left knee. "On the accursed cruise, you mean? The short answer is Romero invited me. He became friendly with my agent when he was trying to acquire the screenplay rights to another of her author's books. She recommended me as someone who could turn the story into a screenplay."

"I thought the book's author did that."

"Turn his own book into a screenplay, you mean? Oh, God no. Not if they value their lives. Much better to cash the check and leave someone else with all the headaches."

"I see. And the long answer about what brought you here?"

"The long answer is that Romero knew from my agent I was researching a bio of Margot Browne, and he thought I might take her off his hands. Keep her busy with interviews and flattery, you know, while keeping her away from him and Trixie—what's her name."

"Tina," Max supplied.

"That's it. What an enormous idiot. I hope Romero knows what he's doing. Anyway, when someone offers you an all-expense-paid vacation on his luxury yacht, you accept, even though I was in the middle of *every*thing and the weather conditions were far from ideal for a pleasure cruise. We spent a lot of time below deck while we were at sea, praying for sunlight and sight of land, like a load of well-fed pilgrims. If you've spent any time with theater or movie people you might know that it's not as much fun as it may sound."

"Oh? Why's that?"

"I suppose because there really aren't that many roles in movies anymore, so they all scratch around like chickens after the leftover chicken feed. It's like Norma Desmond in that movie—you know, *Sunset Boulevard*: 'I am big. It's the pictures that got small.' Imagine a whole roomful or, in this case, a shipful of that sort of look-at-me nonsense. Actually, what's happened these days is the movies got big, bigger, biggest. It's only keeping the stuntmen and the special effects experts employed, filming these action movies. And the lead parts go to the same handful of actors every time. Tom Cruise and his boyish grin will keep appearing until they have to wheel him off the set. It's a cutthroat business—in fact, we need a new word for cutthroat."

"How about murderous," said Max mildly.

"Well, yeah. But surely you're not suggesting Margot was killed because she was threatening to take some other actress's part, are you? That is unlikely in the extreme, if only because if Margot were the last actress standing she'd still have trouble landing a role, any role."

"Because of her age?"

"Well, yes, frankly, there aren't that many parts for mature women." He was picking at the tear in one knee of his jeans, pulling on the loose threads. "But it's more than that. She had a reputation for being difficult. That's poison in this industry—in any industry, I guess. The fans may not care, so long as they get the escapism they paid for up there on the screen or on the stage. They might even think a reputation for difficulty enhances the fantasy—the star so powerful she can bend directors to her will. It adds some spice to their illusions. Margot was never all that. She was famously unreliable: she'd show up late on set three sheets to the wind more often than not. Rumors of cocaine use and even worse abounded, although I really don't think the 'even worse' was true: her chosen poison was booze. If she took drugs it was to help her sleep, and I think she may have been slightly hooked there, yes. Maurice—you've met Maurice?—he's a saint, really. Saint Maurice—I like the sound of that. He was the only one who could put up with her. After a while, he was the only one who even tried. But even Maurice—you don't want to push him too far, saint or no. He'll lose it when he's had enough."

"Do you think he's capable of this crime?" Max asked. "Is that what you're saying?"

"Not really. No." Addy's clear gaze slid away, then returned with the full force of a basically honest nature owning up to the truth.

"Well, sure. Everyone is *capable*. The question is, would he break like that? I think not. He's a decent sort, if a little high-strung."

Max couldn't help but agree: Maurice seemed unlikely, by nature and by lack of motive. But Maurice might have motives that couldn't yet be guessed at.

"Besides, there's an angle the police may be missing. I overheard something one night . . ."

"Oh?"

"Yes, oh. It was Margot and she was below deck talking to the chef. I've no idea what she was doing there but her voice carried up the companionway to where I happened to be standing. She was saying something like, 'Julie was only thirteen, wasn't it?'"

Max grew very still. "You're sure she was with Zaki?"

"That voice, that accent of his—they're unmistakable. Let's say I'm ninety percent sure. If she'd been with anyone else, I might have thought she was rehearsing a play or something. Then she said, 'No wonder you left Hollywood on the next boat out.'"

"And what did Zaki—or whoever—reply to that?"

"About what you'd expect. 'I don't know what you mean.'"

"But you took it to mean . . . What?"

"Given that I never could stomach the sight of Zaki? That he just gave me the creeps so much I didn't even want to eat the food he'd prepared? I think Margot had something on him. At a guess, something involving an underage girl."

However would Margot have got hold of that information? Max supposed the Hollywood grapevine had deep, tangled roots. How foolish of her to confront Zaki with what she knew—if there were truth behind her words, it was an extremely dangerous thing to do.

"When did you first meet Margot?" he asked Addy.

"I met her when she was starring in a play in New York called *Lyre, Lyre, Pants on Fyre*—some kind of Celtic detective musical, as I recall. Don't ask. I was hired as a sort of script doctor to punch up the play book, breathe some life into it. But it was DOA, really, long before I got there. The play folded within a couple of months, and it was an absolute freaking miracle it lasted that long. How it made it out of the fringe theaters is likewise a wonder. And all my rewrites went for nothing. Margot would get out there and ad lib for all she was worth—she was constantly going off-script, wandering around, moving the props. The poor guy playing opposite her felt like he'd wandered onto the wrong set, and would start to flub his own lines. Or his lines would make no sense in the context she'd just created. God, the memories. I'd stand in the wings grinding my teeth as she warbled her way through "Lord of the Wells," flitting hither and yon and upstaging all the actors. If you're looking for motives, you could start with the entire cast of that play."

"She could sing, then? I wasn't aware of that."

"No. No, she could not sing. At least, I wouldn't call it singing. Could Marilyn Monroe do more than sort of breathe and heave and shimmy her way through 'Happy Birthday'? I mean to say, no one was there to learn whether or not Margot Browne could sing. Despite the march of years, she appeared all but topless in that play."

"Did she often appear on the stage? I thought she was more a film star."

"She did both, although she was a better film star. Which is like saying malaria is a way better disease than typhoid—she could barely act in either case. But at least you can do a retake of a scene on film; what happens on stage is ground indelibly into memory."

"Why did she persist in it, do you think?"

"Oh, that's easy. She wanted to be taken seriously as an Actor— that's Actor with a capital *A*. Very early on she badgered some director into letting her appear in his play. The play was called *Shopgirl*—I think that was it. It didn't do too badly, really: had quite a long run in

London—see 'topless' as above. They say she had exquisite breasts then, like the Venus de Milo's or Pamela Harriman's."

"Hmm." Max failed to see how Margot's anatomy could end up being the key that would unlock the investigation, but Addy was a willing and articulate witness so he let him ramble on.

"And then of course there were the porn films. Or perhaps, just the one. Soft porn, I should add."

"You don't say," said Max. Might yet more blackmail play into this? If Margot had been trying to threaten or blackmail Zaki, for example, might he have countered by threatening to reveal something in her own past—if he knew of it? Was Margot likely to say, with Wellington, "Publish and be damned" to a blackmailer? Max thought she might.

"I don't judge her for that, do you? The porn? She was never in high demand and this . . . well, it paid the rent. She only did it because she was young and hungry, and the real parts were so few and far between. I think it's where she learned that if you can't act, you can at least take your clothes off, and you'll get by."

Max felt that in the grand scheme, people had done much worse things for money. The bigger problem with the entire porn industry, in his view, was that it was so exploitative—generally only the men profited from it. He said, "I wonder when all this was? The Celtic play, for example. A chronological telling might help."

"*Lyre, Lyre* was about five years ago. Maybe less. Mercifully, my memory fails me on many of the particulars. But there's nothing simpler than to find out." He reached for his laptop, tapped a few keys, and pulled up his own Web site, "Addywood," where appeared a list of all of Margot's roles throughout the years. It began with *Bad Cattle*, "the Western that made her famous," Addy assured him.

"I don't see how I missed that one," said Max. "I do like watching old films."

"Count your blessings. I was forgetting—no doubt you count blessings as a matter of course."

"I do try."

"Here we go," said Addy after a moment of scrolling up and down the screen. "Here's *Shopgirl*. If you want the dates for that one, you're looking way back: June 1981 to May 1983. God, to have been there to see it, but I wasn't born yet. It ran not quite two years but by West End standards that's practically *Mousetrap*. The play died a natural death once half the males of London had been by to ogle Margot's cleavage."

"After which, presumably, she returned to Hollywood."

"I guess so. There's a gap before she started rehearsals for *El Paso Posse*, another Western—a return to her roots, so to speak. She'd done well with her first Western and this was probably another trip to that well."

"Did it work? Was it successful, I mean?" It all sounded to Max like quite a climb down from her glory days in London.

"It did okay, but nothing like *Shopgirl*. With Margot, the only thing that mattered was the costume, and wearing jeans and a plaid shirt didn't allow her to show off the full range of her talent. She was hardly Barbara Stanwyck, after all. So after *El Paso Posse* she moved on to mysteries—what I believe you call crime stories in this country. The first of those was called *Bad Actress*—and didn't the critics just cry for happy over that title. But that's where she found her métier, in that sort of noir, pulp-revival thing. You know, the dame goes into the PI's office to beg for his help, only she ain't got the jake to pay him. But she's a nice kid so he takes pity and takes on the case pro bono and the next thing you know he's up to his neck in bullets. You know the kind of crap. And it turns out she ain't such a nice kid after all. Cut to the final reel, where she tries to leave him holding the bag from the big bank heist. I swear to God, I could write this stuff in my sleep. Anyway, Margot would take a bullet at the end every time, only to reappear in the next film, looking none the worse for wear."

"Actually, after talking with Maurice, I doubt that is true—the part about her being none the worse for wear. Her private life must have been showing up on her face after a few years, even with his expert attentions."

There was a still pause while Addison considered this. Finally he made a slight *tsk* sound and said, "The rumor mill started working overtime, yes. From the interviews I've conducted to date in Hollywood, and in London, with people who worked with her, she was on a slow but irreversible decline. Apparently, she wasn't too careful about the company she kept, or about where she kept it. Or how many she kept it with. I gather it didn't bother her if her lovers were married— the more married the merrier, in fact. Plus, there was a tangential sort of descent into the opium dens of L.A., if the gossip is anything to go by."

"Do you believe it? The gossip?"

Addy sat back in his chair, crossing his arms in a defensive posture. "It's neither here nor there if I believe it. I'm not writing an authorized biography or even an unauthorized one. And of course now that she's dead . . . well. I've barely cut through the concertina wire around her personal life—some, but not all of it. Anyway, I'm not claiming to write the absolute truth. Who can do that, anyway? You have to leave things out and put things in, and what's left may or may not be a fair portrayal of the subject. I'm writing a 'based on' story, or trying to, but I'm changing the details so much no one can ever come back to me and claim I've held them up to ridicule or caused them harm or something. I'm thinking about the married lovers here—I'm not going to get into some legal imbroglio as easily as all that. Of course, as I say, with Margot dead now it changes things."

"But the book you're writing—it's definitely about Margot. You've said as much, and not just to me."

Addy held up an admonishing finger. "Nope, and nice try. I am writing a story about a terrible actress of minimal talent who is coasting by on her looks until one day, she realizes she's nearly sixty, the parts have dried up long ago, and she's staring a lonely death in the face. But she never realizes it's her own behavior that has brought her to this sorry pass. That, my friend, is a description that could apply to half the people in Hollywood; at least, those of a certain age. And not necessarily just the women, either. It's *not* about Margot, which at some level must really irk the crap out of her—*have* irked the crap out of her—because its being all about her is what she lived for, for so long. It's about 'Everyactress,' if you will. If you want to get really deep or pretentious, we could say my book is about the human condition as much as it is about Margot. In fact, let's just say that it is and be done with it."

"But Margot inspired it," Max insisted. "Why Margot and not some other actress then?"

Addy shrugged. "I'd spent time with her during *Lyre, Lyre*. She really was one of a kind. I don't know—I was just drawn to her as a subject. Writers don't pick their topics; their topics pick them."

"How near are you to completing the book?" Max asked.

Addy replied with a shake of his head. "Honestly, I don't know. The writing's ground to a halt with her death and even I am not sure why. I may have to shelve the thing and go do something else."

Chapter 24

SUSPICION

Max left Addy after another half hour in which they examined some of Addy's online photo stills and video clips of Margot Browne. Nothing relevant turned up.

Apart from a scandal column that had run with a photo of Romero and Margot emerging together from a nightclub. "Reunited and It Feels So Good?" was the headline. Addy insisted the photo had been Photoshopped, and he pointed out the areas that indicated this doctoring. "Her head looks twice as big as his, for one thing. And his hand round her waist doesn't match the size nor the skin color of his other hand." His theory was that it was a story Margot had planted in the media herself. Max was inclined to believe Addy was right.

The true story of her past, Max decided, was not to be found in images of the various stage and film personas she had adopted, but in the personas she had assumed when not in front of a camera.

Max had gained no sense of Addy as a tormented soul hiding secrets, least of all that he was a murderer attempting to cover his tracks. Max had to allow that Addy could be a good actor as well as scriptwriter, but so often the two different talents were at odds with each other. A person operating behind the scenes required a different personality from one who sought the focus of the camera lens. If anything, Max gained the impression that Addy was just anxious for Max leave him alone so he could return to his writing.

Max imagined all the suspects were hoping he would leave them alone. If they made a fuss about having to hang about the hotel, with the Americans threatening to call their embassy ("Like they'd care," had been Patrice's comment), he supposed Cotton would have to release them all unless he could demonstrate more was to be gained by further questioning. Max had wondered why they stayed on, docile as lambs—wondered until he heard about the upcoming party at the hotel, in the planning for weeks. Something to do with the launch of Romero's latest picture, he supposed. No, wait, it was something to do with the premiere of a local film. Whatever the excuse, few of the people in this crowd could resist the siren call of Hollywood magic and the many photo ops the party would provide for the entertainment media. Once the party was over—well, it certainly gave Max and Cotton a deadline to aim for.

But keeping them all in place kept the murderer in place. While that might be convenient for the investigators, there was always the risk that anyone who had killed once might kill again. Might there not be someone besides Margot who, in the murderer's mind, needed to be silenced, for whatever reason?

Was there even a possibility they were dealing with a serial killer, someone who killed out of some uncontrollable bloodlust? It seemed unlikely, but Max supposed it was always just possible.

In any event, he knew that a case solved sooner was always better than one solved too late. Memories faded, witnesses disappeared, innocent people got tripped up—held for decades, sometimes, in a net of suspicion.

Sooner was always better than later.

Max spent the next few hours at his computer, putting his thoughts into coherent order—or trying to. Fighting down a growing sense of unease, he decided on a walk through Monkslip-super-Mare, tempted

by a sun that had by now dissolved most of an earlier drizzle. Before
he left, he had a word with one of the younger constables guarding
the hotel. The police were stretched thin as far as manpower, but
the goal was to keep an eye as much as possible on the inmates of the
hotel and the hallways leading to their rooms. It was an impossible
task in a hotel with such labyrinth passages, but Cotton's team had
been told to do its best. The constable had nothing to report—no
strangers had been seen prowling the hallways, at any rate.

"The baron and his lady are starting to make noises about leaving," he told Max.

"No one is to go without explicit permission. Warn them they
may be detained if they try to leave without authorization."

"That's legal, is it, sir?"

"It is for now." Max patted the constable's shoulder encourag-
ingly. The members of Cotton's team on guard duty had, in a way, the
tougher job, standing alert for hours, waiting for they knew not what.
Max knew from his own early days in MI5 that the duty amounted
to days of boredom interspersed with moments of heart-stopping ter-
ror. "Good man, Constable Robinson. Carry on."

For the next hour, Max Tudor skirted the edges of the harbor,
trying to assemble his thoughts on the case. A light mist clung to his
skin and hair, and masked the sea as it fretted its way along the shore-
line. The pigeons of Monkslip-super-Mare scattered about his feet as
he walked; they were fearless, and made their livings panhandling
from humans.

He stopped and looked at his watch: he wanted to spend more
time going over the files of the case, but couldn't forget the premiere
party that night. The event had been in the planning stages well before the murder had taken place, and the decision had been taken to
carry on regardless—a decision made, apparently, with few regrets.
While Max wouldn't receive an official invitation, he could, so Cotton
had suggested, crash the party with the police force turning a blind

eye as needed. The event's organizers would be the real hurdle to cross, but "you'll think of something," Cotton had assured him.

Max, running down his mental tally of suspects, realized he had spoken with all the main players in the case except Delphine Bee-chum, who had remained elusive and mysterious throughout—as befitted, he supposed, someone practiced in an esoteric art like yoga. When had yoga become so mainstream, anyway? Max wondered. It was familiar to him only because Awena had long set aside space in the back of her shop for classes.

But no connection between Delphine and Margot had come to light, according to Patrice's reports. No angry conversations over-heard, no long-ago ties revealed. Involved with drugs Delphine might well be, but that struck him as being a separate weave in the tapestry of the investigation. Still, there remained a possibility Margot had stumbled across the illicit drug activity on board, making her a threat that had to be removed. He needed to cross Delphine off the list, if crossed off she could be.

He had other reasons for wanting to talk with her. Those like her who had trained themselves to stillness, to tune out the interference of the day-to-day noise, could be the most useful as witnesses. If he couldn't find her tonight at the party, he would get Cotton to pin her to a formal interview in the morning. For she might have noted some strange behavior or other during the voyage among all those people traveling in tight quarters—some buildup of tension culminating in the death of Margot Browne.

In reviewing the other suspects, he felt he had hit a wall. They were a self-involved bunch, but were any of them up for murder? And what could be the motive? Would Tina, for example, really kill Mar-got out of jealousy? It was highly unlikely. Romero had made it clear, and Max believed him, that his relationship with Margot was very much in the past.

There was no discernible motive for Addy, and surely, anyway, it was in the best interests of the biographer that his subject remain alive to be available for further interviews. It would be a reach for Addy to believe killing Margot would help him get his book published— that her murder would somehow create a demand from the reading world worth killing for. An author might be ruthless in pursuit of publication, Max supposed, but in this case that motive would be stretching things a bit too far. Addy was not only already a successful author, but, with a potato chip fortune behind him, he had been spared the sort of financial desperation that might tempt him to such a wild scheme. Besides, did Addy even have a completed manuscript ready in case the worst befell Margot? He said not, and he seemed to be preoccupied with other projects. If his goal was to beat other biographers to the punch, killing her would mean he had acted too much in haste.

Then there was Romero. Would he actually kill Margot because she was an inconvenience, pestering him for a role in his film? Not likely.

And Maurice—would Maurice kill someone of whom he clearly had been fond? Why would he? It had happened before, of course: love could make people do desperate things, but fear could make them do far worse. Perhaps she had something on Maurice, and was blackmailing him over it—but if so, it would be the devil to uncover what it was. Besides, wasn't it more likely to be the other way round—that Maurice would have compromising information on Margot?

Jake? Killing in some jealous, murderous rage? Actually, the more he thought about it, Jake's relationship to Margot seemed distant, cold somehow—not a union of passionate lovers, but an agreed-upon arrangement by two people who found each other convenient. Of course, that was true in any relationship once you scraped the surface, but this union came across as highly calculated. Hadn't Jake said something along those lines? "As long as we were both getting what we wanted"—words to that effect. Hardly a ringing endorsement of true love. Of course, the age difference there may well have tempered the appetites.

The baron and baroness? Those two—he could not put his finger on what was wrong there. They were up to something, but was it necessarily criminal? A minor con, perhaps. A con that had spun out of control, leading them to a larger crime? That he could see happening in their case.

Motive was the problem all down the line. He just couldn't see his way clear around that barrier. On the surface, Margot was a threat to no one, apart from her being a bit of a loose cannon. The threat she posed may have been almost an accidental one.

And those were always the toughest cases to prove: an innocent stumbling into the wrong place at the wrong time, and ending up dead.

That song had got stuck in his head, the one from which Patrice had quoted: "An actor's life for me." It was a song from the animated film *Pinocchio*—this he knew because since his son Owen's arrival, he'd become rather an expert on animated films and bedtime stories, with frequent recourse to the stories of Beatrix Potter and an emphasis on the adventures of Mrs. Tiggy-Winkle. He was also building up a large repertoire of animal sound effects, moos and oinks and meows. Max was constantly amazed to realize the extent to which he was willing to go to raise a laugh from his young son.

The *Pinocchio* tune had haunted him so much the night before, he'd finally done a search for it on his laptop. It is sung by the manipulative con man Honest John as he and Gideon take the puppet Pinocchio to Stromboli's Caravan, promising Pinocchio he will be a star. It was a song of temptation, of seduction into the easy life, a harking to the call of easy money.

Max had paused, looked up from the computer. Pinocchio had been promised stardom. So, presumably, had Margot at some point in her career. At many points, in fact. That was indeed the actor's life. It might be close to being a gambler's addiction. The next film, the next play, was going to be the award-winner, the one that would make the actor live in memory. Was that the connection, the source of the nagging earworm that would not let him go? Margot's constant trying for the brass ring, the hope of success which grew fainter with the passage of time? What would she sacrifice to achieve her goal? Everything and everyone?

Sunk deep in thoughts of fleeting fame, Max suddenly pulled up behind an elderly couple bundled tightly against the cold—wrapped in thick scarves and gloves and woolens, holding hands and leaning into one another, for the woman wasn't too steady on her pins. The man walked with his head thrust forward, a half-smile of anticipation on his lips, like someone looking at the end of a journey. Max wondered if these might even be the Emersons, the couple who had discovered Margot's body.

Max took the conscious decision to slow down to their snail's pace rather than sprint past as if he were late for an appointment. To learn from them, and to take in the sights he'd have missed if he overtook them. He reasoned that they had not reached such a great age without accumulating a certain store of wisdom, and he found himself eavesdropping on their conversation, a charming combination of good-natured banter and concern for the other's welfare. She expressed in a whispery voice a wish for some flowers for their dining room table. "And you shall have them," was his reply. It was said in such a way that Max knew this man's certain joy in life had been in granting his wife's every small wish.

This, he hoped, would be himself and Awena given forty more years. Bundled in wool against the cold and relying ever more on each other for support, more in sync than even now they were, and every passing year bestowing grace along with the wrinkles. Owen would be well out of the nest and on his own by then. Perhaps there would be another child; a girl would be nice next time. Perhaps grandchildren to look forward to . . .

They had survived what Max thought of as the nightmare time. When Awena had been hospitalized and he awoke each day—when he slept at all—to the searing fear that he might yet lose her. Some hospital mishap. Some unforeseen complication. Some new lunatic sent out by a fiendish unknown, bent on revenge. The episode had left a legacy of dread and a deeper love than Max had believed was possible for the human heart to contain.

Dropping behind the couple, he sent them on their way with a silent blessing, watching them turn a corner and begin their slow steep climb up Albert Street. He passed several establishments selling sarnies and pizzas, not all of them open this early in the season. The painted cottages ringing the coastline provided a cheery backdrop of pastel pinks and turquoises and yellows against a sky overcast and mud-gray. Gulls swooped and glided overhead; one carried a hapless fish in its beak. On a distant hill, he could just trace the outline of one of the manor houses that dotted the area, many dating to Elizabethan times, or it may have been one of the ancient abbeys he saw, once nearly demolished beyond repair and now salvaged and converted into private homes. He knew from the brochures provided by the hotel that in summer these establishments opened to the public to share the treasure of their lush gardens, their carefully tended topiaries, and their extravagant follies or summer houses. In winter, the owners would withdraw behind wrought-iron gates to wait beside hand-carved stone fireplaces for the return of good sailing weather.

Passing an ancient church next to the Monkslip-super-Mare Yacht Club, he came upon a sign advertising the "Royal National Lifeboat Institution," the charity established to save lives at sea. The sign claimed the RNLI rescued an average of twenty-two people a day—an astonishing statistic when Max thought about it. Sailors, windsurfers, swimmers—everyone at risk from the fearsome push and pull of the waves.

Max thought the RNLI might have saved Margot if she'd been given half a chance, but of course she'd been dead before she hit the water. He stopped to wonder why her death by drowning had not been left to chance—it was nearly a sure thing, with the yacht's being that far from shore—but of course there could be not the slightest risk taken by a murderer of leaving a live witness.

The weather seemed unable to make up its mind to do anything other than glower erratically. At the moment the horizon was stacked high with sooty cotton-ball clouds, and the harbor was alive with a bobbing fleet of fishing boats. He gathered that in every sort of weather this was a working harbor, with people depending on the sea for their livelihoods, as they had done always. He watched as a group of fishermen unloaded their glistening catch, the men loudly profane as they struggled against the slippery weight. A sign next to a docked ferry assured him that in two weeks' time it would carry passengers from one side of the harbor to the other. Meanwhile an old sailing ship roiled against the tide; it appeared to be waiting for guests to come be regaled by costumed men and women with tales of the hazards of the sea. It was somewhere near this old ship that Margot's body had been found by the Emersons.

He came to the pavilion, gaily decorated with strings of fairy lights. He set the stone pier as his goal, now keeping the harbor to his left. He eyed the yachts in the water, none so fine as Romero's, of course. He also spotted an imposing navy vessel far out to sea. He passed more restaurants and pubs, and fish and chip shops without end, before climbing steep steps to cross the bridge, which at set times of the day would open to allow tall-masted ships to pass beneath. The bridge was illuminated at night, and he could see it from his hotel window; it looked like a structure abandoned by scientists on Mars.

He circled back round to the lifeboat station, and thought of those who go down to the sea in ships in all weathers, the brave ones who unhesitatingly put their lives on the line when sailors and fishermen, wise or foolish, found themselves in trouble.

He stood and watched as another group of local fishermen unloaded a large haul of crabs. He knew the lobsters had come back, too, for the woman at the hotel's front desk had happily told him so. The entire reason for the staff's existence seemed to be to ensure that Max's stay with them was a happy one; in case a lobster dinner were what he most wanted in life, that could be organized.

The staff did not at first connect his presence with that of Cotton and his team, not until they had seen the two men together a few times, striding purposefully across the lobby, at which point the stories had begun to swirl about. MI5 and MI6 consulting on a mission, certainly that was it, they thought, never knowing how close their guesses came.

Before that, what had they imagined? A lone man, recovering by himself from a loss or a breakup, perhaps. The wedding ring symbolizing Max's attached state didn't stop the female side of the staff from romanticizing him over tea in the break room, speculating over what had brought him there and what might induce him to stay. The general hope was that he was a widower (but not *too* recent a widower, for his grief might complicate things) and the further consensus was that he could leave his shoes under their beds anytime he liked.

The object of the women's affections meanwhile stood quietly unawares as dusk fell over the village. Across the harbor, through the furled masts of ships at rest in their slips, Max saw the baron and baroness walking into the hotel. They were hand in hand like the elderly couple, but looking like a magazine ad for expensive timepieces or French perfume. Even the darkening sky cooperated in enhancing the beauty of this pair, the low spotlights that illuminated the garden casting them in a glow like two saints in a stained-glass window. They were perfect. Perfectly formed, perfectly dressed, perfectly coiffed, perfect together in every way.

What was it about that perfection that bothered him so?

Chapter 25

THERE'S NO BUSINESS LIKE
SHOW BUSINESS

Later that night Max stood to one side of the large hotel foyer, watching a large crowd surge its way toward the doors which opened onto the ballroom. He was assessing the strength of the security procedures, and waiting his chance to blend into the throng.

There was no trick to it, really. Gate-crashing a celebrity party was as easy as could be. Everyone charged with security was so busy pretending not to gawk, trying so hard to be cool and blasé, they missed the forest for the trees, every time.

The successful gate-crasher simply attached him- or herself to a large, boisterous group of partygoers as they approached the entrance and pretended to be one with the crowd, laughing and smiling maniacally at whatever was being said. It didn't hurt, of course, that Max looked like a movie star in the first place. He saw people do a double take, wondering who he was and what film they might have seen him in, and he saw the phone cameras pointing in his direction. It occurred to no one to ask to see his invitation; his walk and bearing confirmed his right to be there. As "his" group approached the security station, Max stood aloof, slightly to one side, as if to demonstrate that the security guard was beneath his notice and that Max's precious time was being wasted by such bureaucratic rigmarole—I mean, *really*. Then he swept in through the door with the others, his head thrown back in laughter, his teeth gleaming as they caught the light of the camera flashes. His photograph would appear almost instantaneously online and in the next day's newspaper, where he would be misidentified as Ewan McGregor. There would be widespread Internet pandemonium as bloggers speculated as to why Ewan's hair had turned darker, why he looked even more divinely handsome than before, and why his wife, Eve Mavrakis, was not at his side. Max doubted this case of mistaken identity would fool his bishop for a moment (after all, the poor man was used by now to coming across news photos of his most charismatic and trouble-prone priest) but then again, that was all right these days: Max had been given tacit permission to involve himself "where souls or lives might otherwise be lost." It was an expression that rather reminded Max of the words inscribed on the gate of Hell in Dante's *Inferno*.

Looking around at the goings on, Max felt this party certainly would qualify at least in fulfilling the former condition—it was hardly a Girl Guides convention. Some of the women wore clothes that defied gravity in staying attached to their wearers—some of the men did, as well. The women teetered on six-inch-high heels—again, some of the men did, too. Satins and silks abounded, as did a feathery boa scarf or two. The jewelry alone made the place a natural magnet for a cat burglar working the resorts, and Max spotted a few guests who almost certainly had been placed there by management to keep an eye on things that might otherwise go missing. He recognized a retired colleague of his from MI5 days and, knowing he must be in the room acting as extra security, Max nodded imperceptibly and kept going. In the center of the room was a large fountain that literally spouted champagne, each corner of the room sported a full bar, and against each wall were long tables laden with every sort of tempting delicacy. Max sidestepped the champagne and made straight for a platter of cheese and bread, realizing he'd not taken time to eat that day and was ravenous.

He had talked with Awena earlier on the phone as she'd been preparing a spring salad to go with her homemade vegetable-noodle soup and seed bread. He knew that even with the several types of caviar on offer at the party, nothing here would taste as good. Tomorrow she had a BBC camera crew arriving to film the next installment of *The Pagan Vegan*, her popular organic cooking series, which had reinforced "foraging" as the new catchphrase among foodies. Even a visit to the local market these days was considered foraging, of course, but for those with a real passion for all-natural everything, Awena's show was can't-miss viewing. It had grown in popularity, with advertisers queuing for airtime, and with concomitant offers for publishing contracts and guest appearances. Awena, being Awena, balanced it all with aplomb, declining the guest appearances and sifting through the book offers that, as she put it, "offered the greatest benefit to the greatest number." She held the belief that the planet could only be saved when people focused solely on locally grown fruits and vegetables and eschewed any food that had to be flown in.

She'd held the phone's handset up to Owen, and Max could have sworn his son addressed him as "father." Which made sense, when Max thought about it. It was what the child heard his parishioners call him, after all; he'd have to work on winning him over to a less-formal "Dada." This "father" was followed by incomprehensible shrieks of glee and pretend talk—although Max clearly heard him say the name of his dog, Thea. Owen was eight months old and Max felt his grasp of English was already superior to that of any eight-month-old of his acquaintance. Owen would be reciting poetry in no time. Perhaps they could introduce a few words of French into his daytime routine, which currently consisted largely of napping and eating. That he was now acquainted with a wide range of solid foods was a further source of pride to his parents. Awena was now working on a cookbook that incorporated all natural, homemade baby foods. The working title was *Mush*.

Awena had come back on the line. "Do you know," she said, "I spent some time today looking up Margot Browne online. What a sad life she seems to have led."

"Yes, and one leading to a bitterly sad end. They are trying to locate someone from her family with an interest in organizing a memorial service or at least in giving the coroner instructions on what to do with the body once it's been released. She didn't seem to have anyone who cared what happened to her, except possibly her stylist, and for his own self-preservation, he told me, he'd had to wash his hands of her years ago. Or at least, to keep a safe distance."

"That would be Maurice . . . oh, what's his last name?"

"Maurice Brandon. I suspect he'll be the one to arrange some sort of farewell for her. But how on earth do you know about Maurice?"

"Oh, Max," Awena sighed. It was her "I love you but you are hopeless" sigh. The sigh she used when Max demonstrated once again how out of step he was with what was happening in modern "culture."

"Maurice Brandon—he's known in most circles simply as Maurice—is probably the world's most famous stylist. He's worked on all the biggest stars in Hollywood. They call him the Miracle Worker. Believe me, most of those performers without makeup don't even look like the same person. They look like a shorter, squatter, and balder missing link, if photos I've seen are anything to go by. It's more than that, though: he's their confidant. People trust him. He really does know where all the bodies are buried in the Hollywood Hills but he will never tell all or sell out. Not he. It's how he's built up his clientele and his reputation."

Max suspected Awena was telling him all this for a reason. "Are you saying he would keep these women's secrets, even during a police investigation?"

"Men's and women's," she corrected. "He styles both sexes. But yes, he probably would. I mean, I don't know the man but from what I've read he would want to be absolutely sure of his ground before he ran around spouting his suspicions. He really is the soul of discretion, known for his integrity."

Max had said with a tinge of exasperation, "That's exactly the sort of behavior that can earn you lots of attendees at your own funeral—keeping secrets from investigators in a case like this. It is commendable he has such integrity but if he's keeping something back, it's dangerous for him and for everyone."

"I know. You might try him again, Max." After a pause, she said, "I'm glad you're there to find out who did this. To put a stop to any more of it. She deserved better. Margot had this sort of zany gift, I suppose you'd call it—that star quality . . . people cared about her. Just not enough, it would appear, or in the right ways."

It was odd, reflected Max. While nearly devoid of talent, Margot had managed to build a loyal following of people who could quote at length from her movies—usually exaggerating her already exaggerated manner, it was true. She was still credited with the popularity of things like the Margot haircut: a style of thick waves curling about the shoulders, a style that harkened back to the days of studio stars like Marilyn Monroe and Jane Russell. Possibly Maurice had had something to do with inventing the hairstyle.

"I'll do what I can," Max had told Awena. "Must dash now."

"Have fun, if that's the right term. Oh! And Destiny wants to know where you keep the gluten-free wafers."

Max described where the communion wafers could be found in the vestry. He didn't understand why but more and more of his congregation were asking for the alternate wafer.

"Got it. Catch this person! See you soon," Awena had said, ringing off in a typically breezy Awena manner. Here was her husband surrounded by professional beauties and all the excesses Hollywood could provide—he would be wading this night through a veritable Sodom and Gomorrah—but there was not a question in her mind that Max's presence was essential, much less that he would or could be led astray. She seemed to have forgotten all about Patrice, which also was typical. She knew there was no need for worry, even before learning Patrice was somewhat out of commission in that regard, anyway. Max doubted if anything he'd said on the subject of Patrice had rankled or had remained with Awena for long. She certainly knew her husband had a past—a past that had been at times riotous—but felt, as he did, that his life and hers had not really begun until they'd met in Nether Monkslip those few short years ago.

Glancing now around the glittery ballroom—yes, there was Maurice. Surrounded by sycophantic young people; it was good to see that his star wasn't dimming.

Max rubbed a hand down the left side of his neck, where the muscles were tightening from the strain of the investigation—from days of disturbed sleep and catch-as-catch-can meals. He wished Awena were there with him, with her seemingly magical ability to heal by "channeling energy." He had experienced the truth of her talent himself on more than one occasion. And of course she credited her own miraculous recovery following the explosion with her capacity to attach herself to the swirling light energies that surrounded her. Max pictured this light being drawn to her in somewhat the way lint attached itself to felt. When he had shared this rather prosaic image with her, she had enthusiastically agreed. "Yes," she'd said solemnly. "It's exactly like that." She also claimed that every person carried about them a sort of musical aura, and that some people were chimes and other people were clankers. She assured Max that of course he was one of the chimers, as was Owen. Max had long since given up understanding Awena, but he would love her with his last breath.

Now Max accepted a glass of red wine from a passing waiter—he'd never cared much for champagne, even Veuve Clicquot—and carried his plate of bread, cheese, and olives over to where Maurice held court.

"Of course," Maurice was saying, "Marilyn was everyone's favorite, but even someone like Margot would not be foolish enough to try to go head-to-head with her legacy. There was something about Marilyn—you could see how fragile she was. So very shy, really. Possibly the last person to go into show business but aren't we all grateful she—Oh, hello, Max. Let me introduce you."

Max nodded, recognizing many of the headline names and finding it interesting to see these eminences in person. They looked—normal, for lack of a better word. And shorter than expected. He chatted lightly with them, storing up anecdotes to share with Awena on his return, wondering, as the conversation turned to articles in the most recent issue of *Variety*, what on earth they were talking about. They drifted away, chatting about box office returns. He had Maurice to himself for the moment.

"You can't be old enough to have met Marilyn Monroe in person," he said.

"What a lovely compliment!" said Maurice. "No, no, you're quite right. It was my mother who knew her. She did Marilyn's hair for some of her films, you know, and she was absolutely wrecked by the news of her death. She wouldn't leave her bed for weeks. You should have seen my mother's house before she herself died, twenty years later: it was a positive shrine to Marilyn. My mother never believed for one moment Marilyn died of a deliberate overdose, for what it's worth. My mother was very much plugged in to all things Hollywood, so she would know. But all she ever did was hint darkly: Marilyn was full of plans for the future and never would have done away with herself. My mother held that it was better to say nothing when nothing could be proved, and that gossip wouldn't bring her back, anyway."

Like mother, like son. "Have you," Max asked, "heard anything more?"

"About Margot? You mean, like a full confession by someone to her murder? No, but if I did, you'd be the first to know."

Why did that have such a ring of falsehood about it? Perhaps it was Maurice's expression, that butter-wouldn't-melt look. What on earth was the man playing at?

"I know this goes against your grain," Max said. "And that you're known for your discretion. Most commendable that is, too. We should all have such a reputation. But if you have an inkling, a suspicion, even a wild, fleeting guess . . . Because I don't mind telling you, the police are not finding anything much to go on. There's no real physical evidence that wasn't washed away from the body—no DNA, no fingerprints. Sometimes they can raise prints when the victim has been throttled, you know." The color began to drain slowly from Maurice's face; champagne sloshed over the lip of his glass and he had to step back as a few drops fell onto the tips of his shoes.

"*Please!*" he said.

"Someone needs to answer for her death," Max continued, unrelenting. "It was a horrible, frightening way to go. She was shown no mercy."

Maurice assumed an expression of the utmost severity, a completely changed man from the happy, fawned-over celebrity of just moments before.

"I agree. In this case, I have to agree completely that the seal of the confessional—something about which you may know a thing or two, Father?—will have to be broken. Yes, Addy told me about you— did you really think he wouldn't? I owe it to my clients, in life and in death, to live up to their trust in me."

"This is a special case," said Max. He was growing alarmed. What had seemed an admirable stance amounting to an affectation had grown into some monstrous and intractable position that might do more than derail the investigation. For the first time, Max had a real concern that Maurice was putting himself in danger.

He was also impressed by the speed of the Hollywood grapevine. He hadn't realized Addy was that close to Maurice.

It was as if Max hadn't spoken.

"I have a suspicion, yes, but I need to confirm it," Maurice said. "Because I might be on completely the wrong track and just playing a hunch, a guessing game. With someone's life! It's only fair, you know. If I'm wrong—*quel désastre!* Now, I must bid you good night. I may turn in early. It's all catching up with me."

"Very well," said Max, seeing the man would not be moved, and privately deciding on ways to protect Maurice from himself. He would get Cotton to have someone posted outside Maurice's hotel door and to have him followed. The waste of manpower chafed but Maurice seemed immovably contrary. He considered having Cotton threaten him with a charge of obstructing justice, but turning Maurice into a martyr didn't seem the way to go. He decided on one more try: "But," he said, "can't you at least give us a hint?"

Ah, good! Max could see Maurice hesitate. It was then Max realized that along with Maurice's undoubted integrity he was enjoying exercising a certain sense of power. After years of operating behind the scenes, here was Maurice in the spotlight, and he was going to play it for all it was worth. He leaned over and spoke into Max's ear.

". . . 'The play's the thing, Wherein I'll catch the conscience of the King.'"

Oh, surely not. *Hamlet* now.

"Don't forget, 'One may smile, and smile, and be a villain,'" Max quoted in his turn. "For heaven's sake, do be careful, Maurice. There is such a thing in this world as pure evil."

One of the young sycophants returned just then, and Max allowed Maurice to be swept away. Not without a final warning glare, which was returned with a light-hearted, no-worries smile.

Chapter 26

DELPHINE

Max stood looking about him, hoping to find others from the ill-fated ship. Finally he spotted Delphine Beechum grazing by one of the buffet tables. Delphine—in charge of fun times on the yacht, whatever that job title might entail. A bit more than organizing offshore excursions, apparently. Since she was not a starlet, he wondered if perhaps she, too, was a party crasher.

She stood happily alone, confidently observing the glamorous crowd and taking small sips of her champagne. Max strode over to her side. She brightened visibly at his approach, and once again he was reminded he was operating without the protective shield of his collar. He had in fact dressed down for the occasion, knowing that in a Hollywood crowd jeans and a roll neck jumper would help him blend in.

"Well, hi," Delphine said cheerfully. "I don't recall seeing you in these parts before. You're not one of the actors in Romero's new film?"

"No, no," said Max. "Actually, I've been engaged to look into what happened on board the yacht. To Margot Browne, you know."

"Oh! For real? You're like a private eye?" Max didn't have the chance to correct her before she gushed on, "I was wondering when someone would get around to having a *real* talk with me. I think they assume because I'm part of the staff and below deck half the time I must know very little."

"Oh?" She had Max's attention. As he had noted previously, Delphine's ability to move seamlessly between two worlds made her an obvious source of information. That and her presumed ability to tune in to nuance. She would have made a good spy. "And you think you know something?"

She nodded energetically; her long earrings shimmered in the subdued light from the chandeliers. "Some sergeant or other spoke with me for half an hour but I had scads more I could have said. He sort of gave me the once-over—name, rank, and serial number, you know—and moved on."

"But you think you know something more—something relevant to the investigation?" He didn't plan to question her about her likely drug involvement, nor even mention his suspicions—not before she'd told him what she knew about life on board the yacht. He would leave that thread of the investigation for others to follow up. Margot was his focus.

"Yes and no." With a flutter of one hand, she signaled a passing waiter and, handing him her champagne glass, said, "Could I have some water, please?" To Max she confided, "All this drinking is so bad for the skin. I usually don't indulge, you know, but given the past few days . . . well."

Max asked the waiter to make it two glasses. He wasn't worried about his skin so much as he needed to keep a clear head for what might be a long night ahead.

"I can understand," he said. "It must be quite upsetting."

"Well, there's all the drama—and no one can do drama quite like a troupe of actors, of course—but there's also the fact we're just stuck here. Becalmed, so to speak, until the police say we can go. And they're being very cagey about when that might be. I've offered to host yoga sessions in my room to keep everyone calm, and a few of the people from on board the ship have taken me up on it—you should join us;

you'd love it!—but it's not like it's a full-time job and I'm getting worried . . ."

"You're worried Romero might decide it's time to scale back on the payroll. Of course, I can see that. He's got deckhands and people like that who have to be paid regardless. But I'm sure the authorities will release most of you soon and you can continue your voyage." Max was being disingenuous—Delphine might well be detained, particularly if hard evidence turned up against her. "Where was the yacht headed next, anyway?"

"After Weymouth, we were sailing to Amsterdam and back to France. Romero was waiting for it to get a bit warmer before starting to scout locations for his next movie."

"Which is—I mean, what's the movie about?"

She seemed to pout as she thought this one over, her glossy pink lips scrunching into a thoughtful, provocative moue. She was dressed in a sort of mermaid costume: a tight green sequined number that hugged her curves before flaring out in waves of ruffles at the knees. She had piled her golden hair on top of her head and held it in place with a small tiara. She was, in a word, gorgeous. If you overlooked the slightly calculating cast to her eyes, you'd conclude she was from a higher realm, some sort of angel or goddess sent to earth.

"God, who knows," she said at last. "I can't remember the title, but does it matter? It's the same old thing, except this time set in ancient Gaul. Soldiers raping, pillaging, feasting. Repeat. Sometimes they set fires to villages after defiling all the maidens and toppling all the temples and things. It's pure dreck. He's done the same movie over and over in different settings and time periods. The First Boer War, World War II, the Intergalactic Whatzit."

"People seem to like it."

"People seem to like being stabbed repeatedly in the eye with a needle, if you ask me. It's the anti—antith—it's the *op*posite of everything I stand for, you know. Yoga is about peace and harmony. About Love with a capital *L*." She rounded off this last sentiment with an otherworldly smile and a flutter of thick eyelashes in Max's direction. She was flirting with him, he recognized, but in what seemed a highly superficial way. He recalled Patrice's comment that Delphine flirted just to keep in practice, and he thought he understood now what she'd meant. He gained the impression Delphine would flirt with any male who crossed her path.

"It's interesting that Romero felt the need of a yoga instructor—a good sign, perhaps?" said Max. "Maybe he's starting to feel there isn't much to a life of filming blood and gore all the time."

"He wants to get away from it, I know. But the stupid stuff—that's all they'll let him do, he says. The producers, the money guys. More of the same old, same old. So he uses yoga to, like, balance out his life."

"And how about Tina? Is she a devotee, as well?"

Delphine threw her head back, laughing, making the earrings jingle like soft chimes.

"You could say that. Mainly *Tee*-na"—here she fluttered her fingers about her ears to indicate the general silliness of such as Tina—"Tina likes yoga because it allows her to wear tight pants with a low-cut halter top. I mean, the philosophy behind the whole thing just passes her by. Who does yoga in full makeup with eyelashes, anyway?"

"Hmm," Max said neutrally.

He was about to ask about the night Margot died when Delphine said, "And that is totally why Margot was killed, I think." She nodded darkly. "Karma. It's killer, that stuff. What goes round . . . you know."

He felt somehow they'd skipped over a page here. "How is that?" he asked. "Assuming you don't mean she misbehaved in a previous life." That would make a stunning if improvable defense, he thought.

The court system would grind to a standstill while past-life psychics were brought in to testify.

"Well, probably she did, but I'm thinking it's more about happenings in this lifetime than in any previous incarnations. Margot was a young soul, you know. She was one of those people who kept making the same mistakes and never *saw* it was the same mistake over and over. *Big* duh."

"It's so easy to see it in others, isn't it?" said Max as the waiter approached with their drinks. At this party, it was not mere tap water on offer, but an expensive brand he'd never heard of. Something from ancient glacier melt, no doubt. Something with gold dust settling at the bottom.

"You're so right," she agreed, with a polite nod of thanks to the waiter, who seemed transfixed by the attention from this mythical sea creature. Max wanted to ask her how she'd ended up where she'd ended up—which was at the heart of a murder investigation, far from home and apparently up to no good. He recalled that home was somewhere in New Hampshire, near the border with Vermont.

"We can't see our own mistakes," she went on. "But honestly, Margot had had the error of her ways pointed out to her more than once, sometimes by the international media. Usually, it was the disgruntled spouse or girlfriend of whoever she was 'dating' at the moment, and the pointing out was done at the top of loud voices. 'Dating' being a euphemism for a lot of things, of course, but trying to steal someone else's partner was usually part of the scenario."

"She saw it as a challenge, do you think?"

"I do. Who wants the latest thing unless everyone else wants it—you know that kind of thinking? They chant that mantra on Madison Avenue every day. So the man, whoever he was, had to be rich, and good-looking, and powerful. He had to be the object of attention, a rising star in his field, whatever it was. Usually it was movies or the theater, because of course that's the world in which Margot rolled most often. But if you'd seen her at the races in Monaco—my God. It was like she'd seen whole new worlds to conquer, opening before her very eyes. If the man was already married—that was just the cherry on top. You could see her go after these guys from across a crowded room—separate them from their wives, she would; just cut them out of the herd before the man or his wife knew what was happening."

"Jake Larsson doesn't seem to fit the profile. He's not married, is he?"

"No, and neither is he rich and powerful. Good-looking and ambitious—arm candy for Margot. Younger than her usual, for certain. Yes, this is where the karma part comes in. Margot could no longer command the sort of men who once came running when she crooked her finger. She was reduced to such as Jake."

"Reduced?"

"Yah. Reduced. Jake is no better than he should be. He uses drugs, for sure—why don't they just swallow poison? Same result. Your head explodes or your gut does and then one day: no more Jake."

Max guessed she was being completely disingenuous—holier-than-thou was so often a useful cover. At the same time, she was implicating Jake in the drug scene. Was he one of her "clients"?

"But Jake sees—saw—Margot as a stepping stone to greater things. It was a matter of time before he woke up to the truth. Actually, from watching them together, always in a state of armed siege, he had already woken."

"They weren't getting along?"

She shrugged. "'Course not. Margot had alienated most of her connections over the years. You can't network with that many holes in your net. Poor guy, I could almost feel sorry for him if I liked him better. For both of them."

So. If she'd been seen flirting with Jake it was not, apparently, because she fancied him. Always supposing she was telling the truth.

"So just as Margot used people, so she was being used."

"Right. You got it. Karma—big time." She twirled a ring on her left index finger, a Celtic symbol of infinity with a large diamond at its center. She watched Max drink the high-end water, his wedding band now on full display. Her face crinkled with disappointment, but she rallied quickly. "So, tell me, Max, what's it like being a private eye? Do you need a license and stuff? Because while my yoga practice will always be a part of who I am, I might need to look at steadier employment."

Max wasn't sure that being a private eye would qualify as steady work at the best of times. But he decided not to mislead her further. The news of who he was would reach her soon, anyway. He said, "I'm not a private eye. I mean, I am here in an unpaid, unofficial capacity to assist the police."

"Really?" She looked at him suspiciously, as well she might. "So you sort of investigate freelance? But for no pay?"

Max looked around. There was no one to overhear. No one coming to rescue him from his predicament, either.

"That's more or less correct. I'm the vicar of a small church in Nether Monkslip. I am—"

She snapped her fingers. "Yes! *Yes!* That's where I've seen you before. I knew it! Max Tudor—of course. You've been in the news, haven't you? Murder investigations, suspicious deaths, all that. *Well.* Well, well. It is a pleasure to meet you, truly. My mother and father are both Episcopal priests. You could say religion runs in the family."

You could say that, thought Max, but you'd be wrong. He was having a harder and harder time reconciling Delphine's background with that of a drug dealer, but she wouldn't be the first child of religious parents to run amok. To rebel for the sake of rebellion. The pressure never to put a foot wrong could be intense; it was like being the offspring of a headmaster or prime minister. "Me, I wanted to see the world—*Eat, Pray, Love,* you know; such an inspirational book—and that included seeing what other religions had to offer. And do you know what? I've decided it's all paths to the same place."

"My wife would agree with you."

"Really? Cool. Anyway, it was my dad started following your exploits a while back. I think it's a bit of hero worship on his part, between you and me and my mom. Not that he wants his parishioners to drop dead or anything like that—God forbid; he'd be horrified— but he'd love to solve the crime if they *were* the victims of foul play. Poison in the chalice—you know. So, of course I know who you are; I just couldn't put two and two together."

"You don't say," said Max. "How . . . remarkable."

"Oh, sure. The media in the States picked up on it when you solved that nunnery caper. The 'Canny Cleric,' they call you."

Good Lord. "I hope the name doesn't stick," said Max.

"Oh, just wait 'til I tell my dad!"

Max was still stalled on "Canny Cleric."

"How absolutely appalling," he said, knowing his bishop would never let him forget it if that came to his ears. Nor would Cotton. "I say, I'd rather you—"

"We'll have to come up with something better. What do you think of the 'Saintly Sleuth'? Or—wait, I've got it!—the 'Prying Priest'?"

"God in heaven, no. And whatever you do, don't spread the word about the nunnery investigation to the others. I'm not sure how useful I can be to the inquiry once it's known I—"

"Once your cover's blown. Got it." She tapped one finger alongside her pert nose, which at this point was reddening from excitement or nervousness at meeting her first celebrity priest. Or was he witnessing fear—a fear of discovery? "Your secret is safe with me, Father. I'll take it to my gra—oh, sorry. I mean, I . . ."

Max just then was alerted to a hubbub at the entryway to the ballroom. Turning, he recognized Cotton by the gleam of his fair hair as it caught the lights, and he saw the flash of the warrant card

Cotton was pointing at an officious private guard. Quickly losing his patience, Cotton swept past the gatekeeper and plunged into the crowd. Max pushed his own way through the multitude, heading in Cotton's direction and holding his glass aloft to keep it from the jostling throng. The dazzling hordes on both sides of the room interrupted their laughing conversation as they parted to admit the men, the beautiful and the mighty turning to stare as the two met in the center of the room.

Max could tell with just a glance at Cotton that whatever had happened, it was bad.

He leaned in, and Cotton spoke one word into his ear, just loudly enough to penetrate the noise of the party.

"Maurice," he said. Cotton stood back and shook his head, pale and disbelieving.

"Not—not gone?" asked Max. "But—he was just here. I was just going to ask you to put an extra guard on him."

Cotton nodded. He ran a hand through his hair, disturbing its perfection—a sure sign of his distress. "Maurice," he said again. "I'm afraid so."

Chapter 27

A POOR PLAYER

"I really should have known," Max was saying. "Maurice thought with his heart—he absolutely led with his heart and not his brain. I could have warned him even more strongly to stay out of it."

"Right," said Cotton. "You could have. But you know as well as I do, it wouldn't have made a bit of difference. Most people find it hard to believe they're in danger, don't you find? We all like to believe we're invincible—special and somehow protected from the worst."

They stood in the hallway outside room 202 of the Grand Imperial Hotel, waiting for the coroner's people to remove the body of Maurice Brandon, stylist to the stars. Maurice had been found by Beatrice, a housemaid who had come to turn down his bed for the night. She had knocked and, receiving no answer, used her passkey to enter the room, where she saw Maurice lying face down on the bed. His posture suggested a man who had passed out but Beatrice, having had experience of many such horizontal guests, approached the bed to make sure he was still breathing. It was not uncommon for people on holiday to overindulge. It was also not uncommon for them to take their own lives, as had once happened with a businessman facing bankruptcy. He had rented the poshest room in the hotel, ordered the finest champagne, and used it to wash down a bottle of Seconal.

Beatrice, only in her twenties, was thinking her mother might be right: she needed to get into another line of work, something with a brighter future. Tonight she'd have settled for a job with fewer surprises. Her manager finally had sent her home after she'd reported her discovery, but had said she'd need to be back early tomorrow to be available for further questioning. Not one of these extra hours was going to be on the clock, needless to say. She should have been home an hour before the manager, who was always all up himself to begin with, told her she could leave. Like he had anything to do with it, the pompous git. Anyone could see who was in charge, and it weren't Delwyn Kendrick. It were them two handsome men, the blond one and the dark-haired one. Them and that beautiful pregnant lady, whose role in this Beatrice could not begin to fathom.

She was just taking her cart into the storage closet when she saw Delwyn talking with the men investigating the case, sucking up to them, as she knew he would do. Fat chance of keeping this one out of the papers, she thought, if that's what he was hoping for. He'd be in a right panic over that. Automatically she'd started counting the towels for the next day when she stopped and wondered what the use was of that? She diagnosed herself as suffering from shock—the look on that poor dead man's face, the color of his skin. And his hand—why was his hand held in a claw like that, the veins on the back of his hand so purple and dark? She'd not soon forget the sight. He had been a nice man, ever so considerate, not leaving his kit strewn about the room and flinging his underpants everywhere, like he thought he was the shah of bleedin' Iran, and missing the rubbish bin every time with his nose tissues. Not like them other two, the ones the others called the baron and the baroness—my eye, them two never were royalty, not *proper* royalty. Beatrice had dealt with minor nobs here and there in her job, and she felt she would know the real article if anyone would.

Finally released, Beatrice found her hat and scarf and caught the last bus home, longing for a cuppa and wondering how much she could safely tell her mum. Mum did go on so but this time, she might have a good point worth listening to. It was a glamorous job in its way, working at the hotel, especially with all these film stars hanging about, but when murder got this near—well. And it *was* murder. No one could look at that man and think he had welcomed death. Not like the other poor sod with the Seconal.

Her cousin worked selling tickets in the Cineplex down the road. Maybe a job sweeping the floors there would be glamorous enough for now, just to keep her going until Darryl proposed. He was showing all the signs of being ready to settle down—he'd bought a newspaper subscription for home delivery and all. Maybe if she told him how dangerous her work had become it would be the spur he needed. This could all turn out for the best.

Except for the poor man in room 202, of course. As she rode the Number 12 home, Beatrice made a sign of the cross and said a silent prayer for the peace of his soul. In her world, where neatness rated highly, he'd been a ruddy saint.

It wasn't until the next day during break that Hazel, one of the waitresses, told her she'd seen someone loitering about room 202 the night before. "Behavin' in a most peculiar fashion," she said. "They saw me and scarpered. Do you think I should tell the police and all?"

"Delwyn won't like that."

"I know."

"Did you get a good look at who it was?"

"Oh, yes. From when I was serving lunch the other day."

"You should tell. I guess. Maybe. Maybe Delwyn won't come to hear of it?"

Hazel's face puckered further with concern. "Let me think on it," she said finally. "I don't retire until next year, when I can finally kiss that devil good-bye. Meanwhile, I need the job.

"Besides," she added, "I only saw them skulking about, not

murdering anyone. It's not the same thing at all, is it? I wouldn't want someone banged up for nothing, like they done to my Jonah."

Beatrice nodded understandingly. You didn't involve yourself with the police if you could help it. Everyone with a grain of sense knew that.

"Maurice said he wanted to catch the conscience of the king," said Max. "He was hinting darkly, dropping clues—I really should have threatened him or something."

"Threatened him with what? Excommunication? Max, his reputation as the soul of discretion meant everything to him. You couldn't have prevented this."

"Sent him away then."

"What could we do, in all honesty? Put him in the clink for his own protection?"

Max, who would always feel he could and should have prevented Maurice's death, shrugged Cotton's objections aside and continued with his thought. "That 'conscience of the King' bit could refer to Romero. In fact, that would be the obvious connection. Romero owns the yacht. He's the king of all he surveys."

"There's also a captain of the ship, don't forget," said Cotton. "A kinglike personage. But I'd say the more obvious connection with *Hamlet* is that Maurice was planning to stage something, given his background in theater and film. It's exactly the sort of sideways approach he would adopt. Not stage an entire play, of course, but a scene. Something that would draw signs of guilt from the guilty party."

"It's a big leap to assume the killer here has a guilty conscience, but perhaps. Yes. Let's see . . . *Hamlet*. Could there be another connection? Maurice simply could not make up his mind what to do—in that he was very Hamlet-like. He should have just told us his suspicions but he wanted to be sure."

"Right," Cotton said. "I think we agree, that was Maurice's style. Also, we've got a poisoning here. In the play King Claudius is forced to drink poisoned wine. And the queen, Gertrude—Hamlet's mother—drinks poisoned wine. We have a poisoning of Margot in this case. I suppose . . ."

"There are all sorts of possible connections with the play. Not forgetting that Margot enjoyed a brief strut and fret on the floorboards."

"It wasn't all that brief," said Cotton. "Besides, wrong play."

"Hmm?"

"The strutting and fretting. It's from the Scottish play:

'Out, out, brief candle!
Life's but a walking shadow, a poor player
That struts and frets his hour upon the stage
And then is heard no more.'"

"Right you are," said Max. Cotton was such a treasure, thought Max, his head positively stuffed with lyrics and quotations and other useful tidbits. Typical of him also that he wouldn't say the actual name of the play aloud. It was famously bad luck to do so, at least backstage among actors, where Cotton had spent so many of his formative years. Even quoting from the play was for him going far out on a limb.

"That play," Max went on. "The one Addy told me about, the one Margot starred in, performing on the West End in London. *Shopgirl*."

"I'll have someone on my team look into it," said Cotton. There was a pause, and Cotton cleared his throat before saying, "I'm sorry to have to ask, but what would they be looking for exactly?"

"Costars, producers, money men, disputes, gossip, dates, times, love affairs." Thinking of Delphine, he nearly said, "Karma." "The one thing I can say for sure is Delphine is in the clear for this murder. She was talking with me as Maurice was being killed." But rather than repeat Delphine's "what goes round" theory, he simply added, "Look for motives for revenge, for retribution. Whatever you've got."

"Nothing simpler: on it. Then as now there were gossip columns spreading all the latest scandal."

Max, deep in thought, stared unseeing down the hallway. There were windows at each end, draped in velvet and tassels, and held back by gold ropes. There had been no access from outside through those windows, it had already been determined. Sealed shut by layers of paint, they probably had not been opened for years. "Could I have a look at Margot's autopsy report?"

"Sure. You're still thinking the poisoning may have been accidental?"

"If you mean an accidental overdose, no," said Max somberly. "No, I'm not thinking that at all."

Chapter 28

DEVIL'S BREATH

The following day, Max and Cotton met again with Patrice in the incident room. Once all the technicians and experts released room 202, the three of them did an additional fingertip search.

And for a long while, they came up empty. As Beatrice could have told them, Maurice was a meticulously tidy, organized person. As Patrice put it, in MI5 parlance, "This fellow had all his stuff in the same burn bag." If he'd been the victim of blackmail or something along those lines, there was nothing in his immediate surroundings to indicate what it could have been about; Cotton had the Hollywood police doing a search of his home there. But as Cotton had joked, "It shouldn't take long for them to search. If there's anything in his house, it will be in a folder neatly labeled 'B' for 'Blackmail.'" There was no suicide note or any similar clue, even though the Monkslip-super-Mare police doctor thought the death had been staged rather carelessly to look that way. The heroin had been shot into the back of the right hand, indicating a left-handed user, but Maurice had been right handed. Furthermore, he showed no obvious signs of having been an addict or a habitual user of narcotics.

"And why the back of the hand?" Max asked, looking about him at the meticulously ordered space. Room 202 looked like a page torn from an advertising brochure; even the daffodils in a vase on a table by the window looked freshly arranged. "It may have been staged to look like a suicide, but there is every indication of the killer's not caring if we believed the setup or not. It's a sign our killer is unraveling, wouldn't you agree? If Maurice put up any struggle at all, the hand was an easy target for the needle, and that's what happened, I believe. Getting him to helpfully roll up his sleeve for an injection into his elbow would be out of the question."

"By the way," Cotton said, as they continued turning over every item in the room. "I've got some news about that safe room, but we don't really know what it means. The lab analyzed one of the powders my team found there. It was in a plastic bag inside a mislabeled container, just like all the other drugs. This particular container was a white jar marked 'cacao' and the drug was buried inside, sealed in plastic, under the loose cacao powder. They were baffled by it at first, because at a glance it wasn't cocaine, heroin, or anything else they'd been expecting. The kitchen turned up clean, by the way—nothing in the containers there but what you'd expect."

"Galley," corrected Patrice automatically. She began to kneel to examine a low bureau drawer but then thought better of it: standing up again would be too big a challenge. Max saw her dilemma and began searching the drawer himself.

Sorry, she mouthed.

"No worries," he murmured. "You'd do the same for me."

That made her laugh, and drew a sharp glance in their direction from Cotton.

"It wasn't GHB, either." Cotton paused for effect, making sure he had their attention. "It was scopolamine."

"You're joking," said Max, sitting back on his heels. "Scopolamine? I've only ever heard of it; never seen it . . . but, my God. 'The Devil's Breath.'"

"That's the name, and there was never a name more fitting. The stuff turns the targeted victim into a zombie. There's been a rash of robberies using it. It's a hypnotic drug. The criminals blow the powder into the victim's face and it makes him or her so powerless, so completely lacking in will, that they'll do whatever is asked—hand over money, jewelry, whatever. There was a gang from China using it with great success not too long ago in London. The Met couldn't figure out where they were getting it from. It looks like we may have solved that mystery for them."

"Any chance it was used on Maurice?" Patrice asked.

"We'll find out," said Cotton. "But somehow I doubt it. What Max said about rolling up his sleeve would have been easier if he'd been hypnotized with the stuff. He seems to have been able to put up some resistance. How're you doing over there?" And he went to help her lift a blanket down from a top shelf in the closet.

Max had read an article in one of the broadsheets about scopolamine not long before. He remembered that it was derived from the nightshade family of plants and was produced mainly in South America. It was a scare article, designed to give people something to cluck and worry about over their tea, but it was in fact a frightening drug. A chemical process turned it into a white powder that resembled cocaine. Scopolamine could be used medicinally to treat motion sickness, but in such large amounts, a medicinal use even on board a ship seemed implausible. Besides, why hide it if it were there for innocent reasons?

"This ship has put in to port in South America, am I right?" Max asked.

"Yes," said Cotton. "It's all in the ship's logbook. They were in port in Colombia last year."

"Of course," said Max. "It would be Colombia."

"Colombia was just before I came on board, sailing for two," said Patrice.

"They didn't try to call you in at any point?" he asked, meaning MI5.

"They tried but I ignored them. I was fit as a fiddle and so *very* close to a solve I didn't want to be taken off the case. It didn't all become a problem until recent days. I was planning to leave the ship once we got to Weymouth but—well, you know what happened. Margot happened."

She wanted the glory, thought Max. That was understandable. And that was Patrice all over, when she was on the case, as he well knew—any case. Like a dog with a bone.

"The rest of the drugs could be coming from anywhere, of course," said Cotton. "But in the case of the scopolamine, there's little doubt of the origins. And it's a good bet Colombia is the source for all of it. The yacht rests there quite often."

"Anchors," said Patrice reflectively. "It's odd how so many drugs look much the same. I started thinking 'cocaine' when I saw the chef messing about one evening with something on a pastry board, but it could have been any number of drugs, given what we're finding. It could even have been flour or cornstarch, as he claimed—he told me he was coating the chicken for dinner or some noise like that. But he was nervous as a cat and besides, you'd need far more flour and cornstarch than what he had on that board for coating chicken. I assumed it was just a chef with a habit—that he was worth keeping an eye on to see where he might lead us, no more than that. My bad—sorry. But what was happening on board that yacht was much bigger than a single user or someone who liked to party with his friends. This was a nice sideline in importing stuff—all manner of deadly stuff."

"Could it have been GHB you saw then—the drug that was used to subdue Margot?"

"No idea, really. As I say, it all looks much the same or is cut with the same stuff so it looks the same—until you get it under a microscope. If it were neon pink or something it would be easier to spot and more difficult to hide. I have to say, just going on instinct, that Zaki is the kind of guy who'd carry GHB on him—just in case. He always gave me the creeps. I don't see Romero, for example, going in for that sort of carry-on. Even though he's the no-boundaries, free-spirit auteur type, who manages to inflict no end of damage on other people's boundaries. But why he'd use a date rape drug on Margot, who by all accounts was nothing if not willing, or why he would want to do away with her completely, is anyone's guess. She was a pest, from all we've heard, not a lethal threat to life or liberty."

"And I've no impression Romero has trouble attracting women," said Max. "He's not bad looking. Fame and fortune take care of the rest."

Patrice's reply was muffled. From deep within the closet she emerged holding a thin book bound in red leather.

"What's that?" Cotton asked.

She was flipping slowly through the pages. Max moved to look over her shoulder. "It's a diary," she said. "I found it tucked beneath the padded cover of the ironing board."

Cotton, interest piqued, crossed the room rapidly to join them, saying, "Are you sure it's a diary?"

"It has 'Diary' embossed on the front, so, yes. That was a giveaway. Parts of it seem to be written in code."

"You're not serious."

"Most of it is innocuous stuff. Dental appointments and so on. But then there are pages of coded paragraphs." She pointed to a sample page.

"It looks like a simple substitution code," said Max. "So Maurice, the soul of discretion, confided only in his diary. That fits. Otherwise, he'd burst with all the secrets he was holding for everyone. The diary was his safety valve."

"I don't think we'll even need GCHQ for this," said Patrice. "Give me a few hours and I could crack it. You're right, it's the kind of code a teenaged girl would use to try to get around her parents, to keep secret where she really was last Saturday night."

"Bag it and get it dusted right away. Then get it translated. Tell them to put a rush on it," Cotton said. Patrice opened the door and summoned a waiting constable, relaying the diary and instructions.

Cotton looked around the pristine room and sighed. "So what else have we got?"

"I'd say we've got, as a working theory, the possibility that Margot was killed because she stumbled onto the drug smuggling action on this ship," said Patrice, rejoining them. "Although I don't like Romero for that. Not because he's such an upstanding citizen but because he simply doesn't need the cash. Recreational use, sure, maybe. Whatever's going, probably snorting the occasional line. But smuggling on a grand scale? You don't dirty yourself with that lot unless you're desperate for money. I mean, have you seen the size of that ship?"

"He could be going broke trying to keep that ship afloat, to coin a phrase," said Max. "But when I think of 'hard up for cash,' it's the baron and baroness who come first to mind. And Delphine comes second. Although in her case, while she may like the money, I think the thrill of outfoxing the authorities may be what attracts her most. As you and I were saying, Cotton, there is such a thing as an excitement junkie."

Cotton and Patrice turned to look at each other, then returned their gaze to Max. Their expressions said they agreed. There also was a look of companionable intimacy in the exchange, momentary but unmistakable.

Cotton and Patrice? Max wondered. *Hmm.* It wasn't impossible to imagine. Max thought he might find a moment to tease Cotton on that subject along with others he was storing up, beginning with that Dick Tracy watch of his, but for now he continued. "Returning to the baron and baroness for a moment: there is something about those two that fascinates me. Drifting as they are around the world, both of them so beautiful and so privileged, so connected. They are granted entrée anywhere they choose to go, to the point where they have no need of a permanent address."

"Perhaps they are welcome for more than their cachet of glamour, did we ever stop to think?" said Cotton. "For what they bring to the table besides their good looks? Personally, I assumed people just put up with them, like tiresome relatives at the holidays. One can only stand so much of people who swan around and do nothing all day. But maybe they were welcomed because of what they carried with them in their vast luggage."

"Right," said Patrice. "How likely were these two swans to face tough scrutiny from customs agents?"

"Not too likely. But then how did it all end up with Zaki in the kitchen?" asked Cotton.

"Galley," said Max and Patrice together.

"If I had to guess, the chef was more a customer than a dealer," said Patrice. "Although it's a line easily crossed. He may have been recruited by someone with more brains than he has."

"I'll send Sergeant Essex to ask him again," said Cotton. "In fact, I'll go with her. The chef was softening up nicely, the last I heard. And we need to have a look into the baroness's collection of luggage. And his, of course."

"That may be trickier without a warrant to search for drugs," said Patrice.

"Perhaps," said Cotton, "once we're through talking with the chef, we may have every reasonable cause to search—as part of an ongoing murder investigation."

"You're right about one thing," said Patrice. "We can't ignore the possibility Margot somehow knew too much—that she saw something she shouldn't have seen, like drugs and money changing hands. Something that could put a few people behind bars."

Max nodded, his mood somber. He hated drugs, having seen at

first hand the destruction they inevitably caused. The families and relationships ruined, to say nothing of careers, hopes, and ambitions. People always thought they could handle small amounts without the need escalating, and people were generally wrong. And a dealer? A dealer was close to being a murderer in his mind.

"Yes," Max said to Cotton. "Let us know what you find out. Clearly, we have to pursue all avenues. But speaking of the baron and baroness, I recall now something she said that struck me at the time as odd. She was admiring Addy's work ethic, you see. I thought that was rich coming from her. But when you think about it, what those two have going for them is a very cushy job, but one that they have to work hard to maintain. What, you have to ask yourself, would they do to preserve their status—their job, if you like?"

Again, Cotton and Patrice exchanged glances, this time with mutual shrugs.

"I'd like to see a trace of their movements in, say, the three or four months leading up to their joining the ship. We need to do that with everyone who wasn't already on board, I suppose. But I'm particularly interested to know what those two were up to."

"Getting someone else to peel them a grape, probably," said Patrice.

"Someone else's grape," agreed Cotton. "From someone else's private vineyard. But I'm sure we've collected that information already." Never far from his laptop, Cotton now opened a file or two, and said, "Yes, they were staying for several months with a German couple. The von Rother-Magnums."

"Find out what was talked about, will you?"

"Oh. That's rather a tall order. This is a priority is it?"

"I think it is."

"I'll get someone on it."

"I'll go with you," said Patrice.

"Oh, and by the way," said Max. "There was never a King of Denmark named Claudius. Or one named Hamlet, for that matter."

Cotton, on his way toward the door with Patrice, said something that might have been, "Hmph?" Followed by, "I'm aware of that. Shakespeare took some liberties. We've been fine with it for centuries. What are you talking about, Max?"

"Never mind," Max replied. "But do let me know what more you hear about the drug dealing, and about the visit to Germany of the baron and baroness. And then I think we might also need to learn more about where Margot Browne came from."

Chapter 29

WE ARE FAMILY

Cotton and Patrice joined Max in Camp X to announce that the chef was being held at the station for the allowable twenty-four-hour period.

"Sergeant Essex told me she was afraid he'd vanish otherwise. Of course, if we get evidence linking him to the murder, we can hold him up to ninety-six hours," said Cotton.

Max nodded abstractedly, saying, "I rather wish we knew if the timing of Margot's death—or rather, the exact time she went in the water—were deliberate or accidental. Whoever did this might not have known about the tides."

"Does it matter?"

"If someone is hoping a body will be swept out to sea and disappear, might there be something about the condition of that body the killer doesn't want discovered? On the other hand, if someone does want the body found, might they try to time the disposal of the body so it is swept in on the tide? It is either a small matter or a significant one."

"Well, that certainly covers all the possibilities," said Patrice. "So who, apart from the captain, would know about the tides, and be able to take advantage of following the tide table?"

Max shook his head: *Not sure*. "The baron comes from a shipping family. It's not enough to either take him off the list or put him there. He may not have known these waters. The same goes for Romero. He just owns the yacht. That doesn't make him an expert on tides. Did tides tables show up in a search of their rooms?"

Patrice said, "No. But they all have laptops or mobiles—and Addy seems positively attached at the hip to that laptop of his. We'd need a stronger suspicion of one particular person than we have to warrant a search of his or her computer. But even then—what would finding a tides table in their browser history prove? They could claim they were following the tides as a sort of naff hobby. And if we found truly incriminating evidence in the search for one particular thing, that could bollocks everything up for the prosecution later on."

Max nodded. Evidence of a search of date rape drugs might be more to the point. But the safeguards that protected the innocent also went a long way toward protecting the guilty. It was a delicate balance, always, and a source of keen frustration for investigators. And, of course, for the families of the victims, who so often were denied justice because someone had fouled the case with a clumsy or careless investigation.

"We could start by simply asking to take a look at their computers and mobiles," he said.

"And anyone who refused might just warrant a closer look," Patrice agreed. "No pun intended."

The thought of victims and families led Max to ask, "Is no one turning up in the search for Margot's family?"

Cotton pulled up a file on his own computer with a practiced swipe. "There is a widowed aunt in Providence, Kansas. One of my team spoke with her by phone the other day. The local police found Aunt Sarah—easy enough, since where Margot was born and raised was included in her official studio biography. The dates were wrong, however. It seems Margot had shaved off a few years. It was and probably still is common practice in that field of endeavor."

"Where youth, as we have said, trumps all. So, who is the aunt and what did she have to say?"

"Her name is Sarah Wackenhut," said Cotton, with a verifying glance at his computer screen. "Actually, she was helpful because she and her husband Mr. Bill Wackenhut were the ones who raised Margot, whose parents were killed in a car accident when she was five. Margot was in the backseat, and even though she wasn't wearing a belt it was one of those freak accidents in which not wearing a belt worked in her favor. She was thrown clear, unharmed, and the car caught fire. Sarah was the sister of Margot's mother, Beth, and it was Sarah who arranged a formal adoption. She had three children of her own."

"Had she seen Margot recently?"

"Not in years. It wasn't, Sarah assured me, because she disapproved of Margot's lifestyle, but my sergeant caught strong whiffs of precisely that. I think calling someone a painted strumpet qualifies as disapproval, don't you?"

"I do."

"The name 'Jezebel' was also invoked. So, we can take it that Sarah is deeply religious, if you can call it that: she belongs to a sort of fundamentalist sect most people have never heard of. Reformed Church of the Traveling Sheep or something like that. Perhaps it was Reformed Sheep of the Wandering Chosen—my sergeant had trouble following her, said she spoke quite rapidly in an accent he wasn't familiar with. Anyway, to hear Sarah tell it, the distance between them, her and Margot, was the vast philosophical distance between Hollywood, California, and Providence, Kansas. Sarah and her husband were 'working people'—she told my sergeant that no fewer than five times—and I gather 'money for nothing' didn't sit well with them. Yes, that was how she, at any rate, seemed to view Margot's career—a way of earning piles of tainted money that no decent sort of person would have any truck with."

"She was well off, was Margot?"

"Yes and no: I suppose it depends on your point of view and your own circumstances. Not to mention the cost of living where you live compared with that of Hollywood. I don't have the impression overall that Kansas is a land of fleshpots and opium dens. Anyway, Margot was highly paid at one point in her career for her films—that lasted about a decade. She did not store the money away for the winter as her thrifty family surely had taught her, however—we've seen her bank statements and they confirm she was living a rather lavish lifestyle, one that she had no hope of sustaining into old age. The bills for the facials and facelifts alone were astronomic."

"Which is probably why this part in Romero's movie meant so much to her. She was running out of cash."

"Undoubtedly," said Cotton. "But she did own her own home in Hollywood. Paid cash for a bungalow in the Hollywood Hills during her heyday, which turned out to be a smart move. She may have taken the advice of a financial adviser, as it doesn't sound like something practical she'd think of on her own."

"Or perhaps having lost her parents so young, the one thing she most wanted in life was a secure roof over her head," said Patrice.

Max nodded his agreement. This was Patrice's training showing, as well as her engrained instincts. MI5 drummed into its agents to observe not what people said but what they actually did. What and who they spent their money on and what and who they scrimped on are big clues to personality. Margot's first priority when she came into money had been to try to establish the solid home that had been taken from her when her parents died. "What was she like as a child?" Max asked. "At least, according to Aunt Sarah?"

"Flighty, irresponsible, flirtatious, manipulative—affectionate only when she wanted something out of you," Cotton replied. "Given to meltdowns and drama when she didn't get what she wanted. Pretty, of course, as even Aunt Sarah grudgingly admitted. 'Then she had to go and spoil it all with the tantrums.'"

"It would appear not a lot had changed," said Patrice.

"Aunt Sarah is the disapproving type, so we can season what she thinks with a grain of salt. She is not someone you'd turn to later in life when you'd made a hash of things, expecting a sympathetic hearing. These two may have made a poor pairing—Sarah and Margot—but it sounds as if Sarah and Bill were Margot's only option for guardians when she was orphaned. Not that, at that young age, Margot had any choice. As Aunt Sarah put it"—here Cotton swiped to a different page of the interview document—"she 'saved Margot from the orphanage and from having to make shoelaces in the workhouse,' proving that Margot came by her sense of melodrama legitimately."

"Yes. I doubt there is a shoelace factory in Providence, particularly one that ever used child labor. And Bill?"

"My sergeant came to perceive Bill as much less unyielding than Sarah, when he was alive, that is. He died when Margot was still in her teens."

"What a bleak picture. How long did Margot live with them, then?"

"Let's see . . . Margot kept on living with her cousins and her aunt until she turned eighteen and graduated from secondary school. One cousin, a girl, was similar in age, and there were two boys, one three years older than Margot and the other five years older. I gather that without the leavening influence of Bill's more open-minded approach, the real estrangement from the family began. That's a nice way of saying they all grew to cordially loathe one another. Margot was on the first bus out of town, literally—she left the day after graduation. In her official bio, this was her turning point—the die was cast and she was never coming back, and she never did. That much we can take as true. She'd studied drama in secondary school—they call it high school over there—and a teacher encouraged her dreams. So Margot, quick as she could, joined the flock of hopefuls that descend on Hollywood each year. All the clichés about waiting tables and parking cars while waiting for the big break are true. The dreams of acting start to fade at different times. I have always gathered that the odds of making it in show business are astronomically against, almost regardless of looks or talent."

"This was about forty years ago," said Max. "Are any of the cousins still around?"

Another swipe of the screen. "The two male cousins both died not long ago, about a year apart. The family on the male side seems to suffer from sudden heart problems. There is a sister, Clarice Merriweather. She still lives nearby with her husband."

"I'd like to talk with her," said Max. "It sounds like your man got everything there was to be got out of Aunt Sarah."

"Blood from a turnip," agreed Cotton. "Certainly, I can organize a call for you."

Minutes later, Cotton left to hand out assignments to his team, as well as help put the pressure on the yacht's chef. Max stood as if to leave also, but Patrice held out a hand to stop him.

Awkward. They hadn't been alone since the case began.

Max found he was at a bit of a loss. There was really only one thing he wanted to know, apart from whether or not Patrice was happy in her life, facing the momentous changes ahead. But the direct route— "So, who's the daddy?"—didn't seem quite the best way to go about asking.

Patrice, he knew, could sense what was worrying him. That perception had always been her strength, which she used to great advantage working for MI5—as shown in her guess about Margot's need for a home of her own. She also could read the bad guys as well as the good, seldom tainting observations with her own prejudices.

"I made up my mind, Max, that the father might go or stay but that I would keep the baby. Not everyone has that luxury, of course. I feel very lucky."

"Does he know? He does know—right?"

Typical Max, that honest concern suffusing his face. No wonder she had loved him. And loved him still. He looked like he might go and fetch a shotgun and perform the ceremony himself.

"He does. He would, he thinks, make a lousy father, and his first instinct was to bid me adios. I agree with his assessment, although he seems to be changing a bit lately. He's a lovely man but I'm still not sure he would be an asset to the situation. We're taking it a day at a time."

Max looked at her. Competent and serene as always—yes, she was all that. But there were many single mothers in his parish, at all different levels of education and income, who were struggling. His own housekeeper was one of them. Her two children were raising themselves most days, despite all the resources of the village being made available to help them out.

"I'm glad, then, Patrice," he said. "I guess things work out the way they're meant to, even if we can't see it at the time."

"And you, Max. I drilled out of Cotton your current situation. Awena—of course, I know her from that *fantastic* cooking show on the telly but I'd no idea she was yours. What can I say? She is absolutely charming. You have my permission to live happily ever after." A beat, and then she added: "I'm truly happy now, Max. Happier than I deserve to be. I know all this"—and here she waved a hand across her stomach—"all this will come right."

How Patrice thought this would come right, in her line of work . . . it was absurd, really. They'd likely take her out of undercover work after the birth and put her on a desk job—something in analysis was likely, and it was something she would be good at. But her real strength was in bridge-building, and in being able to coordinate with MI6 and GCHQ to get things done, to get answers to the questions political leaders in Whitehall needed to have answered, to head off the next looming threat to security. She might become a reports operator, passing information in a chain leading to the desk of "C"—the chief, the only person ever allowed to sign papers in green ink. But Max suspected she would hate all that. Patrice was designed for undercover work, not for pushing papers along. She might, he guessed, be put on recruiting at some point to take advantage of the charm and gift for improvisation that might otherwise go to waste—so much of the job was pure theater.

Financially she might be stable, but . . .

But what could he do? Offer to talk to the "boyfriend" in some older brother capacity? Hardly. What a cringe-worthy thought. For one thing, she didn't seem to mind whether he decided to stay or go. And that had to speak volumes. Patrice was nothing if not a sterling judge of character.

"I'm sure you will make a lovely mother," he said, and he was sincere in saying it. "Perceptive and kind." Again, that consciousness of other people and their needs would serve her well. It was the practicalities that might bedevil her. He and Awena had a nearly perfect system going, whereby Owen could be handed off to one or other busy parent, and they'd all be together at the end of most days. Owen generally spent his daytime hours in a cot either in the vicarage or in Awena's kitchen or her shop Goddessspell. This time away in Monkslip-super-Mare was the exception to their little domestic routine, and Max was chafing to get home and pick up his predictable, happy schedule where he'd left it off.

He wished the same sort of home life for Patrice—a partner who was anxious to see her and their child at the end of the day. And he was annoyed with the fellow for not seeing it that way immediately.

She smiled. "Max, I am one of the lucky ones. I can afford to hire help when and as I need it. I'm even thinking I can swing hiring a nanny, at least in daytime. I have a large extended family. My own sister has two of her own and says she'll be right there to help."

"It's not the same," he said stubbornly.

"What's not the same?"

"This fellow of yours—does he have a name?"

"Byron."

"Seriously?"

"Yeah, I know."

"Well this Byron will be missing out on the best thing that has ever happened to him. You be sure and tell him that from me if you like."

"Okay. Will do. That will certainly bring him round."

"Listen, Pat. You may think you've got it sussed but you've no idea. Even good and well-behaved babies like my Owen are nonstop." He was thinking that the child of anyone named Byron was unlikely to be well-behaved. But he recognized his bias, too.

"Are you really happy?" he asked her. "Truly? Because I can't think of anyone who deserves it more than you do."

"I'm ecstatic," she said simply. "I'm thirty-five—hardly over the hill, but they told me years ago I couldn't have children, and I just built my life around that belief. No problem, no big regrets. But once I found out I was pregnant—everything in my landscape just shifted. All the neatly labeled bins of how my future would look— gone. Everything I believed or thought my life was going to be changed. Overnight, and for the better. I've never looked at the future before with so much hope. And, trepidation, yes. But hope running right alongside the worry."

She paused at the sound of a gull outside, and stopped to watch it sweep by. She was glowing, breathtaking in her beauty, her profile a cameo carved into the sunlight from the window. Light spilled across the folds of her dress, and made her luxuriant hair into a nimbus of highlights. She turned her attention back now to Max.

"Whether Byron comes round or not is up to him. It makes no difference to me, and I am well on my way to deciding I'm—we're—better off without him. Yes, I'm happy. Never better. And I can see that is the case with you, as well. You should see your face when you talk about your little family. I expect I'll be the same. Photo albums everywhere, my wallet stuffed with pictures of the little one. Grabbing complete strangers on the street and forcing them to look at the drooly pictures on my mobile phone."

He nodded. "Life is passing strange, isn't it?"

"Yes, it most certainly is. What is that, more *Hamlet*?"

"No. *Othello*. It's just that Cotton has got me thinking." He turned aside for a moment, his thoughts chasing a scenario that had just come into his mind. He said, "Sit down a moment."

"I am sitting down. And I'm not moving again until the midwife comes for me and my great whacking stomach."

"Okay. Perfect." He pulled up a chair closer to her. "Let me run an idea by you."

Chapter 30

CLARICE

Clarice Merriweather turned out to be one of those people who believed that because the phone call came from across the Atlantic she had to shout in order to be heard. Or perhaps she was hard of hearing, even though she was no great age. She was in fact fifty-eight years old, the same age as Margot; the two cousins had very nearly shared a birthday. Margot's mother and her Aunt Sarah must have been pregnant together, perhaps in a friendly competition over who would deliver first.

It soon became clear, however, that the nearness in birthdays Clarice shared with Margot had been one of several grievances—unforgiveable crimes for which Margot had been found guilty, particularly by this member of her family.

"I never had a birthday party of my own growing up," Clarice shouted at Max. He had been introduced to her in advance by one of Cotton's men, the same sergeant who had talked with Margot's aunt previously. Sergeant Jones had rung Max at the hotel to relay the number and to tell Max the woman had agreed to accept the call.

"Good luck, mate," the sergeant had said. "She's not what they call in the States a happy camper. More a professional whinger. Don't, if you value your own life, ask about her health. You'll never get her off the line if you do."

"I never even had my own birthday cake," Clarice continued now, in a theme that had gone on uninterrupted for several minutes. "They gave us one cake with both our names in frosting on it, and her name always came first, although alphabetically my name should have been first, and the cake was always chocolate, because 'chocolate is her favorite.'" Clarice was mimicking someone with the last phrase, it wasn't clear who, the adult who had provided the offending cake, presumably. It was a ridiculous theme for a woman of her age. It was difficult, in fact, to think of the last age at which such a childish diatribe might be forgiven. Max had already recognized a situation not uncommon to him in his vicarly calling. He had learned to cultivate great patience with such people, people who spent too much time alone, some with no friends or family, people who were finally getting the chance to be in the spotlight for a moment—these were the people who were unstoppable. They had years of outrage to offload.

"It was always all about Margie, Margie, Margie," she told him. "That's what my father called her. 'My little Margie.'" That mimicking voice again. "It used to make me sick, I tell you. What was so special about her?"

Max felt they had quickly arrived at the nub of the problem, for which injection of Godspeed he was grateful. Good old jealousy, rearing its ugly head. Two little girls, close in age, one thrust upon the other by a tragic loss of parents, thrown into the other's house, the accident making her an object of deserving pity. Initially, young Clarice might have been sympathetic to Margot and her wrenching tale of loss. But that may have been the problem—Clarice was very young, too young to sort out the emotions her cousin's arrival would stir up. Bad enough she had to share her parents with her siblings; now she had to share them with this beautiful stranger.

He would be willing to bet also that Clarice had been less beautiful than her cousin—most women were, so that was a safe enough bet. And it sounded as if Margot had been taken under her uncle's wing, quickly becoming a favorite—at least, that may have been Clarice's perception. How had Clarice's brothers reacted? They, too, were close in age to the young girls.

Max breathed a little inner sigh, head bowed as he continued listening, like a man praying or doing penance. He was seated at his desk in the hotel, and he picked up the promotional pen provided by the hotel ("Make Waves with Us") and began doodling with it on the pad of paper embossed with the hotel's logo in matching sea-blue ink. The logo involved some sort of stylized representation of a fish and Max began adding fins to it, until he'd created a lionfish of monstrous proportions. Clarice, meanwhile, had arrived at, "This is all her fault. I've got reporters calling, you know. Day and night."

Max somehow doubted that. Margot's death, however mysterious and dramatic, would have unleashed little more than a brief media flurry in a town she'd left behind decades earlier. Unless the Kardashians had gone into hiding, the media had bigger fish to fry on any given day. But on the subject of media attention, Clarice sounded as if she might secretly be pleased. At last! A chance to tell her side of the story. Perhaps the media would care to hear her saga of injustice and hardship.

Poor Margot. No wonder she'd taken the first chance to leave.

Clarice seemed to be one of those people forever watching a film called *It's All Their Fault*, thought Max: As long as that's the only movie playing in her personal Cineplex, that's all I'll get out of her. It's always going to be someone else's fault.

Max managed to insert a question into the narrative, although because he had to blurt out the first thing that came to mind, it might not have been the smoothest or most well-phrased question. In a voice with a desperate edge to it, in fact, he asked, "How did Margot get along with your mother and father, then?"

A sniff. *That* had shut her up for a full five seconds. Then, on a deep sigh: "My mother was put upon from day one. She had lost her own sister and brother-in-law in the crash, you know. That was bad enough. Then to be saddled with Margot, who was such a little snot—never grateful for anything. Well." Sniff. "It nearly *killed* my mother."

"Why do you think that?" Max asked quietly, wondering if the sense of grievance was somehow inherited, passed down from one generation to the next, like tarnished silver. "I mean, did she often complain?"

"My mother was a *saint*," Clarice replied hotly, as if he'd suggested the opposite. "She never complained. Not even after the way Margot brought nothing but disgrace into the family."

"I'm sorry," began Max. "I don't—"

She cut him off. It was as if, having led them down this path, she was suddenly having second thoughts about the wisdom of her route. Her mouth had been running too fast, not allowing time for her brain to catch up. "Water under the bridge," she said firmly.

Max wondered if he could use her victim psychology to get the story out of her. Make it all somebody's fault, and the truth might slip out.

To stall for time, meanwhile, he asked about her health, as the sergeant had specifically warned him against doing. But this gave him at least five minutes to come up with a strategy. It was clear nothing she said about her vertigo and her blood pressure was going to require a response from him; he may as well set the phone down on the desk and go for a walk on the promenade. Or at least focus on drawing his fish scales. Politely, however, he hung on the line, inserting sympathetic grunts and murmurs given half an opening.

Finally, she began winding down. "But that's nothing compared to the heart palpitations. I get them all the time now. It doesn't half frighten you to death in the middle of the night. You ever get that?" She didn't stop for an answer. "It's like mice have nested in your heart valves but my doctor says not to worry. I should just take a vacation.

If I made the kind of money he makes, the old sawbones, I'd be able to take a vacation, I tell him . . ."

Max could think of few careers more frustrating than being Clarice's doctor. A panda fertility coach, perhaps.

". . . and furthermore, if you're calling looking for someone to pay for Margot's funeral expenses, you've got the wrong number. Yes sirree. My husband and I are on a fixed income now, you know. Not that he ever made much money. We're not rich Hollywood types, not all la-di-dah shenanigans like Margot. We're simple working people."

And on that simpering note of piety she finally shut up. Max carpe diem-ed for all he was worth, plunging into the brief opening.

"And besides, what happened may have been her fault," said Max, hating himself for it but knowing that was the only chord he could play with Clarice.

"I'm sure it was. She fell off the boat, right? Three sheets to the wind? 'Wine is a mocker, strong drink a brawler.' That's in the Bible."

"I know."

"And now there's all this fuss. It's like I told you."

"Some people have a gift for causing trouble," said Max.

"That's exactly it!" Clarice exclaimed. *This was more like it. Praise the Lord. This man understood her at last.* "She walked into the room, and all the men, it was like they'd lost their minds. Even when she was little, and of course it got worse as she got older."

"And she didn't have to lift a finger to get their attention," said Max. "I'll bet she didn't need makeup and things to make herself look attractive." He wanted to stab himself with the hotel pen for being so double-faced, so duplicitous. It was this kind of thing, this easy playing with people, that had made him want to get out of MI5 in the first place.

"Oh, but she did!" Clarice insisted. "When my mother said she was too young for makeup and some of the clothes she wanted to wear, slit all up to here and down to there, didn't Margot just take herself down to the department store, lie about her age, and get herself a job to pay for what she wanted?" (Apparently in Clarice's world there were working people and then there were people who worked to get what they wanted—a fine distinction at best.) "Then she'd smuggle the stuff into school—leave the house dressed like a Puritan and change into these practically Las Vegas *show*girl outfits. Or like a cheerleader from the Dallas Cowboys. She asked for it, yes she did. No man stood a chance up against that."

"I can see how that would be difficult. And of course she was lying to your parents."

"Yes!" Max had the sure knowledge she would have hugged him if she'd been in the room. "She was a liar and a fantasist, always flirting, looking for ways to ensnare the boys, who were too dumb to see through it."

"Boys?" Max inserted mildly. "You don't mean, your brothers?" Carefully, he put down the pen, listening intently for her answer, willing the gardener, who he could hear clipping hedges down below in the hotel garden, to stop.

"The boys," she said, softly, for her. He thought she might have started to cry. "They never stood a chance."

Oh, my God.

Chapter 31

HOUSE OF HORRORS

An hour after his talk with cousin Clarice, Max still felt like he needed a hot shower and a scrub with lye soap. He couldn't wait to try to wash the entire Wackenhut family down the drain, and out of his memory if he could. For now, as he waited in his room for Cotton and Patrice, he skimmed back over the reports on the suspects. The answer must be in there somewhere.

Cotton and Patrice arrived with news. "They've cracked the code of Maurice's diary already," said Cotton. "I gather the tech people were insulted to be asked, it was so simple as to be beneath them. But the contents are powerhouse stuff, and not just the entries about Margot. You wouldn't believe the bits about Dick and Liz. But first let's hear what you've learned."

"It seems Margot escaped a house of horrors, poor kid. And she *was* just a kid, still in her teens when she left. Correction: when she ran for her life from her tormentors."

"Clarice just came out with it?"

"Oh, yes. Her version of it, anyway. The very repulsive thing is, Clarice is so determined to protect her brothers' reputations even posthumously that once she got going, she spoke quite openly about the despicable and vile exploitation of Margot—speaking 'openly' being the only way to place the blame squarely on Margot. Who was only a child, mind. In Clarice's telling, Margot was some vampy teen-age temptress leading her brothers astray. All the while, Clarice and her parents, her mother in particular, completely ignored the fact that when the abuse started one brother was three years older than Margot and the other brother five years older and technically an adult. And of course they remained older, throughout years of this mistreatment. She was coerced and threatened, you can be sure of it. There were two of them, and only one of her. It's a crime however you look at it, and her age and vulnerability make it particularly heinous. But Clarice sees it as a 'boys will be boys' situation. And then, when it couldn't get any worse, it did, and Margot fell pregnant."

Cotton nodded. "Everyone in town thought she'd just fled gaily to the bright lights of the city. With this creepy family ranged against her, she couldn't tell the truth about her pregnancy. They would never let the truth come out—never. It explains her estrangement from them—more than that. She hated them and as she was such a threat, the loathing was mutual."

"Is it all in Maurice's diary?"

"Yes. It's enough to make you ill, it really is. According to Maurice, Margot was never sure which brother got her pregnant. For Maurice, it was always a matter of sleeping dogs, and of 'protecting her reputation'—even though she was the innocent party, she never wanted the truth to come out, except to her one confidant. Margot trusted Maurice to keep quiet. He did—he wrote down every word, but he guarded that diary with his life—literally, it seems. Even when Margot got to be such a handful for him—and you can see why she was as disturbed as she apparently was, can't you?—he kept her secrets. What cousin Clarice told you confirms it, even though, as you say, she is putting her own spin on things. What an unspeakable family."

Max shook his head in disgust. "The father was decent to her, but only up to a point. And of course he had died by the time she became pregnant. But if he knew of or even suspected the abuse . . . Well, for Margot, that must have been the final betrayal. He had loved her like his own daughter, there seems to be no question about that, but he could not see that his own sons were the monsters they were. Neither could his wife accept it: Margot was her blood but not in the way her sons and her daughter were her blood. She had, she felt, to protect her 'real' family, and the only way to do that was to get rid of this beautiful, disruptive influence."

"Margot had five people ranged against her," put in Cotton. "Two adults; Clarice, who had always been jealous of her; and two male cousins who would certainly go to prison if the case could be proved against them. It was imperative to crush Margot's story. This was before DNA could have proven paternity, of course. And even then, it would always be her word against theirs that she wasn't a willing participant. At the age of thirteen, which was when the abuse started, and with her parents dead!"

The gorge rose in Max's throat; his face was suffused with anger as he said, "Margot had to know she wasn't loved in all quarters by this family. The father, though, had seemed to be honestly, well, fatherly toward her. That he was cowardly enough to turn a blind eye, to just go along—and I do see this as cowardice on his part—that was the final straw. That is what broke her. She washed her hands of them all—just imagine, she was pregnant, frightened, alone. Having to deal with everything, alone."

Patrice had remained silent throughout this recitation, as if dumb-struck. The look on her face was one of pure grief—and anger. Max thought it probably matched his own expression. He also thought he saw a tear in the corner of one eye before she roughly brushed it away, her fair face mottled with emotion.

"So," she said. "We may never find out which cousin was the father, but she was sexually abused by both brothers in that mad household.

No wonder she looked upon Zaki with a particular loathing. Most anyone would, but given her background? Abused at thirteen? It's a wonder she didn't try to drown him."

"Agreed. We can't put him aside as a suspect for Margot's murder. Perhaps they quarreled again, and in a final sort of way."

"That is the vilest, most disgusting . . ." Patrice took a breath to steady herself. "And so, she came to Hollywood. And she quickly found work somewhere. Something to keep her going."

"Not in film or theater, of course, although that followed quickly, within a couple of years," Cotton said. "This also is from the diary, Max: She worked as a waitress to pay the bills, until her condition began to show. This was before the word 'accommodation' was part of the employment world. Once she could no longer hide her condition, she had more and more trouble finding work. Meanwhile, however, she'd met Maurice. He used to come into a restaurant where she was waiting tables. He was sympathetic and before long he came to understand what a mess she was in. She didn't tell him the whole story at once; it came out in dribs and drabs. But he let her stay with him. When the baby was born, she gave the child up for adoption. That, according to Maurice, is when the trouble really began—the drinking, the abusive boyfriends, the whole trauma of her young life catching up with her. Maurice helped as much as he could, put up with it as long as he could, and then eased her out. He felt guilty about it but he shouldn't have, in my view. He was a true friend, the only friend she'd got, really. He did as well by her as he could while keeping his own boundaries and sanity intact. And certainly he kept her secrets well."

"So," Patrice wanted to know, "what happened to the baby?"

Cotton, who had been doing some complicated maneuver with his computer, looked over his shoulder and said, "I've got some people on it now."

"The problem is," said Max, "adoptions in those days were a big secret. It's nothing like today, where as a matter of course it is understood that people might want to contact their parents, whether or not the parents want to be contacted. To learn something of their families and medical histories."

Cotton said, "Maurice wasn't there for the birth and claimed not to know where the baby was taken from the hospital. He did know that Margot signed away all her rights to the child—that was the arrangement. There was no question of her raising it herself—she didn't have the financial resources in those days, and honestly, one has to wonder how she could have overcome her natural, well, revulsion—knowing how the child was conceived."

"Right," said Patrice. "What was she going to do, maybe ask the lunatic Wackenhuts to take the baby into their asylum, to be raised by them? No way. At least with the adoption, she was giving the kid a chance that neither she nor her so-called family could offer." She shook herself visibly, as if casting aside all thought of monster families. Max wondered if by comparison, her own situation didn't look shades brighter. It was not a question he could or would ever ask her.

"I hope this isn't distressing you," said Max. "It's a rotten conversation at the best of times."

"Not at all," Patrice replied stoutly. "It just makes me more anxious to see Margot vindicated, poor woman. Do you think there's any connection? The creepy Wackenhuts and this whole sad adoption story?"

Max shook his head. *Not sure.* "Let's see if we can find out."

"We've just got an answer from Hamburg," Cotton put in. "From that German nob the baron and baroness stayed with. You wanted to know what they talked about."

"Yes?" said Max. "And?"

"Nothing important. What these people always talk about, I would imagine. Hunting, fishing, tax evasion, their ancestors. The Count and Countess von Rother-Magnum are distant cousins of the baron—fourth or perhaps fifth cousins. It would seem they have taken to the study of genealogy in a big way—they had their DNA tested using one of those online kits, and were delighted to learn they are not predisposed to glucose intolerance, for example. It's all quite boring, the way they tell it."

"Tell me more," said Max.

That evening, while jotting down notes at one of the antique desks Cotton had requisitioned for Camp X, Max saw that he'd missed a message from Awena on his mobile. They had spoken an hour previously, when he'd filled her in as much as he could on the state of the investigation.

He stepped into the hallway, away from various members of Cotton's team, to ring her back. When she answered he could hear all the usual background chaos of filming taking place in the airy kitchen of their Nether Monkslip cottage—men and women shouting, the director hysterical ("For the hundredth time, can we move the cable so she doesn't trip over it? Is that too goddamn much to ask?"), the sounds of several mobiles going off at once, creating a symphony of electronic pings and jingles.

When Awena had first agreed to do the show, the BBC film crew had wanted to take out a wall in the cottage to enhance the ability to wheel large cameras about ("Absolutely not"). Then they had insisted all the filming take place on a set in a London studio ("Sorry, but of course I can't leave the baby"). A compromise had been reached of using portable cameras in the small space. Awena, acting as her own agent, always seemed to get her way in these matters, using a beguiling blend of steadfast good humor and a take-no-hostages manner. Max pictured her now, wearing one of her trademark embroidered gowns protected by a snowy white chef's apron, her glossy dark hair perhaps braided into a loop framing her face. He had never known her to be flustered or overwhelmed by her newfound celebrity. Feeling she was providing a needed service, she had quickly established her boundaries: there would be no compromise—not in her time, in the ingredients she used, or in the honest portrayal of how the food was prepared. Max thought of it as cooking with integrity. It went without saying that no animals were harmed in the making of any film that featured Awena and her kitchen.

The background cacophony faded as she moved into the sitting room and closed the door behind her.

"I'm glad you were able to call, Max. I've had a sort of epiphany." This had been triggered, she told him, by cracking open eggs for the spring-vegetable quiche—that day's featured creation. Her recipes were in the main vegan but she offered vegetarian options for those so inclined.

"It was a double-yolk, as it happens. That's a good omen, you know. Tremendously good luck and a sign of fertility, particularly twins. But it sent my mind down another path, and I wondered: could it be a female killer you're looking for? I had been thinking in terms of a male because a date rape drug was used. But that drug or any other could be used by anyone of either sex, to render a person unconscious or unable to fight."

"Yes, we had considered that possibility," Max said. "But a woman acting alone—it is difficult to see how she could have hefted the body over the side. That's become the sticking point every time."

"I see. She would need an accomplice. Or . . ."

"Or?"

"Leverage. Some sort of leverage. Like, I don't know, a rope-and-pulley system. Ships always have ways to lift things overhead or over the side so the sailors don't have to rely on brute strength." Awena's father had made his living as a fisherman in Wales: she would know, Max reflected. It was so obvious, but with his own experience of ships restricted to traveling undercover on luxury cruises, what he'd mostly observed was that passengers on a cruise were like cats, sitting in the sun, just waiting for their next meal. It made them oblivious to their surroundings, creating a situation where unscrupulous people might take advantage. Max once had been seconded to help Scotland Yard follow a couple to Riga—a couple suspected of smuggling arms into the U.K. He had posed as a crew member, handing them towels and drinks as he eavesdropped, recording their conversations when and as he could, conversations transmitted live to his compatriots. Apart from that, rowing a scull on the Cherwell at Oxford was the closest he'd come to a knowledge of floating vessels.

Cotton's experience of water was even more limited. Possibly he'd had a bathtub overflow once.

"That may well be," Max said. He sighed. "Motive is still the big question, as much as the ways and means."

"I think for anyone basically unstable like a killer, there is always motive aplenty, if only illusory motive. That is true if it's a killer made or a killer born. You're going on the assumption after talking with Clarice it could be someone biologically connected with Margot, aren't you? So put yourself in that person's shoes. You've learned your mother gave you away—she didn't want you in her life. That may or may not have been true in varying degrees but a troubled personality might let that image of himself—or herself—gnaw away at the core, making that person feel disposable somehow. Unloved. Whatever Margot's reasons for giving the baby up for adoption, her side of the case was never heard. At least, not by the person who most needed to hear it."

"Or her side *was* heard, and that was how she talked herself into being murdered."

"It's a theory. But you're assuming an impulsive act, in that case. A sudden surge of hatred. But if the murder was planned—that rather requires even *more* motivation. For the killer to stay the course in such a cold-blooded way. Look, I have to run. It was just on my mind. The eggs, you know."

Max didn't question this process of thought from eggs to abandoned children. If the thought came from Awena, there would be a perfectly rational explanation, and it would evolve from a chain of ideas tightly linked.

There was certainly logic in what she had said. An adoption might be "avenged" years later by an unstable personality—particularly if that person had been adopted into an unloving or even abusive family.

But avenged by whom? There were candidates aplenty of the right age for Margot to have given birth to them. Everyone but the captain, Maurice, and Romero fit the bill, in fact.

And the father of that child? That, Max reflected, was an entire other kettle of fish. Even if his identity could be determined, what purpose would that serve after all these years?

Chapter 32

WATER EVERYWHERE

As Max talked with Awena, Cotton had found for himself a quiet nook in which to sort through his own notes on the case. The hotel was full of such places: bay windows cushioned and curtained for privacy, and corners with good lighting, plush upholstered chairs, and small polished tables. He stopped at the hotel bar and ordered a glass of mineral water to take with him to his chosen nook. As he waited, he studied the voluptuous room. It was like a stage set, the sort of place that looked as if Prince Albert might wander in at any moment, leading with his broad, cumberbunded stomach, and with a lovely damsel leaning on each arm.

The bartender placed Cotton's water on the bar, quite near another waiting order of sparkling water. A young waitress swept by just then and picked up the glass. Cotton was almost certain it was the glass that had been intended for him and started to protest, but no matter. Water was water. He picked up the other glass.

He started to take a sip and stopped, the glass halted halfway to his lips. Of course, one drink was like another. One glass of water. One glass of wine. One poisoned glass of table red, versus another unsullied glass.

Slowly he put his glass down onto the bar, as if it were suddenly too heavy to hold. He thought through the ramifications as he stared at the polished wood of the bar, his eyes tracing the burl of the grain, the deformity of wood that created such a beautiful pattern when the tree was sliced open. He, usually the most fastidious of men, looked unseeing at the water mark left by his glass.

Water, water, everywhere.

Blood is thicker than water.

He and Max had been talking about Hamlet and Gertrude and the entire messy crew, the whole dysfunctional Danish lot of them, plotting and scheming and avenging old wrongs, never allowing bygones to be bygones, stabbing and poisoning until hardly a soul was left standing. Poisoned blades, drownings. Poisoned drinks. Poison poured in ears, for heaven's sake, which always had struck Cotton as one of the most inefficient ways in the world to do away with someone. For if you had poison handy, surely the easiest thing was to put it in someone's glass.

But *Hamlet* was a play full of the wrong people being killed, and that thought was what had stilled Cotton's hand. Polonius, stabbed accidentally by Hamlet, who had mistaken the concealed Polonius for the hated Claudius. Gertrude, Hamlet's mother, accidentally poisoned when she drank from a glass intended for someone else. When she drank from a glass intended for Hamlet, in fact.

It was there the pieces started to come together for Cotton.

The play's the thing.

Leaving behind the unfinished drink of water, he went to find Max.

An hour later, within the fringed and ormolued confines of Camp X: "The report just came in," Cotton told Max.

"We were right?"

"Yes. It was a process of elimination, really. After verifying everyone else's origins, he was the only one it could be. It turns out he was adopted, making him the only viable candidate for this role. At least, the only candidate who was on board the ship."

"What do you mean?" Max asked.

"Romero has a daughter he formally adopted at her birth forty years ago. Her name is Frances."

"Frances Farnier. I saw her picture in his room. Of course."

"Why 'of course'?"

"It explains the hold Margot had over him, as nothing else does. Why else would Romero put up with her—take her on board his luxury yacht, no expense spared, and try to find a spot for her in his movie? Because he was such a nice guy? Not if his treatment of Tina is anything to go by. He didn't need Margot—he could have any actress to play any part he chose, any big name he wanted. Margot needed *him*. And because she did, she played him. She let him believe he had fathered a child on her years before. Fortunately, he was devoted to the child, but still he let Margot play that guilt card, right up until the end."

"It was Maurice who arranged for the child to be adopted," said Cotton. "Maurice knew everybody in Hollywood, including the nuns at Catholic Charities. Although the nuns kept to themselves the details of exactly *who* had ended up adopting the child. It was a different time."

"This is all in Maurice's diary, right? The nuns, the adoption—everything?"

"Yes. But with mere guesswork as to Romero's role—Maurice only knew Romero was in the picture, in Margot's life, at the relevant time. And that she never seemed to quite get out of Romero's life. Do you think . . . well, is it possible Romero just got tired of playing the game? Of feeling guilty for something that, after all, is no crime. Besides, he had done the honorable thing. He had taken the child in, and he had raised her as—I nearly said, he had raised her as his own. But in his mind, that's what she was. His own greatly loved child. Did Margot ever tell him the truth, that he almost certainly could not be the biological father? Knowing her nature, it is doubtful."

Max nodded. "She would lose all leverage over him if she told."

There were so many brands of parenting, Max reflected. His own mother had been a kind, loving, and good-hearted scatterbrain who would never have given him over to the care of others. Max was not certain, however, she'd have noticed if her child had fallen down a well, although by mealtime she'd have noticed he was missing. She was so easily distractible, her head always in the clouds, "where things are beautiful." Max thought her absent-minded brand of mothering might be the reason he'd grown up to be self-reliant, the sort of child who would one day work undercover, with no one to call on when a mission went south. He'd credit her with his streak of idealism, too. The streak that had led him to be recruited—twice, now—into working for MI5. She wanted the world to be a nicer, safer, gentler, and more beautiful place, and so did he.

Max added, "But it is Frances's half-brother who is our concern now."

"And that would be Addy. The only one who fits the bill."

"Margot never having learned her lesson, apparently."

"Ah. Well, it does happen. However, according to her medical records, she had a difficult delivery with Frances and she probably thought it had left her infertile. Any doctor of the time would have told her that was the case—according to our own doctor, who has looked at the old records. So she may have felt she had rather a free pass in that department. Then, Addy came along."

"None of this proves Addy killed her. In fact, I doubt he's capable of such a thing."

"Let's go and ask him," said Cotton. "See what he says."

"While we're at it, let's have a guard posted on his room. I think it much more likely his life is in danger than that he is a danger to anyone." Off Cotton's look, Max said, "I'll explain later."

They found Addison Phelps laboring once more over his screenplay, having given up entirely on the story of Margot. As he explained to the DCI and his vicar pal, it was likely the truth of her life would never be known, and he wasn't sure he was the one who could tell it, anyway.

He was much too close to his subject.

"From my research, I suspected I was on the right track," Addy told them. "There was so much that added up to exactly the right places and times. A few photos, also, that were suggestive if not conclusive: Margot corseted up to her eyeballs in an attempt to hide either a pregnancy or a serious eating disorder.

"Of course, I always knew I was adopted. My parents—the people who raised me—were progressive types. All very avant-garde in their thoughts on child rearing. They hired a foreign nanny who was commanded to speak to me only in French—that sort of thing. I think they told me the truth well before I understood what in the world they were talking about, to be honest. But all they said was I had been the love-child—their term—the love-child of a famous actress and some unidentified but terribly important man. He was British and that's all I knew for sure. I was apparently conceived at the same time Margot was here in the U.K., doing that play in the West End. I still don't know who the man was, exactly. I mean, I don't know the *sort* of man he was. Someone who was smitten by her performance, came backstage, and swept her off her feet—I'm guessing, but that's likely what happened. I had my DNA tested not long ago using one of those online kits that are so popular now. All it could tell me was that I was free of markers for certain dreadful diseases, which was good to know. When you're adopted, you worry about that sort of thing. But you see, the more I looked into Margot's life, the more I was sure she was the actress my parents had hinted at."

"You didn't know this, before you started writing about her?"

"No." He shook his head firmly. "I really didn't. Subconsciously, perhaps? Had I picked up hints along the way from my parents? I'm not sure, because I wasn't one of these children you read about, desperate to learn their origins, frantic for any clue. I was happy where I was, and very lucky to have ended up in the lap of luxury. I like to think I had the sense to know that, to shut up and be grateful.

"But I was always an old movie buff and maybe, just maybe, I saw the similarities in her face and features to mine. Something in her gestures, something I responded to. My parents loved watching these old films of hers, too. And then I met her, and of course . . . the attachment I felt was undeniable. I can't prove it, and you need not believe me, but I had had only inklings of the truth up until then. I wasn't totally sure up until this moment, in fact, now you tell me you've seen the birth records."

"I believe you," said Max simply. "Do you happen to have with you a copy of your DNA test?"

"Well, no. Would you expect me to? But the results are online."

"Might I have a look?"

"I don't know," Addy answered warily. "What are you looking for?"

"To be honest, I'm not sure," said Max. "Anything that might codify your relationship to Margot."

Addy pulled up a screen, logged in, and stepped back while Max in his turn sat down before the screen.

"You're distantly related to Napoleon, it says," Max remarked a few minutes later.

"I know," said Addy. "How cool is that? Also to Marie Antoinette. And to Prince Philip and Susan Sarandon."

Max had been scrolling quickly through the pages, most of which contained coding that was incomprehensible to a layman. He shook his head: *nothing*. Addy, looking over his shoulder, said, "I found quite a close relation before. But there was no way to connect with whoever it was. You can opt in or out of revealing more than just your first name or your initials. You can also be completely anonymous if you don't want your DNA relatives getting in touch. Then the test results only list the predicted strength of the relationship."

Suddenly Max stopped scrolling and peered closely at the screen.

"Look at this," he said to Cotton.

Cotton walked over and saw Max was pointing to one of the anonymous listings.

"Well, that's suggestive," Cotton said. "Not conclusive, but— what are the chances?" He turned to Addy, saying, "We must warn you: you could be in some danger."

"How's that?"

"We think the intended victim was not Margot. We think the intended victim was you, because of your relationship to Margot. Your blood relationship."

"What were you drinking that night, the night Margot died?" Max asked.

"The same as everyone, really, not that I was keeping tabs on people. Red wine was what I had to drink, is all I can say for certain. There were several bottles decanted. I think that's all anyone was having."

"Margot was drinking the red wine as well?"

"Yes. Yes, I'm fairly sure I saw her with a glass of the wine."

"Is it possible someone switched your glass for hers? That she picked up the wrong glass, and drank from it?"

"It is more than possible," said Addy. "She was drinking whatever was there, whatever you put in front of her. But why—who would . . . I mean, why me? Who would want to poison me?"

"For the usual reasons," said Cotton. "You were a threat to some-one. You stood between them and something they wanted very badly."

Addy shook his head sadly. "I don't know how you do the job you do. Too much reality, much of it sordid. Me, I'd rather deal in fantasy. Like Margot."

Chapter 33

HOLLOWAY

Cotton and Max were leaving Addy's room to discuss their next move when a uniformed constable came at a run down the hallway.

Reaching a clumsy halt, and gasping for air, he said, "One of them's done a runner, sir. I'm sorry, sir. That dark, skinny one. Looks like a movie star. He were running scared, like a man fleein' hellfire. And he ignored me when I yelled at him to stop." The constable looked ruefully down at his protruding stomach. "I tried to give chase but he were in better shape."

"Which way?" Cotton asked tersely. The constable, still breathing heavily, pointed behind Cotton's head. "I'm sorry, sir," he said again. "It happened so fast."

Max turned to Cotton. "You know the area better than I. What's north of here? Which way would you go to avoid capture? Up that holloway, right?"

Cotton agreed, "Yes. Up the holloway. You could hide an elephant in there and no one would notice. A man could easily use the trees and overhanging branches to hide behind. If he heard someone in pursuit, he could just scamper up a bank, and wait until the coast was clear."

"But he could be routed."

"Eventually. If I stationed my team in a string along the path, he could."

"How long is it?"

Cotton shrugged. "Half a kilometer?"

"'No time is to be lost.' I'll meet you in back of the hotel."

Max stopped into his room only long enough to exchange his runners for boots. The death of Maurice had been the unhinging factor; he felt the door was flying off the case now. It was a murder too carelessly executed, a sign of the disintegrating personality behind it.

Tossing a scarf round his throat and shoving his arms into a jacket, he headed out of the hotel by the back entrance. There he found Cotton pulling an immaculate pair of green Wellies from the boot of his car. He reached far into the boot to retrieve his torch.

"Believe me, we'll need this."

The southern coast of England is a region of soft sandstone. It is riddled with sunken roads or "holloways" whose origins stretch back to the Iron Age. These winding paths were made originally by animals being driven to market, and became codified by pilgrims walking to nearby abbeys to pay their respects to the relics of their favorite saints. In the case of Monkslip-super-Mare and other sea villages, they were used mainly by farmers and artisans—and the occasional smuggler— to carry goods to and from the seaports.

These sunken roads began as mere ruts in the road but hooves and feet and cartwheels turned them into steep ditches, and running water turned ditches into gorges. They can be as much as thirty feet deep, their beauty and drama arising from the tree branches that meet overhead to create a shadowy canopy of leaves. Walking through a holloway is like walking down the vaulted aisle of an ancient and long-deserted abbey church from which all the monks have fled.

These paths are dark, mysterious, and somewhat dangerous, and are largely disused today except by nature lovers, and by lovers gen- erally.

But on this day, the holloway the locals call the Devil's Trail was nearly a path to freedom for a murderer.

Max and Cotton plunged into the gloom of the holloway like divers entering a pool. Max was glad he'd thought of the boots, for spring showers had turned parts of the stony bottom of the path into a slurry of mud.

Cotton, via his smart watch, had sent several members of his team ahead to block the ends and exits of the holloway. In theory, their quarry could scramble up the steep sides of the path almost anywhere, but in most places it would require unusual strength, the agility of a goat, and a great deal of noisy thrashing about. He would be easy enough to hear and spot even if he were able to reach the top.

The path was lined with bluebells and wild garlic, and was permeated by a ghostly aura of dank fog. The two men hadn't walked but a few yards before they were eclipsed in gloomy darkness, bounded by gnarly shadow—it was very like entering a moss-sided cave, the banks on either side exposing a rich tangle of undergrowth. Only the torch and intermittent sunlight prevented them stumbling headfirst over rocks or knotted roots. The torch illuminated the few feet in front of them, and was otherwise inadequate to the task. Max was comforted to think their quarry was probably facing all the same obstacles they were, and wondered if he'd somehow had the foresight to bring along a torch.

He tried to peer ahead even as he minded every step. The pathway formed a natural green tunnel that in the distance emitted a space-age sort of light, like a half-life dream; the walls on either side had trees growing at their tops, the roots of the trees helping to hold the wall in place. The air itself was a soupy dark green which made it difficult to breathe. Max dared a glance at Cotton, who in the gloom resembled one of the ghostly forest creatures rumored to inhabit the area.

A scuttling sound, and Max was in time to see a hedgehog caught in the rays of the torch. Probably it was just out of hibernation and scouting a building site for a nest. Now it scampered to safety beneath the leaves and roots.

They hadn't gone far when a cry ahead made them stop, their senses as alert as those of the birds and animals, who scattered now with renewed energy, signaling to each other the news of a foreign invasion.

"That was human," said Max. "Up ahead."

They ran as fast as the roots and slippery moss would allow. Their quarry had recovered from his fall, only to tumble again in taking the next hurdle. His lace-up dress shoes weren't designed to cope with the wild terrain. Cotton could have told him that.

Max reached out and collared him by the scruff of his jacket, and Cotton moved in to pin his arms behind him.

The soiree was over for the Baron Sieben-Kuchen-Bäcker.

Chapter 34

DENOUEMENT

"Let me get this straight," said Patrice, speaking again from her throne of cushions and pillows, her swollen ankles resting atop a rounded pouf she'd requisitioned for Camp X. "Addison or Addy as he's called—he was Margot's natural son."

"That's right. Also, Frances was her daughter, her firstborn. Most likely conceived in the horrible circumstances we've described, when Margot was a teenager in Kansas. But that didn't stop her plans for a glorious future. She left town at the first opportunity with what money she'd saved from her after-school jobs."

"Okay. So she goes to Hollywood, gets some sort of menial work to keep body and soul together, and then perhaps eight months later, Frances is born. She is given up for adoption. Is that right?"

"So far so good, yes."

"Where does Romero come into this?"

"Margot met Romero right after she arrived in Hollywood," said Max. "Romero misled me about when they first met. Like Maurice, he was taken with her. Unlike Maurice, he launched headlong into an intimate relationship with her. He was very much in love, by the way, and followed her to London later. He lied about that: it made him look rather a fool, if not a complete stalker."

"I'm sorry, I don't . . ." began Patrice. Then: "Oh. Frances. He thought Frances was his."

Max nodded. "Margot let him think so, certainly. We have to remember she came from the sort of shattered background that doesn't encourage what today we would call bonding. Or honesty, for that matter. Given her losses coupled with her dreadful upbringing, Margot no doubt had a rather shaky idea of the entire concept of family. And of love. She may simply have presented to Romero that he was the father and, because he loved Margot, he jumped at the chance of parenthood. Maybe he saw it as a way to cement the bond with Margot. Or he simply accepted the responsibility, and made doubly sure he could keep the child by going to the trouble of a formal adoption. I don't think we'll ever know, to be honest. He seems to regard Frances as his daughter, whether by birth or by choice. I'll let someone else break the news to him of the true situation. I'm not sure it's our place to do so."

"One question," said Cotton. "Does this have anything to do with why you wanted to see the autopsy results?"

"I wondered whether Margot had ever given birth. The coroner was concerned only with how she died and so didn't highlight all the aspects of her medical history. But as you know, we rather lucked out. The autopsy actually showed she'd given birth *twice*. One was a natural birth: Frances. The second was a Caesarean—no doubt necessitated by complications from the first birth."

"Wait," said Patrice. "Caesarean? Second birth?" Her eyes narrowed as her mind knotted all the ends together. "Addy," she said, "So if we think the baron was trying to poison Addy—"

Max cleared his throat, looked over to Cotton, who made an "after you" gesture.

"He was."

"But why?" She pushed back her hair in frustration. "Why would he do that?"

"Try to poison his own flesh and blood, you mean? For that, we'd have to revisit the story of Cain and Abel. Although, in this case, we are dealing with two *half* brothers. Both born of the same father but of two different mothers."

"Max," said Patrice, and her voice carried a warning note. "What on earth are you talking about?"

Max, smiling, relented. "All right. The young baron as we know him is no baron at all. He was born out of wedlock to one of his father's paramours, and that illegitimacy, all very hushed up, is the great secret of our young baron's life. Just imagine, the people who have hosted him and his wife all these years finding out he never was born to a great title and wealth. Imagine *her* finding out that he is not the rightful heir to the estate of the Sieben-Kuchen-Bäckers. That honor goes to none other than Addy. Addison Phelps, as he came to be called by the people who adopted him."

"That would mean—are you saying—Margot and the old baron were married?"

"Yes. She seems to have talked him into marriage in time to legitimize Addy. Her pregnancy with Addy may have been unintended and unexpected, given her medical history. But this time she had a baron in her sights, not a struggling would-be director like Romero had been."

"Or worse," said Patrice. "One of her disgusting cousins."

"Right. This time, she was going to change the course of her own history. Write her own fairy tale of a movie. She and the baron were married in Scotland. He had a remote hunting lodge up there, and that is where she delivered Addy."

"Why keep things so hidden?" asked Patrice. "Why would she go about it like that?"

"Because there was no hiding the fact that the baby had been conceived out of wedlock and that was still something people liked to cluck over in those days. They would count up the months to nine and come up a few months short. But Addy was legitimate—according to the National Records of Scotland, his father married Margot in a valid ceremony. She hustled her baron to the altar just in the nick of time."

"But then she gave Addy up for adoption?"

"Yes. Once again, she felt she had to. The old baron died shortly after the birth—he probably knew he was dying when they married, and that may have added to his wish to leave a legitimate heir. But Margot was in the same position as before, really, as she had been with Frances. She, the least maternal of women, had a child on her hands she had no wish to raise, and she had few means with which to raise it—especially when it turned out the baron was land poor. He had land and a title but little money to sustain either. He had gambled away much of his wealth, a fact of which she was no doubt blissfully unaware when she took up with him."

"But Addy was the real thing. He was the true heir to whatever was going."

"Yes." Max had spoken briefly with Addy, who was having a hard time adjusting to his revised status. He was also grieving, in his own way, the loss of a mother he'd never known.

"So, she gave up her child for adoption to clear the path for a success she never really achieved," had been Addy's reaction. "There is a sad irony there. I was traded in for a sort of fool's gold, wasn't I?"

"Margot chose to bring you into the world," Max had reminded him. "I believe you did mean something to her."

Addy's reply had been a scoffing, "Do you really think so?"

"I do, actually. The thing about Margot is, she knew her own weaknesses, at least when it came to motherhood. Her own limitations, given the trauma of her past. She knew or feared she'd be no sort of mother to you, and she wanted you to have a better chance than she could offer."

"She wanted stardom, is what she wanted. To not be saddled with me."

He would feel that for a long time, thought Max. But Max hoped that one day, for his own sake, Addy might change his mind, or at least make his peace with what he believed.

"Addy was the legitimate heir, yes," he continued now to Patrice and Cotton. "But the fact of Addy's legitimacy made him dangerous to the young 'baron'—the fraudster who had spent years trading on a title to which he was not, to coin a phrase, entitled. I think it likely his own mother fueled his sense of grievance about what he'd lost, about what would rightfully have been his, had his father married his mother. He had no trade, no skills, nothing to fall back on but the family name, remember, which he had taken—stolen—as his own. That was his way of making a living, in a manner of speaking. And when he learned the identity of a genuine, verifiable heir, he saw that heir as a threat to his livelihood, a threat that must be disposed of."

"Was her ladyship aware of the imposture?" Patrice asked.

"We may never be sure. She won't admit any knowledge now, that much is certain. She may not have been aware of his true situation when they married. But once they *were* married, if she began to suspect, or if he told her the truth—well, she may have found after a number of years that she was in too deep. It may just have been easier to go along than risk a scandalous divorce."

"But how did *he* come to know all this about Addy?"

"Through another relative of his, oddly enough. Remember the German couple he and his wife were visiting? This German couple had taken up online DNA testing almost as a party game, and they persuaded the 'baron' to be tested, also. It would appear the fun part of this testing is in learning you are related by blood, however distantly, to someone famous.

"Let's start using his first name, Axelrod, in order to be clear. Well, as there seemed to be no harm in it—Axelrod knew he was a blood relation of the old baron, his father—he went along. Remember that his role as a houseguest was to keep his hosts happy, and the German wanted to see the confirmation of the blood tie. Very often, with this testing, the conclusions can be fortified by a cross-referencing with another blood relative. That is why these services allow all the participants to interact with one another, if they choose to, or at a minimum, to see other relatives with whom they share a connection. They can also see the strength of that connection—first cousin, fourth cousin, whatever. Well, lo and behold, Axelrod saw that he shared, through his father's line, an extremely close tie with someone named Addy Phelps. And this Addy, being the open and transparent sort of person he was, had provided his contact information—home town, e-mail, and so forth—so others sharing bits of his DNA could get in touch if they wanted. This information was enough for the baron to do some research of his own online, find Addy's year of birth (a matter of record, because of the copyrights on his writings) and confirm Addy must indeed be the true but unnamed heir his own mother had complained about. From there, it was a matter of finding Addy, and thanks to Addy's online blog, nothing could be simpler. He was, by happy chance, in Monte Carlo, sailing around Europe with Romero."

"With Margot on board."

"Yes, Addy had of course mentioned this on his blog, too. He was traveling with the once-well-known actress Margot Browne. Writing about her, in fact."

"The two people in the world who were a huge threat to the fake baron, Axelrod, were tidily collected in one place," said Patrice. "Isn't that rather a coincidence?"

"Not when you consider the industry they were in, no. It is often said that Hollywood is a small town. Margot, Romero, and Addy were all connected via agents, and producers, and past collaborations in film and on stage. The odd thing about it is that this was the *first* time all three of them were together in close proximity."

"Did the baron realize how close Addy was coming to the truth?"

"I think he must have done. Addy *was* getting closer to the truth. And while the baron quickly altered his online profile with the DNA service to hide his close relationship with Addy, here was Addy, researching like mad, and wanting to show off his research in a book—well, Addy had to go. Poor Addy didn't know he was a threat. He thought it was all just an interesting and growing possibility that he was Margot's child."

"Addy didn't realize the danger?"

"Not for a minute. He's an American, remember. Even had he begun to glimpse the full truth of his origins, he simply did not think in terms of having a title, and there was so little money and property attached to being the legitimate heir to the Sieben-Kuchen-Bäcker dynasty, anyway. Not compared with the vast sort of wealth he was used to. He may have found the whole idea preposterous—at best, a bit of a lark."

"And for the baron, it was no lark," said Cotton. "He was about to lose everything once Addy made all these connections, which, given his inquisitive nature, he was bound to do."

"Correct. But when it came to the murder, Addy thought Margot was the actual target, just as we did. That she had been killed for some incomprehensible reason, just as we did. He didn't realize he himself was first in line to be eliminated. Margot was probably in line for removal later on, although she had kept her secrets so long, she posed no immediate threat."

"That's what I don't understand," said Patrice. "She must have recognized the baron's name from the start: Sieben-Kuchen-Bäcker. I mean, really. Why did she say nothing? Did she not realize he was an imposter?"

"Not at all. Axelrod took the first opportunity to tell her he was the rightful heir—that his own mother had married his father, the baron. And that they had never divorced. Not true, of course, they had never married. But what was one more lie? He let Margot believe her own marriage was invalid. From what she knew of the old baron's dubious character, she would not have questioned it. He'd lied to her about his finances, too, remember—I think a novelty in Margot's life would have been a man who *didn't* lie to her. Anyway, Axelrod further told her—just to make sure she shut up and stayed shut up—that he had had a younger half-brother he'd stayed in touch with, but that this half-brother had died. Of course she thought he meant her son. The man we know as Addy.

"Still, the baron must have felt the scheme was unraveling around him. He tells us he saw Addy and Margot in conversation all the time, and he was sure the truth would come out. They were probably talking about old movies but that is where his paranoia kicked in. There could be no chance of the world learning the truth, or the baron would lose what little he had. Not just the title but the small income from the property he'd also been cashing in on. All that would go to Addy if the truth were known. I have a suspicion losing the title was what really rankled, though. It was that title that gave the 'baron' entrée. It made him *some*body. Without it, he was just another mooching house-guest who brought nothing to the table, not even bragging rights. Plus, he'd be made a laughingstock in the upper-class circles in which he orbited. The whole tawdry story of his origins was bound to come out. He'd have done anything to prevent that happening.

"So on the night of the murder, he—having full access via Delphine to every drug going on that ship—doctored Addy's drink. Margot, already three sheets to the wind, scooped up the glass and knocked back the contents, to his initial horror. That was not how this was supposed to go down. He followed Margot out onto the deck, where she had collapsed into a deck chair. 'Dead to the world,' as he told us. The combination of so much alcohol with the drugs was deadly. He decided he had to hide the body with its telltale stomach contents, and the time-honored method was at hand: to send her overboard. Making sure she was dead first.

"He probably could have managed everything himself but his wife came along just then, and together they made short work of things. It's rather chilling, when you think about it. With no more thought than a sort of, 'Oh, dear, we've killed the wrong one,' they got rid of the body and swanned off to think again how to get rid of Addy. But then poor Maurice had to be dealt with first. Maurice, who knew too much."

"Of course," put in Cotton, "Addy remained the primary threat. He knew everything or was well on his way to uncovering everything. He just didn't recognize the significance of what he was turning up. But worse, as far as Axelrod was concerned, he was *writing* about what he knew—always scribbling in his Moleskine or banging away on his laptop, as his wife told Max. Addy may not have been motivated by greed—probably he was not. There was money to be made by his tale, but he had money. The fact he was a real-live baron—that may have been too good to keep to himself, American or no. He certainly could not write his book without mentioning who he was, who his father was, and the whole story of his parents' meeting and secret marriage. Addy had to be silenced, and as soon as the police let everyone go, that is what would have happened. A little accident, a car driven off a cliff into the ocean when the brakes failed, whatever could be arranged. Within a week or so, a month or so—before he finished his book, Addy had to be eliminated. More breath of the devil."

"He confessed—the fake baron, I mean? Axelrod?"

"As good as. Once his wife learned that he'd tossed her into it—we never would have known of her help that night without his telling us—she became most helpful. Just an unstoppable flow of information. It is likely we will look the other way when it comes to a thorough review of her role in the scheme. Just so long as she continues to tell us every detail, she'll get off lightly in this."

"Oh, my God," said Patrice.

"Yes, it's distressing, but it's for the best. In the interests of justice, we—"

"I don't mean that. I mean 'Oh, my God, the baby's on the way.' Call the midwife, will you?"

In fact two midwifes from the local catchment area arrived, both young women bristling with a starchy, calm efficiency, like nurses from the Crimean War. With their takeover of the scene, there was nothing more for Max to do. He gave Patrice's hand a squeeze and took himself off to notify Addy of the danger having passed. Then he put in a call to Awena. As usual, she had been right, about the eggs and a few other things. Right in her rather sideways, amorphous, piercing-the-veil way, but right nonetheless. How he missed her. He would be home the next day, he promised. Just a few loose ends.

Patrice? Oh, Patrice was fine. Baby on the way now. All was well. Cotton was staying at her side for moral support.

"Cotton?"

"Yes. I'll explain later."

Max looked back on the sort of comfortable, collegial familiarity Cotton and Patrice seemed to have established early in the investigation, before Max himself came on board, and found he was not surprised at the way events had unfolded.

Cotton had in fact insisted on staying with Patrice, a choice that would have astonished anyone but Max, who had taken a moment to savor the comic beauty of Cotton's helpless panic. He had stood literally wringing his hands, hoping someone would ask him to boil water or wrap bandages or find a clean newspaper or do *some*thing useful. But there he stood, seemingly rooted to the spot—a reaction that spoke volumes, a reaction familiar to Max from the day his son Owen had been born. That churning fear had something—everything—to do with love.

The midwives, finally understanding that Cotton was not the father, tried to shoo him from the room, particularly as he was, for all intents and purposes, useless. He countered by holding up his warrant card, only to be told he held no sway in these matters. They did not care that he was a DCI. He was a civilian and in the way as far as they were concerned.

It was Patrice who finally intervened and persuaded the women to relent.

"Let him stay," she said. "There's no one on earth I'd rather have with me now."

Chapter 35

IT'S A WRAP

If this were the close of one of his films, Romero Farnier might tack on a series of photos before rolling the end credits, so audiences could learn what happened next in the lives of the key players. This he found to be a particularly useful story-telling device in the case of historical dramas, to show viewers what fate had in store for the real-life principals.

Romero himself went on to be an auteur, and to make the sort of art-house film he had always longed to create: films with subtitles produced in snowy places like Sweden and Iceland. These efforts are generally panned by the critics, who have dubbed Romero the Woody Allen of Scandinavia, but Romero shrugs that aside, for he is content. Whenever he needs extra cash to fund his experimental films, he spends a year directing the sort of spectacle that made him famous. He sold the *Calypso Facto* to fund his most recent effort, the title of which can be translated as *A Long Story of Nothing*. He recently gave his daughter's hand in marriage to a film grip. Romero never learned the truth of Frances's origins.

A frequent collaborator on films with Romero is Addy Phelps, now a world-renowned Academy Award–winning screenwriter. He spends most of each year living in a French farmhouse in Provence.

He seldom uses his title except to get better reservations in London restaurants.

Sometimes appearing in Romero's films is Jake Larsson, originally cast because of his Swedish last name and because he was willing to dye his hair blond for the role. But because of his scene-stealing role in *Attilius* Jake developed a large Twitter following, and finds himself in demand for the sort of toga dramas Romero now eschews.

Tina Calvert likewise enjoyed a brush with fame after appearing in an interstellar film shot in Australia, a role Romero had found for her. She played Talisman Dragol of Planet Minerva 6 and she is currently married to a stunt double (Chad Briggs/Lurgo Zalzebana) from that film. Her publicist has announced her next role will be to star in a biopic of Margot Browne, for which Addy Phelps declined to write the screenplay.

Maurice Brandon's partner, Frank, moved to a vineyard north of San Francisco, where he sells wine from an award-winning vineyard, and is collaborating on a new varietal with Francis Ford Coppola. Margot's body was laid to rest near Maurice's on a sunny hilltop overlooking the vineyard. Romero, Frances, and Addy attended the services.

Captain Smith continues to ply the waters of the English Channel and the North Sea as a captain-for-hire of private yachts. He has no fixed abode and has often expressed the wish to be buried at sea.

Former sous-chef Angel Torres owns a restaurant and bakery in New York City called Angelcake. He is happily married to an immigration attorney, and has sworn he will never again board a ship.

Of course a sad fate was reserved for Axelrod, formerly known as Baron Sieben-Kuchen-Bäcker. While Great Britain has no death penalty, it does offer a life sentence to murderers, and many of Axelrod's former acquaintances felt he would have preferred the death penalty to a life spent among what he always referred to as lowlifes. For a short while he shared a prison yard with Zaki Zafour, awaiting trial for his role in conveying and dealing Class A drugs. Sadly, or not, Zaki was the victim of a prison riot not long after Axelrod was transferred to a larger but safer prison near London.

The fate of Axelrod's wife, Emma, no longer allowed to style herself the Baroness Sieben-Kuchen-Bäcker, is nearly as tragic as her husband's, for once Emma's role in disposing of the body of Margot Browne became known, as well as the cover-up to the crime that followed, her life on the royal circuit came to an abrupt end. Penniless, she became a buyer for a women's fashion boutique in London, and spends her days being condescended to by society women as they select their frocks and accessories for evening wear. She divorced her husband, whom she never visited in prison, anyway.

Delphine could have told the pseudo-baroness that what goes round comes round. After being sentenced to prison for her role in drug smuggling, Delphine turned to religion, eventually becoming an ordained priest of the Anglican church and an advocate for prison reform. She has made many converts to the faith.

Hazel and Beatrice, former employees of the Grand Imperial Hotel, pooled their resources and opened a fish-and-chips shop in Monkslip-super-Mare. It is called the Sign of the Whale and is frequently mentioned in travel guides as a locals' favorite.

DCI Cotton and Patrice Logan share a home in Monkslip-super-Mare with their daughter, Alexis, whom Cotton has officially adopted. They are frequent customers of the Whale, where a great fuss is made over Alexis and her extravagant ringlets.

Max Tudor has resumed his rightful place in the village of Nether Monkslip, with Awena and Owen at his side. But before long he will become embroiled in solving a case of murder at nearby Wooton Priory. Max and his bishop wonder where it all will end.